Sisters of the Roaring Twenties

Flappers finding love in Hollywood

By day, the three Dryer sisters, Betty, Patsy and Jane, are dutiful and obedient daughters, doing chores insisted on by their tyrannical father.

But what their father doesn't know is that his daughters lead secret lives—as flappers who dance all night in Hollywood's speakeasies!

Their father insists they will marry wealthy men of his choosing, but these independent sisters are determined to find love on their own terms!

Read Patsy's story in
The Flapper's Fake Fiancé

Read Betty's story in
The Flapper's Baby Scandal

And look out for Jane's story
The Flapper's Scandalous Elopement
coming soon!

Author Note

Welcome to another Roaring Twenties story. While I was writing Henry and Betty's story, my husband asked how the book was coming along. I told him that I couldn't wait to see how it ended. He gave me one of those dumbfounded looks and pointed out that I was the author. I nodded and said, "I know."

That's how it is sometimes—the characters take over, and I'm just typing the story they are laying out for me, right up to the end. That's what happened with this story. I thought it would end with a wedding. They proved me wrong.

There are two things I'd like to point out. The FBI wasn't the Federal Bureau of Investigation until 1935. Prior to that, it was the Bureau of Investigation, therefore agents were not referred to as "FBI" during the Roaring Twenties. However, I termed Henry's occupation as an FBI agent and hope you don't mind.

The second one is that childbirth changed drastically in the 1920s. There were fewer "home deliveries" with the rise in hospitals, and maternity wards became more commonplace. So did administering ether to women in labor so they "slept" through the entire process, not remembering anything when they woke up. Yes, it was known as "modern medicine."

I do hope you enjoy Henry and Betty's story!

LAURI ROBINSON

—

The Flapper's Baby Scandal

HARLEQUIN
HISTORICAL

**HARLEQUIN®
HISTORICAL™**

PLEASE RECYCLE

Recycling programs
for this product may
not exist in your area.

ISBN-13: 978-1-335-50560-6

The Flapper's Baby Scandal

Copyright © 2020 by Lauri Robinson

This edition published by arrangement with Harlequin Books S.A.

For questions and comments about the quality of this book,
please contact us at CustomerService@Harlequin.com.

Harlequin Enterprises ULC
22 Adelaide St. West, 40th Floor
Toronto, Ontario M5H 4E3, Canada
www.Harlequin.com

Printed in U.S.A.

A lover of fairy tales and history, **Lauri Robinson** can't imagine a better profession than penning happily-ever-after stories about men and women in days gone past. Her favorite settings include World War II, the Roaring Twenties and the Old West. Lauri and her husband raised three sons in their rural Minnesota home and are now getting their just rewards by spoiling their grandchildren. Visit her at laurirobinson.Blogspot.com, Facebook.com/lauri.robinson1 or Twitter.com/laurir.

Visit the Author Profile page
at Harlequin.com for more titles.

To Diane S. for always being one of the first people to read my books as soon as they are released. I appreciate your support so very much!

Chapter One

1928

Betty Dryer sat at the bar on the outskirts of the dance floor, tapping the toe of one black patent leather shoe against the foot rail to the beat of the music while scanning the crowded room. The Rooster's Nest was a hopping place tonight and her sisters were already taking advantage of that. Exercising the freedom that only came when the three of them escaped into the night, became the women they could only dream about being.

Her youngest sister, Patsy, wearing a cute blue dress covered with layers of fringe and a matching hat, was nearly dragging a guy onto the dance floor, while Jane, in her red-and-white-striped A-line dress was over by the piano, pinning numbers onto the backs of couples for the dance-off that had just been announced. Jane wore a hat that matched her outfit, too. They all did. Betty's hat was silver, with a purple feather, the same shade as her purple dress, trimmed with double layers of wide silver lace at the hem, neckline and sleeve openings. She'd sewn it herself. They all had sewn their dresses and wore hats to cover their blond hair. In order to keep people from recognizing them as William Dryer's daughters.

This was their secret life. One their parents could never learn about or they'd be locked away in the top floor of their house like a trio of Rapunzels.

Betty scanned the crowd a little harder, looking for a dance partner. She'd already turned down two men, because she'd danced with them earlier tonight. That was one of the rules she'd set for herself and her sisters. To never dance with the same man too many times. They were here for one reason. Fun. Getting paired up with someone could ruin that for everyone.

A knot formed in her stomach. She breathed through the tightening, wishing she could make it go completely away, but that wouldn't happen. Just like not marrying James Bauer wouldn't happen. The man her father had chosen for her to marry. Other than seeing him at one of the houses he'd built in partnership with her father, she didn't even know James.

She didn't know many people in general. Due to a life of being locked up in her father's house, knowing her only taste of freedom was this—sneaking out at night to visit speakeasies—which would stop as soon as she married James.

She used to have dreams, when she was younger, of growing up and getting married. She'd thought that would be the most wonderful thing on earth. Having her own house, her own children, who she would take to the park, to the beach, on picnics, just all sorts of different places and have all kinds of fun.

Then, she'd grown up and discovered the real world. That had happened three years ago, when she'd been up in Seattle visiting her grandmother and aunt. Her aunt had fallen in love with a man, one who had run out on her, left her pregnant and alone.

It was the next thing that had solidified how wrong Betty's dreams had been.

She'd met a man. A man who proved how easy a woman can become besotted and how fast a man can disappear.

That thought was enough to anger her all over again, and she wasn't here to be angry. She was here to have fun and dance.

Dance the night away.

She scanned the room again, and as it had before, her gaze landed on a man sitting alone, at a table in the far corner behind the piano. He'd been there since she'd arrived, and she'd wondered if she'd seen him before, here or at one of the other speakeasies she and her sisters visited regularly. There was something about him that was familiar, but she couldn't say what.

He looked like an average Joe, as did most of the other men in the room. The Rooster's Nest attracted those types, working men. Day laborers and dockworkers. Men who had their sleeves rolled up and their boot strings double knotted. Those were the type of men who wouldn't know her father.

There was something about that guy in the corner that made him stand out to her. She wasn't sure what, except that his flat, newsboy-type hat partially hid his face, making her even more curious.

He'd watched her earlier, when she'd danced, and she'd expected him to approach her, ask her to dance.

But he hadn't.

A slow smile built on her lips as she rose to her feet. She'd just have to ask him.

That was part of the fun about being a flapper. They

embraced life with gusto. They weren't shy, nor did they worry about what others thought. They tossed the conventional standards of female behavior out the window and embraced life with newfound freedom.

The same freedom she and her sisters embraced during their nights out on the town. They had all come to love the liberty their nightlife gave them. It was the exact opposite from the stifling life they lived during the day. Every day.

Skirting around the line of people waiting to have numbers pinned on their backs, she saw him stand up. Her heart thudded, and she wasn't exactly sure why, until he turned, as if he was going to walk away from his table before she arrived.

She cut through another line of people between him and her and stepped in front of him, stopping his escape, if that was what he'd had in mind.

"You aren't thinking about taking a hike, are you?" she asked while batting her mascara-covered lashes at him. That was a trick Jane had read about in one of the magazines she'd snuck into the house, and it always made men smile.

He didn't smile. Instead, he tugged the brim of his flat brown leather hat up a touch. "I was."

She peered up at him harder, and the moment she caught sight of the eyes his hat had been shadowing, her heart stopped. Right then and there. At the exact same time her entire body started to tremble. "It's you!" she gasped. The very man who'd—who'd—who *was* the reason she'd set down another rule for her and her sisters. No kissing. Absolutely none!

"And it's you," he said. "Imagine that."

Imagine! She didn't have to imagine! She knew! Those blue eyes were too unique to forget. Pale blue, like the sky first thing in the morning, and darkly rimmed with black lashes. She'd never seen another set like them and knew she never would, either.

Her heart started to pound and she was nearly gasping for air. It was him. The man who'd kissed her on the beach, right where anyone could have seen, and then walked away as if nothing had happened.

Anger, a level she'd never hit before, struck hard. "What are you doing here? How did you find me?"

"Right here!" someone shouted. "We have the final couple! Lacy and her Reuben!"

Betty recognized Jane's voice and twisted as her sister grasped the back of her dress to pin a number to her back. "We aren't entering the dance-off."

"Yes, you are!" Jane said.

Betty twisted, trying to keep Jane from pinning on the number. "No, we—"

"Yes, we are," the blue-eyed man said, grabbing her hand.

"You two are number three," Jane said, moving to pin a piece of paper on his back.

"I'm not dancing with you," Betty said, trying to pull away.

"Yes. You. Are." His voice was deep, low, and under his breath.

Betty's insides quivered at the seriousness of his tone.

"Clear the floor!" someone shouted. "Give the dancers room!"

Jane slapped his back. "Hit the floor, Reuben!"

"Come on, Lacy." He drew her toward the dance floor.

"My name's not Lacy," she said, gritting her teeth.

"And mine's not Reuben."

Of course his name wasn't Reuben, that was just slang for a stranger in town. His plain blue shirt, black suspenders, and tan pants made him look like he wasn't a man-about-town. She and her sisters never used their real names while on the town. They used whatever name took their fancy. Jane had called her Lacy because of her lace-trimmed dress.

They stepped onto the dance floor and he spun around, facing her. With a grin that revealed he had nice and straight, white teeth, which made him even more handsome, he planted his free hand on the small of her back.

She tried to move, get away, but between his hold and the people crowding the dance floor around them, she had nowhere to go.

"Dig any clams lately?" he asked.

She pinched her lips together, refusing to answer. Too bad she couldn't refuse the memories from flooding forward.

While in Seattle three years ago, she'd been digging clams, and had wandered out too far. Before she'd realized what was happening, the tide had been rolling in. She'd panicked, having never experienced how quickly the water was rising and had climbed up on some rocks, but the waves had soon covered the rocks. Out of nowhere, he'd shown up and carried her to shore. Then he'd kissed her! More than once! Until she hadn't been able to breathe, or think, or move, and then…then he'd walked away! Like nothing had happened.

A bandit. That was what he was, and she was not going to dance with him. Mad all over again, she turned to run away.

He spun her neatly back round again.

"Nice try, Lacy, but you're dancing with me."

"No, I'm not," she hissed. "I was hoping to never see you again!"

"Then you need to find different company."

"What?" That made no sense. None whatsoever.

The piano man struck the keys, and they were suddenly moving across the floor. Her and this…this kissing bandit!

His movements were smooth, flowed perfectly with the music, even as she held herself stiffly.

"No wonder you didn't want to enter the dance-off," he said. "You don't know how to dance."

"I do, too!"

"No, you don't."

"Yes, I do. I just don't want to dance with you!"

"Too late. We're couple number three and we are dancing," he said, his hands going to her waist and lifting her up. "Until you get us disqualified."

Another flash of anger rose up inside her. She couldn't get them disqualified, that could cause a scene, and that went against another one of her rules.

"No wonder you couldn't find a partner," he said. "They all must have known you can't dance."

They were dancing the fox-trot, and she was excellent at the fox-trot. "Put me down."

"Why, so you can prove you can't dance?"

"No!" She glared at him. "So I can show you how to dance."

He laughed. "I know how to dance."

She was going to prove who knew how to dance. Her. "No, you don't, you're supposed to be bending at the knees."

"Like this?" Grinning, he bent his knees until her heels barely tapped the floor, then straightened upright again.

"Oh, for heaven's sake, put me down!"

He lowered her to the floor but kept his hands on her waist. She kept hers on his shoulders and, determined to prove him wrong, took two steps back, slid one step to the side, bent her knees, and straightened. He'd matched each of her steps, nearly perfectly, but still, she said, "That's how you do it."

"Oh, so you mean like this."

He led her through the steps so quickly, and so perfectly, she nearly forgot she didn't want to dance with him.

Nearly.

"Somewhat," she said.

"Let's try this, then."

Once again, his steps were quick, smooth, and in perfect time with the beat. He then released her waist, grasped her hand, twirled her around beneath their clasped hands, and pulled her back into his arms so swiftly, it almost made her dizzy.

"And?"

"And what?" she said, pretending not to know.

"How am I doing now?" He twirled her again. "Or do I need more instructions?"

She huffed out a breath. "You are doing fine."

"Just fine?"

She was not going to compliment him on his dancing. Absolutely not. Even if he was one of the best partners she'd ever had. She didn't need to concentrate on the steps at all; they were gliding around the floor as if they danced together every day.

While continuing to glide her through the steps, he asked, "How long have you been in Los Angeles?"

"My entire life," she answered. "What are you doing here?"

"Working."

"Do you live in Seattle?" She'd dreamed of going back to Seattle to look for him, just because he'd made her so angry by kissing her and then walking off, she'd wanted to… Oh, she wasn't even sure what she'd wanted to do to him, but no one had ever made her so angry. Not even the way her father kept them locked up at home. Him, this kissing bandit had made her believe that maybe her father was right. That he had to choose husbands for them because most men couldn't be trusted.

"No, I was only in Seattle for a short time three years ago. Working." He spun them around at the edge of the floor and started back in the other direction. "What were you doing there three years ago?"

"Visiting family." She wasn't interested in learning more about him, but talking kept her mind busy on something other than how handsome he was. Especially when he smiled. That nearly took her breath away. "What type of work do you do?"

"This and that," he said.

Her heart skipped a beat. Could he know her father? "Construction?"

"No. I'm not very good with a hammer and nail."

Thank goodness. She'd always feared they might run into one of the men who worked on the crews building houses in Hollywoodland. She and her sisters were never allowed near the building sites until the homes were done and the crews all gone, but she still worried.

The music ended and she questioned escaping his hold and leaving the Rooster's Nest altogether, but Patsy was dancing and Jane was helping the piano player, and the rule was they all left together.

He was looking at her, as if waiting for her to decide.

She lifted her chin and gave a small nod as the music started up again.

They were off, with him leading them around the dance floor all over again.

The bright overhead lights with their stained-glass lampshades made his blue eyes stand out even more. They truly were unique. Captivating.

She pulled her eyes off them because she certainly didn't want to be captivated. Not by him or any other man.

He was tall, so tall she couldn't see over his shoulders—very broad and firm shoulders. She eased backward, trying to put more space between their bodies, but his hold on her waist tightened, keeping her right where she was at, close to him. Very close.

She'd danced with many men since she and her sisters started sneaking out, and she'd never been this aware of a single one of them. Her heart was thudding, her insides tingling, and she didn't dare look at his face again, because every time she did, she remembered the way they'd looked at each other for a moment, just before he'd kissed her.

She remembered kissing him back, too. That was another part that had made her so mad. It had probably been because she'd been scared of the water rising. The water he'd carried her out of. She'd been happy, so happy to be on dry ground, she would have kissed it.

"We are going to have to do better than this if we want to win," he said, and twirled her about.

The next thing she knew, they were dancing past the other couples, to the edge of the dance floor, where he dipped her, twirled her, and then they were heading back to the other end of the parquet floor to do it all over again.

Between the fast music, the gaiety of the other dancers and onlookers, and his gracefulness, she couldn't help but be drawn in, and was soon challenging his every move with one of her own, including kicking a leg high in the air each time he dipped her.

The onlookers were cheering loudly when that song ended and the next one began. She let out a gleeful laugh, recognizing the fun, fast-paced tempo. This was a favorite of hers, because she didn't need to even hold her partner's hands. Not only his, but any man she danced with. "Do you know how to shimmy?"

"It looks like I'm about to learn," he replied as he released her hands.

"Oh, yes you are!" Full of excitement, she crouched down, like all the other dancers, and then arms held out at her sides, she playfully shook her torso, making the lace on her dress flip and flop as she rose back up.

He followed suit, but when he was standing straight again, he grasped her waist and lifted her high in the air and spun around before setting her back on her feet.

The crowd cheered loudly, and it was a moment before she realized they were shouting the number three.

"They are cheering for us!" she shouted above the roar of the crowd and the music. She'd never had this much fun dancing.

"I believe they are!" He grasped her hands. "If we want to win, we have to give them a show."

Excitement flared inside her. "Let's! Let's give them a show and win!"

They crouched down together, hands held, and rose back up, shaking and shimmying, toward one another until their torsos touched before shimmying away from each other again. Laughing as the crowd cheered louder, they did it again. And again.

The enjoyment inside her grew as they continued to dance, as the crowd continued to applaud. He was a spectacular dancer and led her through a course of dips and twirls, jumps and shimmies that had the crowd cheering and clapping louder and louder.

During the next song, which was a tango, they gained more cheers while dancing cheek to cheek, chest to chest, up and down the floor. On every turn, he'd add in several overly flourished dips and bows that kept the crowd shouting their number.

When the beginning chords of the final song struck, he threw his head back in laughter while grabbing her hand, leading her backward several steps, and then forward. Having the time of her life, Betty kicked up her heels to the fast beats of the Charleston tune the piano man was playing.

She pranced back and forth next to him, with the hem of her purple skirt flapping against her legs as she tapped the heels of her shoes with her palms, slapped the floor with her fingers and crisscrossed her ankles. It was so fun, so exhilarating, she danced faster and faster.

So did he.

He grasped her hand when a couple fell down in front of them, and then another. Without missing a beat, he pulled her forward. They leaped over the fallen dancers and kept on dancing.

Her heart was pounding in her chest faster than the piano man was striking keys, and she loved it. Loved dancing. Loved the freedom of not caring about anything except having a good time. No other partner had ever made her feel this carefree, this alive. Every time she looked into his eyes, saw them shimmering, the exhilaration inside her grew even more.

At the edge of the dance floor, rather than turning

back in the other direction, he grasped her waist and lifted her high in the air so she was looking down on him, and then he swung her downward, alongside his right hip and then his left hip before setting her feet back on the floor at the precise moment the music ended.

She was so light-headed, so dizzy, she had to grasp on to his shoulders with both hands. The roar of the crowd echoed in her ears as she looked up at him. He was so handsome, his eyes so unique and striking, a warmth swirled inside her, and grew as he brought his face closer to hers. A memory, a hope, filled her so quickly, she barely had time to contemplate it, other than the recognition that she wanted to kiss him again. Kiss him like she had on the beach three years ago.

The moment his lips touched hers, that hope came to fruition, and she looped her arms around his neck to kiss him in return.

The fun, the excitement, he'd been caught up in came to a crashing halt the moment Henry Randall realized what he was doing.

Kissing her.

In the eight years he'd been an agent for the Bureau of Investigation under the federal Justice Department, since the day he'd turned eighteen and his uncle had assigned him the position, he'd never once forgotten who he was, or what he was doing.

Until tonight.

Until the sea nymph he'd carried ashore three years ago had reentered his life.

What the hell had he been thinking? He was working undercover, on a major case. A case that seven years ago, when he'd still been a rookie, had propelled him to the top. Made other agents look at him as an equal, not his uncle's nephew.

Henry pulled his lips off hers, which were as soft and sweet as he'd remembered and took a step back. Telling himself not to look at her. Not to meet the gaze of those dark blue eyes again because that had been his first downfall tonight. He'd thought his eyes were playing tricks on him when he'd first noticed her. Thought it couldn't be her. But it was.

The investigator in him rose up. She'd been in Seattle, and now she was here?

That couldn't be a coincidence.

He glanced around the room, beyond the crowd that was encircling them. Congratulating them.

His attention snagged on a man, one who he'd leaped over on the dance floor a short time ago. A wave of dread washed over him and kicked his senses back where they belonged. At least his common sense.

Lane Cox. If anyone would recognize him, it would be Lane. Cox was not only the owner of the local newspaper, he was the best reporter in the state. If not the nation.

Although his instincts were to stay at her side, find out who she knew and why she was here, Henry knew what he had to do, and took a step back. Then another.

He bumped into someone, and shifting aside, to see who it was, he nodded at the piano player.

The guy nodded toward the other side of the crowd. "They are bringing your trophies. Two mugs of beer, one for you and one for your partner."

Henry shook his head and stepped behind the man. "Accept it for me, will you, pal?" As deeper regret filled him, he added, "And tell my partner…" Tell her what?

He needed information from her. Find out why she

was here and why she had been in Seattle three years ago. So had the mole. She could know the mole, could confirm he was right about which agent had been defying the oath he'd taken.

The piano man was looking at him like he'd just lost his mind. Maybe he had, but Henry couldn't do anything about it right now. He couldn't take the chance of his cover being blown by Lane Cox.

A cigarette girl was making her way through the crowd, carrying two mugs of beer over her head. Trophies for the winners of the dance-off.

Him and Lacy, or whatever her name was. He'd have to find that out, too.

She was twisting left and right, looking around. For him no doubt. A hint of remorse struck.

"Tell her what?" the piano man asked.

"That I'll see her tomorrow night," Henry said, slipping into the crowd behind him. As he neared the wall behind the piano, he took a final glance around to make sure no one was looking at him, and then ducked behind the curtain that hung along the wall. He would come back tomorrow night. Find out everything Lacy knew.

He opened the door that the curtain kept hidden and hurried through the long and narrow storeroom that was lined with shelves and crates full of various types of alcohol. If he was a prohibition agent instead of an investigation agent, the owner of the Rooster's Nest would already be in jail and the contents of this room confiscated and destroyed.

Some of it destroyed. Some of it would be shipped elsewhere, where it would be consumed during secretive parties that the American people would be shocked to learn about.

Actually, not that many people would be shocked.

In a lot of ways, prohibition had created more drinking than it had reduced. People seemed to love the idea of sneaking around, of drinking behind closed doors. It had become one of the most popular things to do. Throw in music and a dance floor, and joints across the nation were packed full every night.

Prohibition wasn't a part of his job, and he was glad of that. That was a fine line the government was walking right now. He couldn't see it lasting much longer. The Volstead Act hadn't brought about the end results the followers imagined, and other than a select few, the number of people still supporting the act had dwindled over the years.

At the corner of the end wall, he found the little catch on the side of the shelf and swung it away from the wall. Opening the secret door the shelf kept hidden in the wall, he crossed over the threshold and pulled the shelf back in place. Then as he stepped onto the first step of the stairway that led down to the tunnel, he pulled the door shut behind him.

He stood there for a moment, on that first step, shaking his head. He'd never expected to see her again.

Never.

The odds of that had to be one in a million, which meant it wasn't a coincidence.

Their past encounter had only lasted minutes, yet it had stuck with him.

Three years ago, he'd been in Seattle, undercover, which had grown into his specialty, and he'd just made a major break in the counterfeiting case by having gained access into a beach cottage where the perpetrators had been printing bills, when he'd seen her walking along the sand in the secluded bay.

She'd been wearing a pair of dark knickers and a

white blouse and carrying her shoes in one hand and a bucket and clam-digging shovel in the other. Her long blond hair had been blowing in the wind as she'd walked, swinging her arms as if she hadn't had a care in the world.

The tide had already been rolling in, and at the time, he remembered hoping she knew what she was doing. High tide in that small bay quickly flooded the entire area.

He hadn't wasted any more time contemplating if she did or didn't, because he'd known he'd only had minutes to complete his survey of the house and equipment.

He'd found what he'd needed to find, and made a hasty exit before being discovered, but upon leaving the cottage, he'd seen her again.

The tide had caught her off guard, and she'd been perched upon a cluster of rocks, clearly frantic at the water that had been sloshing around her shins and growing higher and higher.

He hadn't even bothered to take off his shoes, just ran out through the rising water and plucked her off the rocks. She'd been crying and clung to him so hard she'd nearly strangled him by the time he'd carried her to shore.

Sobbing, she'd thanked him for saving her life.

He'd considered telling her the water hadn't been waist high, but that had only been a part of it. The currents of the tide could have easily tripped her, and all the rocks made the water dangerous no matter how high it had been.

The first glance he'd gotten of her hadn't prepared him for how pretty she'd been up close, even while crying. Her delicate features, dark blue eyes gazing into his, and her rosy lips had nearly taken his breath away.

Much like it had tonight.

As she'd started to explain what had happened, he'd seen a car pull up to the beach cottage.

At a risk of being caught, he'd acted quickly, and had done the only thing he could think of. Kissed her. A long, deep, passionate kiss that would convince anyone who might have noticed them that they were merely lovers taking advantage of the secluded beach.

They'd kissed until they'd both been breathless, and then they'd sucked in air, and kissed again.

By the time he'd lifted his head a second time, the men, having found the cottage empty, were climbing back in their car. He'd released her then.

She'd been gasping for air again, much like when he'd hoisted her off the rocks.

He'd told her to be more careful in the future, and to go home. Then he'd walked away, up the beach, to where he'd parked his car behind a cluster of trees. From there, he'd watched her hurry up the trail that led away from the beach, the opposite way of the cottage, and onto the road that curved around the hill and led to several houses.

Another woman had met her on the road. He'd driven away then, to report his findings and set up the capture of the counterfeit ring, which hadn't happened that night. Someone had tipped them off. The crooks were eventually caught a week later.

In Oregon.

Tasting those lips again brought everything back like it all had happened yesterday.

Coincidences didn't happen in the intelligence world. He should have paid more attention to the fact she'd been at the beach next to that cottage.

She could be one of the missing pieces he was searching for.

Perhaps *the* piece.

The sounds behind him, although muffled by the walls, still entered his ears. The laughter, the music. He weighed his options, and the chance of Lane recognizing him was too great. The outcome of this case was too great. There was a mole in the agency. An agent who was tipping off criminals, gangsters, about busts that were imminent and leaking other aspects of vital information that only few knew.

That was why he was undercover right now, pretending to be Rex Gaynor, a train robber who had been offed while in prison. Someone had snuck bootlegged whiskey into the prison. That wasn't unusual. Things, all sorts of items and contraband, were smuggled into and out of prisons on a daily basis. But Gaynor had been given widow-maker juice. The first cup of shine out of a still was a deadly concoction of pure methanol.

A dead inmate who'd been tried and convicted usually wouldn't raise awareness, but this case was different. It had been seven years since Gaynor had robbed that train, and though Gaynor had always claimed there had been someone else involved, someone he didn't know, there hadn't been any proof of that.

Back when he'd been working that case, Henry had suspected there was either a piece of information left uncovered, or, what he truly thought, was that it had been covered up. He suspected that train robbery had been the mole's first crack at leaking information, and because it had worked, the mole had continued doing so.

Henry had been assigned to investigating Gaynor's death because he'd worked on the case seven years ago. He'd had no reason to suspect another agent back then of covering up information, but because that feeling had stuck with him, he hadn't stopped looking. He'd found what he'd been looking for. A manifesto of passengers on the train, one that had supposedly been thoroughly examined seven years ago to attest that all passengers had been accounted for, and whoever had examined it back then had also covered up the truth. Henry had suspicions about who had covered that up.

All the passengers hadn't been accounted for. Another man had been on that train. Vincent Burrows, a two-bit member of a crime family from New Jersey who had bounced back and forth across the county but had never been involved in anything big enough to have the Bureau looking into him.

Until now.

Gaynor hadn't known who Burrows was seven years ago, so why would Burrows have him offed now? Someone had put Burrows up to it, and Henry was certain it had been the mole. He just wasn't sure why.

The prison had kept Gaynor's death a secret. Other than the warden and the guard who'd found Gaynor, only intelligence agents knew Gaynor was dead. Burrows might have ordered Gaynor's death, but the only way he'd know for sure if his order had been followed out, was if an intelligence agent had told him. The ploy Henry and his supervisor had established was to let the public, and others, believe that Rex Gaynor had escaped, and for Henry to pretend to be Gaynor, in order for Burrows to seek him out, whereas in reality, the true mission was to draw out and nail the mole. It was one of the three other agents working on the case, and Henry had his suspicions on which one.

Convinced tonight had not been a coincidence, he locked the door behind him.

He had more reason to believe the woman he'd danced with tonight and seen on the beach in Seattle three years ago was connected to the mole. The prison warden said a young blonde woman had visited the prison, hours before Gaynor had died.

People, the general public and those in all levels of law enforcement, often refused to believe that women were capable of doing dirty deeds. In his mind, women weren't any more righteous or just than men. Society just wished they were. He'd discovered that during one of his first major cases.

His insides grew dark at the memory.

Scarlet O'Malley had duped him. Seduced him. She'd almost gotten away with it. Almost. He'd eventually seen through her. When he'd arrested her there had been an uproar of anger toward the Bureau. Scarlet had been loved by many, because she'd read nighttime stories to children over the radio every night. Those stories had been codes for bootleggers and rumrunners to know where the blockades had been set up to thwart the efforts of law enforcement.

He still hated himself for the fact that she'd obtained, seduced, information out of him. That was a lesson learned he'd never forget. Scarlet was a lesson he'd never forget. She'd been attractive and fun, and he'd been young and stupid. Had thought he'd known everything there was to know. He'd gone to college, had become an investigation agent for the Bureau. Scarlet verified none of that had made him smart.

Because of her, he'd almost lost that job. All because she'd told him that she loved him, and he'd been foolish enough to believe her. No one had ever loved him, and he'd never loved anyone. Scarlet had proven that to him all over again. She'd only wanted what she could get out of him.

No woman would ever do that again. Fool him again. He'd be here tomorrow night, meet *Lacy*, and wouldn't hold a single qualm in using her to get to the mole. *Lacy* would soon learn that it would take more than a set of sparkling blue eyes, perfect curves, and a set of sweet lips to fool him.

Anger at himself made his jaw tighten. Those blue eyes. When she'd looked up at him, he'd almost been able to read her mind. She'd wanted to be kissed. He'd complied. This time. But wouldn't again.

Henry walked down the steps into the long tunnel that eventually ended up at an abandoned house in a neighborhood near the base of the Santa Monica Mountains.

From there, he'd walk up a long trail into the woods and up the mountainside before he'd finally arrive at the cabin that was his hiding base for this assignment.

His thoughts, his determination to solve this assignment, continued as he walked along the dark tunnel. He took pride in being a federal investigation agent. Took satisfaction in how his hard work had made his uncle, his adoptive parent, proud. This job had given him something he'd never had before.

A place where he belonged. Where he fit in.

Orphans rarely fit in anywhere.

He'd learned that at an early age.

Being adopted hadn't helped.

But the Justice Department had.

He'd finally found a place where he could be alone. That was how he liked it. Scarlet had almost ruined all that for him. That would never happen again. No one, man or woman, would ever jeopardize the oath he'd taken as a federal agent. Especially no little blue-eyed flapper.

one man or woman would ever remember that she
had a heart as a beauty yet, especially, so that their
eyes flutter.

Chapter Two

Long after she and her sisters had met in the alleyway,
ran to catch the trolley, walked through the yard of the
abandoned house on the edge of Hollywoodland, hiked
up the road, and snuck through their own backyard to
climb up the trellis and into the bathroom window, Betty's heart still fluttered.

She had truly believed she'd never see him again.
Had most certainly thought she'd never kiss him again.

But she had.

Met him and kissed him. Right there in the middle of the dance floor. It had been like before, on the
beach. Her lips, her body, had instantly reacted to his
lips touching hers and kissed him back.

Her heart began to thud.

She had broken more than one of the rules she'd set
down for her and her sisters.

Neither Patsy nor Jane had questioned her about kissing him, and she hoped like she'd never hoped for something before that they hadn't seen that happen.

If they had, she'd blame it on the dancing. She hadn't
had to think about the steps of any of the songs, just follow his lead up and down the dance floor and around

and around. The dancing might have made her dizzy, light-headed. She hadn't even realized what was happening, that they were kissing, until his lips left hers.

Yes, she had. She'd wanted him to kiss her, and when he had, she hadn't wanted it to end. But it had, and then, just like he had on the beach, he'd left. Disappeared.

It hadn't been until someone had handed her the mug that she'd spun around, expecting to see him at her side.

He hadn't been there. The piano man had been, and told her that her partner had left, but that he'd be back tomorrow night.

Tomorrow night.

Well, she wouldn't be there. She'd convince her sisters that they needed to visit a different joint. One *he* wouldn't be at.

An odd sense of disappointment formed in her chest, right behind her breastbone.

Disappointed or not, she couldn't take the chance of ever seeing him again. That, too, was against all the rules she'd set down that she and her sisters had to follow in order to continue sneaking out at night.

As the oldest, she'd always been charged with setting a good example for her younger sisters. Although she hated the strict rules they'd always had to live by, she did understand that rules were a part of life. If everyone was allowed to just go about doing what they wanted, the world would be in chaos. Therefore, she rarely broke rules and when Jane had first come up with the sneaking-out plan, she had strongly forbidden such an idea.

Which hadn't helped. Jane had snuck out anyway.

When Patsy had joined Jane the second night, and they'd both come home exuberant, Betty had known she wouldn't be able to stop them from doing so again. A part of her had been envious, and wanted to see the things they'd seen, do the things they'd done, but she'd also been concerned about the consequences that could arise.

The first few nights she'd joined her sisters in sneaking out, she'd observed, listened, and anticipated all that might possibly go wrong. She'd then taken all she'd learned, paired that with predictions, and came up with a solid set of rules that if any were broken, their night excursions would end. In order to make her sisters understand why they needed the rules, she'd pointed out things such as going blind—or, worse, death—from drinking certain beverages, as well as going to jail if a joint they were in was busted.

In the end, her sisters had agreed to follow the rules she'd set down and had.

She was the one who had broken rules tonight, and going to the Rooster's Nest again tomorrow night would break another one—because he'd said he'd be there.

Therefore, it couldn't happen.

Satisfied with her conclusion, she rolled onto her side, telling herself it was time to fall asleep. Her gaze, though, caught sight of the mug on her dressing table. The moonlight coming in through the window seemed to be shining directly on it. She'd set it there earlier, and dropped her hairpins into it.

A wave of guilt churned in her stomach. That was another rule she'd broken. If Patsy or Jane had won a mug, she would have made them leave it at the joint or discard it on the way home. She hadn't been able to do that. Instead she had clutched it to her breast all the way home, telling herself her parents would never see it because they rarely came upstairs.

Frustrated at herself, she got up and buried the mug in the bottom of a drawer.

Once back in bed she told herself to completely forget about the mug, the dance-off, and the kissing bandit, and willed herself to fall asleep.

She fell asleep but awoke with her heart pounding due to dreams where she and the bandit danced, laughed, and, of course, kissed.

That frustrated her, how her dreams had deceived her. Made her feel as if all her efforts of trying to be dutiful, of following all the rules, were for naught. She still didn't have any control over any part of her life.

She lay in bed for a moment, eyes closed, and chided herself for ever thinking that she did have any control. Not even of her future.

Last week Father had requested her presence. That was how he'd put it—her presence was requested in his office. Like their family was royalty or something. Some days it felt as if she lived in a dozen different worlds, and she got dizzy hopping back and forth between them.

There was Mother's world, where the sky was always blue, everyone spoke softly, did their chores, and pinched pennies wherever possible.

Then there was Father's world, where he was the ruler of all. He'd owned all of Hollywoodland at one time. Inherited the land from his grandfather, who had tried to farm it, but it was too hilly. Father first sold acreage to several film studios who needed space to film their movies, and that was what had given him the inspiration for Hollywoodland. An elite real estate division that only the rich could afford to live in. He had a large sign erected that could be seen from downtown and took out advertisements in the newspapers about the elite property for sale. In his world, he was a land baron—called himself that all the time—whereas in reality he was a land tyrant. He had so many rules and regulations about everything, not only the property he sold, but life, that Betty truly felt sorry for him because no one liked him. He didn't allow them to.

Which led to her world of being one of his three daughters. There was no fun in being one of William Dryer's daughters. On the outside, it appeared as if they had everything. A beautiful home, more than ample clothing, a new car, plenty of food—after all, they were rich. But what no one on the outside knew was that she and her sisters were practically held prisoners in their own home. Being the oldest, the one where his hand lay the heaviest, was so stifling there were days she dreamed of running away from it all.

She couldn't do that, though, because that would bring down Father's wrath on Jane and Patsy and she couldn't do that to them. She was the oldest; protecting them, keeping them safe, and orderly at times, was her burden to bear.

So she'd set down her own rules in order to make her life more bearable. One of those rules was to accept what was and to not dream about what would be better because that only led to disappointment.

Although they were the daughters of one of the richest men in the county, she and her sisters had already had plenty of disappointments. They had the clothes, closetfuls, but they were demure housedresses, suitable for shopping and attending church. The ones they wore for their nightlife were homemade from material they'd secretly purchased while on their weekly shopping trips with Mother and hidden in the backs of their closets. Coming out only at night, after her parents were asleep.

Dressed as flappers, in fashionable short skirts, wearing makeup and strings of pearls—which also had secretly been purchased—they'd climb down the trellis and hightail it to the nearest speakeasy to laugh and dance the night away.

They were all aware that their nights out wouldn't last forever. They couldn't. And last week had proven that. When Father had requested her presence in his office, it had been to inform her that she would be marrying James Bauer before the end of the year, which was only five months away.

Her sisters knew about that meeting and despised the idea of being married to a man of Father's choosing.

They also knew they couldn't defy him. None of them could. Especially her. She had to set a good example.

She climbed out of bed, and dressed, checking her reflection in the tall mirror carefully to make sure there were no traces of mascara or lipstick on her face from last night.

Then, wearing the somber, controlled expression that she'd mastered years before, she left her room. She'd mastered her decorum as a child, having discovered her place, her role, as the oldest to be a serious, studious one. That had been her role all through school and beyond, having graduated five years ago, and it would continue to be. Even though she loved her nights out with her sisters, she knew that was only playacting, like she used to do when she was a child, pretending Patsy and Jane were her children instead of her sisters. Someday it would all come to an end. She would miss it, but she would accept it. That was life.

It was baking day, which meant they were all in the kitchen, along with Mother for the majority of the day. Staying busy helped, but her mind kept drifting off, to last night, the dance-off, and...to him.

Despite her best efforts, her determination of not going to the Rooster's Nest again tonight dwindled. She couldn't help but think about seeing him again. Find out more about him. When Patsy secretly announced that would be their destination, Betty didn't disagree.

Instead, as soon as the baking was completed, and the kitchen was in order, she slipped upstairs to press the dress she'd wear tonight. A royal blue one, trimmed with white piping. She also plumped the white floppy-brimmed hat, fluffed out the white feather boa, and shined her white shoes.

She would find out more about him, simply because that would make not seeing him again easier. Just like she'd found out more information about the speakeasies, and alcohol. Knowing more about him, she'd have a reason as to why the Rooster's Nest should be taken off the list of places they could visit.

Supper was as somber as ever. That was how Father liked it. Silent. No one spoke unless spoken to. Not even Mother. She was a beautiful and kind woman, and a dutiful wife. She not only followed every rule Father set down, she reinforced them.

Betty had once asked her mother about that, about being a dutiful wife. Mother claimed that Father had provided her with far more than she'd ever dreamed of having and that she couldn't possibly be happier.

Once the meal was complete, she and her sisters cleaned the dining room and kitchen, and as soon as the last dish was done they bade their parents good-night. Adults or not, they were expected to be in their upstairs bedrooms by seven thirty every night.

Father and Mother were in their bedroom by eight. Downstairs. Which played into her and her sisters being able to sneak out at night. As did the large fan Father used to keep his bedroom cool throughout the night.

As soon as they were upstairs, she and her sisters entered their bedrooms, to change their clothes, apply makeup, and prepare to sneak out by eight thirty.

Betty found herself more excited than usual. Her heart was thudding and she had to keep taking deep breaths to settle her trembling hands enough to apply mascara and lipstick.

She finally dropped the lipstick in her pocket and took a long look at herself in the mirror as she draped the white feather boa around her shoulders and flipped one end around her neck. The blue dress was one of her favorites. Blue, all shades, was her favorite color. That may be part of the reason she'd never forgotten the bandit's blue eyes.

Concluding tonight would be the last night she'd ever have to think about those eyes, she clicked off the light and quietly opened her door.

Patsy was already in the bathroom, and Jane entered the hallway a second after Betty had shut her bedroom door.

Betty gave Patsy a nod as soon as they were all three in the bathroom, with the door locked. Her youngest sister silently stepped up on the stool, slipped out the window and disappeared.

Jane went next, just as quietly, and then Betty. She slipped out the window and quickly climbed down the ivy-covered trellis that went from the second floor to the ground.

As always, she gave both of her sisters a quick once-over, to make sure that they were dressed appropriately, including that their blond hair was completely hidden beneath their stylish hats, before giving a nod of approval. Then, excitedly, they all three scurried across the backyard, and through the line of trees that grew alongside the road. Patsy and Jane chatted quietly as they walked down the hill to the abandoned house.

Betty listened, and nodded now and again, but for the most part, she kept an eye out for headlights, so she could instruct all of them to jump into the trees.

There was no traffic tonight, and soon they were crossing through the yard of the boarded-up house that had once been owned by a mob boss, but had been confiscated in a raid and was now owned by the government. Father had tried to buy the house several times, even protested against it being abandoned at city hall meetings, which had gained him more enemies.

The red line of the city's electric streetcar system stopped at the corner across the street from the lot the house sat upon. She and her sisters arrived just as the trolley rang its bell, signaling its approach.

There was no talking now, not to each other, or anyone else. That was another one of the rules she'd set down. No one could know they were sisters. There were people who knew Father had three daughters and they had to be careful to not be recognized.

Several blocks later, they stepped off the trolley, one at a time, and in single file, as if they didn't know each other; they walked down the block to the Laundromat. The door led to an entranceway that had another door that led down a set of steps where they had to knock and give the password.

The Rooster's Nest was busy again tonight, and Betty scanned the area, looking for a flat brown hat, black hair, and blue eyes. He wasn't at the table in the corner, nor sitting at one of the many stools along the bar.

She moved slowly, searching the people sitting at

tables and those on the dance floor. Not one of them was him. A sickening feeling formed in her stomach by the time she'd made a complete round of the room, including the narrow hallway that led down to the powder rooms.

There was no reason for her to be sick over not seeing him, or even disappointed. She hadn't wanted to see him. Not ever again.

She sat down at the nearest empty table, the one that was behind the piano player. That just so happened to be same one he'd been sitting at last night. She'd sat at this table because it was handy and not because she could see if he walked through the door.

Actually, if he did walk through the door, which she could clearly see from where she sat, she would move. Find someone to dance with so she wouldn't have to talk to him. That was what she was here for. To dance. Have fun.

Thinking that was exactly what she was going to do, she stood, and jolted slightly as someone laid a hand on her shoulder. Twisting, her heart somersaulted and started pounding at the set of unique blue eyes.

"I was beginning to think you wouldn't be here tonight," he said.

Willing her heart to slow down, she said, "It was a last-minute decision."

"Why?"

How? was the question in her mind, specifically how he'd suddenly appeared at the table. She'd searched the entire joint for him. It wasn't that large of a place, and there had been no sign of him anywhere. She'd been facing the door since she'd sat down and he had not walked through it. There was another door, behind the bar, but it led into a narrow alleyway and only deliverymen used it. Murray, the bartender, kept it locked.

Too curious not to, she asked, "How did you get in here?"

"A door."

She shook her head. "I was watching the door."

"I said a door, not the door." He grasped the back of her chair. "Would you care for a drink?"

"What do you mean 'a door'? The only other door in this joint is behind the bar and it's locked."

He lifted a brow. "You seem to know a lot about this place."

"I made it my business to."

"Why?"

"I have my reasons." She was trying her best to act aloof, because that was what he seemed to be. Aloof and mysterious with how he'd suddenly appeared.

"I know."

A shiver rippled down her spine. "You know what?"

"About you."

Her insides shrank and so did she, but she managed to land in the chair as her knees gave out. All she could hope was that he hadn't yet told her father. That had to be what he meant. There was nothing else to know.

"I'd like to talk to you about that," he said while lowering himself onto the adjacent chair.

Her sisters were going to be so upset. So very, very upset. Betty closed her eyes and swallowed the lump in her throat. "What about it?"

He glanced around the room, then leaned closer. "Perhaps we can make a deal."

It was over. Her father was going to be so angry. Her mother so disappointed. Her sisters so mad. Betty glanced past him, at Jane on the dance floor and Patsy sitting at a table talking to Lane Cox.

Sorrow filled her insides. This, going out at night, was the only fun they'd ever had, and they'd deserved to have that fun. She had, too, and she hated that it was all about to end.

"We need to find a quiet place to talk," he said.

She glanced up as he stood. The music had started up again and the crowd was lively and loud. There wouldn't be a quiet place anywhere in the room. She shook her head and shrugged.

"I know of a place." He held out his hand. "It will be of your benefit to hear me out."

Nothing had ever been to her benefit, but if it would benefit her sisters, she would listen to what he had to say. She was responsible for them, right down to their happiness.

Henry wasn't surprised she followed without question. He'd seen her expression when he'd said he knew about her. Besides the way she'd gone white and sank into the chair, her eyes had been as big and round as silver dollars. A sure sign she knew she'd been found out.

He'd felt bad for a moment, at shocking her, but he wanted answers and she had them. Nothing was going to stand in his way to get them. The tunnel was his only option for a place to question her with Lane Cox sitting at a table near the door. Lane had been there most of the night, and that had Henry wondering if Lane was looking for him. Lane was a good guy, but he couldn't tell him anything; there was too much at stake.

Making sure that no one saw them, Henry led her behind the gold brocade curtain that went from floor to ceiling next to the wall, and into the storage room. The two lightbulbs hanging down from the ceiling shone on the shelves and crates full of bottles containing various forms of alcohol from wine to gin and whiskey.

She tugged on his hand, whispering, "We can't talk in here."

He understood her apprehension but wasn't going to let that stop him. "We aren't—we are just passing through."

"Passing through to where?"

"A quiet place to talk." Still holding her hand, he led her through the long room, then pulled the shelf away from the wall. As he opened the door in the wall and stepped through it, he said, "It's safe. I promise. Just dark, but I have a light."

She shook her head.

"You're used to sneaking around."

Her lips pursed but she didn't budge, until a thud sounded behind her.

Knowing someone was entering the storage room, he quickly pulled her forward, through the door and onto the top step of the short set of stairs leading to the tunnel. He pulled the shelf back in place and the door shut just as the door to the storeroom flung open.

The area was instantly dark. He released her hand and pulled out his flashlight and clicked it on, shone the beam upward, lighting up his and her faces as he held a finger to his lips.

Trepidation was in her eyes, on her face. He took ahold of her hand and gave it a gentle squeeze, hoping that eased her fears. Hurting her physically was not in his plan, but he understood she didn't know that.

A moment later, he heard the thud of the storage room door closing, and knew whoever had entered it had left it. He released the breath he'd been holding and handed her the flashlight.

"Hold this, please."

She took the light and held it as he removed his jacket, stepped down the stairs, and tossed his jacket over the top two steps.

"There," he said. "You can sit on that so you don't get your dress dirty."

"Sit on it why?" she asked.

He sat down. "So we can talk."

"Where do these steps go?" she asked, holding the flashlight so the light shone down the long tunnel with wood-planked walls and a ceiling.

"It's a tunnel." There was no risk in telling her the truth. In fact, he was going to tell her plenty, and expected her to be just as truthful. "It goes for several blocks, through basements and under streets until it comes out at a house near the Santa Monica Mountains."

"What house?"

"Just a house."

She was still standing and shining the flashlight down the tunnel.

"No one knows about it but me."

"Why?" She shone the light on him. "Why are you the only one to know about it?"

"Because I work for the government—the government owns the house." Just like he'd been a ward of the government. The day he'd been adopted, he'd thought that would end for him. It had in some ways, but not in others. He'd been fifteen when John and Esther Randall had adopted him from the orphanage. A shocking event because no one wanted older children. The headmistress had tried to convince them otherwise, stating a younger child would be much more suitable, but the Randalls had insisted he was who they wanted.

He had soon discovered why. John Randall had needed an experiment, and due to his academic grades during his time at the orphanage, he'd been exactly what John Randall had been looking for. Instrumental in starting a newly formed junior college in Virginia, John had wanted proof that this new opportunity at higher education was exactly what the majority of the youth in America needed. What better proof than a son?

So Henry had gone from living behind the walls of an orphanage to living behind the walls of a college. In truth, there wasn't much difference.

Then he'd gotten a job for the government. In the Department of Justice, as an intelligence agent. For him, the circle of life, all included the government.

"The government?" She shone the light back down the tunnel. "I know that house."

"You do?" He hadn't expected that, but should have. Being an agent, the mole could know about the tunnel and the house and could have told her.

"Yes. It's abandoned. The windows are boarded up."

He patted the jacket he'd laid over the steps. "Sit down so we can talk."

She was still uneasy, but sat and scooted close to the wall.

"The original owner of the house, a mob boss, had it built so he had an escape route if his business was raided." He shifted slightly, leaned a shoulder against the wall behind him as he continued, "He owned this joint at the time. It wasn't the Rooster's Nest then, and this tunnel is exactly how he was busted. Prohibition agents discovered it and raided his house and business at the same time."

"How did they discover it?"

He kept his eyes on her, watching for her reaction, as he said, "An insider."

Her face scrunched up as she frowned. "What's that?"

A tiny tingle raced over his shoulders. She either truly didn't know or was a very good actress. "An insider?"

"Yes."

"Someone who is privy to information and, at times, provides it to someone else who shouldn't have it," he explained, watching for her reaction.

"Oh." She bowed her head and huffed out a breath. "Is that how you learned about me and my sisters? An insider?"

Sisters? He leaned the back of his head against the wall and let that sink in. Sisters… The woman she'd met on the road to the beach? "Were your sisters in Seattle with you?"

She still hadn't looked up. "No, it was just Mother and I." Shaking her head, she let out a very sad-sounding sigh. "When I came home, I promised my sisters I'd never leave them again."

Mother? How many other people were involved in this? Or was that why she was involved, to protect her family from the mole? "Why?"

There were tears welling in the bottoms of her eyes as she looked at him. "Because of our father and his strict rules. He keeps all three of us locked up like Rapunzels. That's why we sneak out at night and come here." She shook her head and closed her eyes. "I was so careful to make sure that no one knew. That no one recognized us."

He still wasn't sure if she was acting, or if she totally thought she'd been caught. Not in sneaking out. That had to be an excuse. Had to be. "How old are you and your sisters?"

"Twenty-two, twenty-one, and nineteen." She huffed out a long, frustrated-sounding breath. "Plenty old enough to go out, but to hear our father talk, you'd think we are still two, four and five."

"Which one are you? Oldest? Youngest?"

"The oldest, Betty. Jane is next and Patsy is the youngest." She sighed again. "Despite what people might think, being one of William Dryer's daughters is not much fun at all."

William Dryer? Henry had only been in town a couple of days, but already had learned more about William Dryer than he cared to know. The old cabin he was staying in was on Dryer's land, but that chunk of land was too hilly to develop, so his supervisor, a man he'd worked under for years, LeRoy Black, was convinced he wouldn't be discovered, not even by the other agents working on this case.

During his briefing, LeRoy had mentioned that Dryer had daughters. Three of them. But from what LeRoy had said, they were little girls. Children. Not women. Did she know that, and was pretending to be one of Dryer's daughters? If so, why? Was she hoping to learn if he knew who the mole was or, more precisely, whom he thought it was?

Normally, he had an easy time reading people and his gut said to believe her, but the fact she'd been in Seattle, where the counterfeiting ring had gotten a tip that they were about to be busted, and here, where Burrows was now setting up a bootlegging operation after having Gaynor offed, his mind said that was just too much of a coincidence. She had to be working with the mole.

The very person he was here to stop, and anyone who might also be involved.

He just had to figure out how best to use her to get to the mole. Flat out asking, demanding she tell him all she knew, could send her straight to the mole. However, a little finesse, get her to leak enough that he could point out the danger of her being arrested for her participation, could make her flip sides. Then he'd have a direct line to the mole, learn the motivation, and gather enough proof to send the mole up the river for the rest of his life.

Finesse, especially when it came to a woman, wasn't his specialty. He'd avoided women after the Scarlet incident, as much as possible, and it goaded him that he didn't have a backup partner to turn her over to. Normally he did, but this case was too risky to bring in anyone else except for him and his direct supervisor.

"Who told you?" she asked again.

He leaned forward, rested both hands on his knees. He was at an impasse of sorts on whether to use the mole's name or not, and whether he should say he was Henry or Rex and see her reaction. If she knew Rex Gaynor was dead, then she was a part of things for sure.

"I guess who doesn't matter," she whispered. "It's what happens now that does."

Henry mulled on the what-happens-next portion of her statement for a moment. LeRoy, who had been a Texas Ranger before going to work for the department, oversaw the operations from the Mississippi River west, and was as thorough as he was stern; he was one hell of a supervisor, and rarely, if ever, wrong.

Yet, LeRoy's information about the Dryer children being young and Henry's own gut instincts weren't matching up.

Because his gut wasn't the only thing sending out signals. She was pretty.

Very pretty.

His body had been reacting to her closeness since he'd sat down at the table beside her. Her perfume was light, but heady. Intoxicating far more than any whiskey he'd ever consumed, making him believe parts of what she was saying were true.

He'd been fooled by a pretty face before, and had sworn that would never happen again, and it wouldn't.

She could bat those long lashes all she wanted. It wasn't going to affect him. The mole could have already told her who he was, so it didn't matter. "My name is Henry, Henry Randall. I'm an intelligence officer, for the Department of Justice, looking for an escaped convict."

Her head snapped up. "Rex Gaynor?"

Chapter Three

"You've heard of him?" Henry asked. Her reaction had been immediate. As soon as he'd said *escaped convict.* "Rex Gaynor?"

"There was an article about him in the newspaper, that he'd escaped from prison. I didn't read the article, but my sister Patsy did." She pressed a hand to her chest. "Oh, dear. Is he near? Here? Patsy said the newspaper said to keep all doors locked." She jumped to her feet. "I have to go. I have to find my sisters and tell them. I—I have to get them home, now!"

Henry took ahold of her wrist, felt how fast her pulse raced. "No. He's not here. You aren't in any danger from Rex Gaynor. Neither are your sisters."

"How do you know? You just said you are looking for him."

Lying could make a person's pulse race, but it usually didn't make a person tremble the way she was trembling. He stood, and though it was unlike him, he laid his other hand on her upper arm. "You're safe, Betty."

"Why should I believe you?"

There was no more reason for her to believe him than there was for him to believe her. If he wanted to find out if she was being truthful, he was going to have to gain her trust. Not so unlike Scarlet had convinced him he could trust her. Maybe he had learned more from Scarlet than a lesson. She'd been an expert at seduction. "Rex Gaynor has already been captured, but he had a partner in that train robbery—that's who I'm looking for now."

Her dark blue eyes widened. "There were two escaped convicts?"

He rubbed her arm softly. "No. The one I'm looking for was never arrested."

"But he's here? That's why you are here." She gasped. "Oh, dear."

She was trembling so hard the white boa around her neck was shaking. He rubbed her upper arm again. "Yes, he's here, in Los Angeles, and that's why I'm here, but you are not in danger. Neither are your sisters." If there truly were any sisters. He still wasn't convinced she was telling him the truth. He wasn't convinced she was lying, either, and that bothered him.

"Is that how you found out about us?" she asked. "Because Patsy was trying to get information about Rex Gaynor?"

"Patsy, your sister?"

"Yes."

"Why is she trying to get information on him?"

"Because she wants to write an article about him." She shook her head. "She wants to be a reporter so badly she even convinced Father to let her attend secretarial school so she could learn to type."

Henry nodded, mainly because he was taking this all in, and trying to figure out his next steps. Ultimately, he needed more information.

"Are you going to tell our father?"

"No," Henry said.

The relief in her eyes did something to his insides, but he ignored it. He wasn't going to fall for anything.

"Why not?" she asked.

"Because…" He contemplated a reason. A believable one. "Because I need your help."

"My help?" A hint of a smile touched her lips as she shook her head, then shrugged. "How? What could I do?"

He had no idea, but would come up with something. That little hint of a smile was enough for him to know this was a case of keep your enemies close—even potential ones. "First I have to know if you're willing to help me."

Her eyes scanned him, up and down, and up again, to his face, as she remained silent. It made his skin tingle, his blood warm, but he kept his gaze on her. Somehow. It was harder than holding eye contact with a criminal holding a gun on him. That had happened before, more than once—a criminal with a gun. He'd handled it, and could handle her, too. Even if she had the bluest eyes he'd ever seen. Even in the muted light from the flashlight, they were striking.

She blinked, nodded. "I am willing, but I would need to know exactly what help you would need."

He held silent, giving himself a moment. That moment turned into a minute, and he still hadn't come up with an answer. She was very pretty. And likable. And kissable. Dang it! What was it about her that…that affected him in ways he shouldn't be affected?

"I'll tell you tomorrow," he said, taking a step back and releasing his hold on her wrist and dropping his hand away from her arm.

"Tomorrow?"

Unlike many of the other women he'd met over years, there was an innocence to her. She might dress like a flapper and dance like a flapper, but that too was something he questioned.

She was different from most of the dames he'd met in joints like this. Her outfit—the blue dress, white feather boa, and white hat—was fetching, fashionable, but it was her face that he couldn't stop staring at. Heart shaped, with a perfect little chin, big blue eyes and rosy lips, she was more than pretty. She was adorable, and made him want to shield her in a way he'd never quite experienced. That baffled him.

"Yes, tomorrow," he said. "You came here tonight to dance."

She looked at him from beneath those long lashes, almost as if slightly embarrassed.

Damn, he wished he knew if she was faking that, too. Either way, he was going to use it to get what he wanted.

He brushed a knuckle along her chin. "To dance, not sit in a dark hallway."

She blinked and pinched her lips together. "It—it's not so bad, and I—I have a flashlight."

Was she testing him? Playing demure? He'd find out. "Listen," he said. "Do you hear that?" It was muffled, but the song the piano man was playing filtered into the tunnel.

She nodded.

He took the flashlight from her hand and laid it on the top step, so it shone light on them. "I need to remain hidden, but I'd be honored if you'd dance with me."

"Here?"

He stepped down the two stairs. "Yes, here."

Biting her bottom lip, she nodded and stepped down beside him.

His heart thudded, only because he knew this was the route he needed to take. What he needed to do in order to convince her she could trust him. "There's not a lot of room," he said, while looping an arm around her waist and resting his hand on her back. "But we don't need a lot of room, do we?"

"No." Her answer was barely a whisper.

He grasped her hand and stepped closer. Every part of his body rose to full awareness, like it had last night, while dancing with her. Like it had three years ago, on the beach, while kissing her. His mind, however, knew this was all in the line of duty.

The beam of the flashlight barely reached beyond them, into the tunnel, and he carefully led her around the small area between the tunnel walls. The faraway tune was faster than what they were dancing, but she didn't seem to mind.

The curve of her waist beneath his fingers made his hand tingle, imagining the skin beneath was as smooth as the silk of her blue dress.

Her eyes never left his, and that put him in some sort of trance. His body, his mind, were focused only on her. The dance seemed to stretch time, and when the music finally ended, their feet stopped, they were chest to chest, eyes locked. He saw the want in her eyes again, and despite all he knew about himself, that same want filled him. It shouldn't. But it did.

By mutual agreement, with full understanding, their faces merged and they engaged in a kiss that was as natural and slow as the sun rising in the morning.

Her lips were so warm, so soft and sweet, he couldn't get enough of them. The desires racing inside him coaxed him to use his tongue to part her lips and slip inside her mouth. His pulse pounded at the heat, the sweetness of her tongue dancing with his.

The kiss would have lasted a lot longer, he was sure of it, if a crash in the storage room hadn't rattled the door. He pulled his mouth away from hers and instantly pressed her up against the tunnel wall.

A plethora of cursing filtered through the closed door, and several of his own silently crossed his mind as she pressed her face into his shirt. He kept his arms around her until the thuds and muttered cursing ended, and then took a step back.

"Are we going to be able to sneak back out that way?" she asked.

"Yes, the bartender must have been collecting more booze." That was why he hadn't seen her walk in the tavern earlier. He'd been watching from behind the curtain, because he'd already spied Lane. Upon seeing the bartender round the bar, he'd hurried into the room and then into the tunnel. When the coast had been clear for him to return to the curtain, she'd been sitting at the table.

Mirth shimmered in her eyes. "I think he broke a bottle or two."

"Sounded like it," he agreed.

She sighed, and then laid a hand on his chest, right over his heart. "You really won't tell my father?"

Reality, of what he was doing and why, returned. "No, I'll uphold my end of the bargain as long as you uphold yours."

"I will."

"No one else can know."

"They won't." She let out a sigh. "What time do you think it is?"

He moved to the steps and picked up the flashlight.

As soon as the light hit his wrist, she gasped. "That can't be right."

He read the time. "Yes, it's eleven fifty-five."

"It can't be. I was supposed to meet my sisters ten minutes ago."

The urgency in her voice was as real. He grasped her arm. "Where?"

"Between two buildings up the street." She rushed up the steps. "I have to go, Henry. Now."

He stepped up beside her. "All right. Stay there, let me check." He clicked off the flashlight and tucked it in his pocket before opening the door a crack and peeking through the bottle-lined shelf to make sure the storeroom was empty.

The area was free of anyone else, and he pulled the door all the way open and then pushed the shelf aside. "Come on. I'll walk you to the alley."

"No!" She slapped a hand over her mouth. "Sorry," she whispered as she stepped into the room. "I have to go alone. They can't know about you."

"I won't let them see me." He pushed the shelf back in place and took her hand. "I'll just make sure you meet up with them."

"I'll meet up with them just fine."

Holding her hand, he walked to the door and opened it, peeked out. "What if they've already left?"

"They won't leave without me."

He stepped out the door and pulled it closed behind her. "I want to make sure."

"There's no need." She flashed him a hint of a smile. "I'll see you tomorrow night. Same time."

He released her hand. "I'll be here."

She peeked around the edge of curtain, then shot out around it.

He waited a couple of seconds, and then walked out. No one was looking his way. They were all too busy dancing and drinking, smoking and laughing. He watched as Betty skirted around the floor and then scurried toward the door, her white boa flipping in her wake.

Slowly, to not draw any attention, he followed her. As he rounded the corner and pulled open the door, all he saw were the heels of her shoes as she ran up the steps and out the other door.

He took the steps two at a time and hurried out the two sets of doors and onto the street.

Once again, he barely got a glimpse of her running along the sidewalk before she shot into the space between two buildings.

Staying in the shadows, he walked to the spot where she'd slipped between the buildings and eased around the edge to peer into the narrow space. Three women were hurrying toward the alley on the other end.

He followed them along six city blocks, and then past two film studios before they entered the lawn of a house he knew well. The mob house where the tunnel ended.

Keeping well in the shadows, he watched as they continued walking.

They crossed the lawn near the far edge, where a row of trees marked the property line, then down through the ditch and up on the gravel road that led into Hollywoodland.

Here, like they had while walking along the buildings and the trees, they walked near the edge of the road, so they could slip into the ditch and the trees if a car came along.

They turned off the road after walking up the hill. He followed, staying in the trees, ducking around branches, and walking on the balls of his feet so he wouldn't make a sound.

There had barely been a snap or click of heel from them, either. They were good at this. Used to it.

From the trees, he watched as they made their way across the backyard of a large brick home. He then held his breath at the sight that played out. One after the other, they shimmied up an ivy-covered trellis and into a window.

Betty was the last one up the trellis, and he waited, watching as lights turned on in three of the windows on the second floor. The last light had been in the room on the far right. That had to be her room.

He stood there for a long time, questioning all sorts of things. Besides her, he'd recognized one of the other women with her as one who had danced with Vincent Burrows last night, before the dance-off, before he'd noticed Lane Cox at the speakeasy.

Burrows had been at the bar, talking to the bartender, and Henry had walked past him, hoping to be noticed. LeRoy had been convinced their plan would work because Henry's and Gaynor's builds and black hair had been similar enough for someone who hadn't known Gaynor that well to believe Henry was him. Burrows hadn't noticed, though, because he'd been talking to a little blonde.

Burrows had left after that dance, and that was when he'd noticed Betty sitting at the bar. He'd seen her dancing before then and recognized an uncanny likeness to the sea nymph from Seattle, but it hadn't been until she'd approached him that he'd known it was her for sure.

What he still wasn't sure about was what to do about it. The lights clicked off in the house and he turned, walked back down the hill, along the road, and then to the house. As he'd known, the front door was locked. The back one, along with all the windows, was boarded up.

Returning to the front door, he pulled out his pocketknife and used it to pick the lock. The jacket he'd left on the stairs was of little concern, except that the keys for the house were in one of its pockets. The door to the storage room was unlocked, and that was a concern, so he made his way through the house, down to the basement, and into the tunnel that would lead back to the Rooster's Nest. The entire way, his thoughts were on Betty, and the other woman, and just how deeply involved they were in all this.

Betty lay in bed that night, trying to make sense of all that had happened. She'd broken so many rules she couldn't even count them. That wasn't like her. She'd not only snuck into a dark tunnel, alone with him, she'd danced there, and kissed him again.

Kissed him in ways she'd never imagined. Her heart was still thudding over that. It was all for her sisters, to make sure their father didn't find out about them sneaking out.

Except, she was having a hard time believing that. If it had been another man, other than Henry... Henry Randall. He was so handsome, just looking at him made her heart throb, and he was so mysterious, an odd sense of excitement filled her.

She rolled onto her side. What could she do to help him? She didn't know anything about Rex Gaynor or the other man he mentioned. Didn't know anything about anything, but she had to help him. Had to do anything she could to keep her father from finding out about their nightly escapes.

The thing she could not do again was kiss Henry.

Or dance with him. That made her forget everything, and the next thing she knew, they were kissing. That had happened twice now, and could not happen again. She would have to keep her wits about her at all times.

No more sneaking into the storage room and into that tunnel, either.

That had been thrilling, too, sneaking away, hiding.

Everything about him was thrilling, and that filled her with the most unique sensations.

She flipped onto her back, disgusted with herself. She was the oldest. The responsible and sensible one. The one to set a good example. If that had been Patsy or Jane, she wouldn't allow them to go back out, not until they'd learned their lesson.

Patsy or Jane couldn't find out about how she'd done that. Not ever.

No one could.

She was going to have to make sure her sisters were being extra careful, too, without them knowing about Henry. Or what he knew. She had to find out how he'd discovered who they were, and make sure that didn't happen again, too.

It was going to be hard to not tell Patsy what she'd learned about Rex Gaynor. Patsy was nearly obsessed with the story, convinced that becoming a reporter was her ticket out of their father's house.

Betty didn't want to shatter her sister's dream, so she never said much about it to Patsy, but deep down, she knew Father would never allow one of his daughters to get away that easy. Marriage was the only way he'd let any of them out of the house. Marriage to a rich man.

He wanted his daughters to marry men with money. Lots of it. So they would no longer want his. He cared more about his money than he did any of them.

But she didn't care about his money at all. It was how he thought that money was the most important aspect when it came to any of his daughters getting married. That their happiness meant nothing.

Father was sitting at the dining room table, reading the morning paper and waiting for breakfast to be served, when Betty entered the room the following morning. She wished him a good morning while making her way into the kitchen.

Patsy and Jane were already there, collecting items to carry into the dining room to set the table. Betty crossed the room and lifted out three serving platters for the sausage, eggs, and potatoes that Mother was cooking.

Other than the obligatory good-mornings to each other, there was no talking while breakfast was cooked, served, and eaten. Father's rules again.

As she sat there, hearing only the occasional clink of silverware against a plate, she once again thought how her house would be nothing like this. When she was married and had her own home, it wouldn't be silent. She'd encourage conversations and laughter at every meal because that was what she wanted most in her life, laughter, happiness. For everyone to be happy. That was all she'd ever wanted, which was the only reason she had agreed to help Henry. Not because she liked him.

Later that night, her sister Patsy was very happy that Betty and Jane were entering the Rooster's Nest without her. Lane had met Patsy near the street corner where the trolley had stopped to let them off. Betty had serious concerns about that and that Lane was taking Patsy to a party downtown, but she herself had broken so many rules that ultimately, she had to let Patsy go with Lane.

There were times when Betty wished that she wasn't the oldest. That she could be more carefree when it came to breaking rules.

Her stomach hiccupped with excitement, and she knew why. Whether she was breaking a rule or not, the idea of seeing Henry again was exciting.

Following Jane down the steps of the tavern, Betty ran her hands over the skirt of the cream-colored sleeveless dress she'd chosen to wear, making sure that no wrinkles had formed during the streetcar ride. The dress had an overlay of light pink lace and long silky fringes of the same color along the hem. She'd also chosen to wear a black hat and black shoes and a set of black pearls.

A moment later, her heart skipped a beat when her gaze settled on a table behind the piano player. Henry was there, saw her, and gave a slight nod in recognition. She bit her lip, knowing she shouldn't be so happy to see him, yet truly couldn't help it. Everything about him was thrilling, from his looks, to him being an intelligence agent, searching for a criminal, to asking her to help him.

It shouldn't be. She should be frightened to death, knowing he knew about her and her sisters, but she wasn't, and that was as odd for her as breaking rules. It was almost as if there was something about him that made her want to break rules. Made her want to be someone she'd never been before. Even while sneaking out, she hadn't been as boisterous and outgoing as her sisters. She had danced and had fun, but she'd also spent a lot of time watching, mainly her sisters, making sure they weren't breaking rules that would get them in trouble. Like dancing with the same man too often, or sneaking outside with one, or drinking too many glasses of wine.

At least that was one rule she hadn't broken.

"Hello," Henry said, holding out a chair for her as she arrived at the table.

"Hello," she replied, breathing through how fast her heart thudded.

He sat down and slid a glass in front of her. "I ordered you a glass of wine."

A lump the size of an orange formed in her throat. She couldn't even say thank-you.

He picked up a glass in front of him and held it out to her.

She picked up hers and flinched slightly as their glasses clinked, because she'd probably break yet another rule tonight.

She did.

She'd barely been there five minutes when she was already on her second glass of wine. He asked her where her third sister was, and when she said Patsy hadn't joined them tonight, he said he'd seen all three of them leave the house.

She finished her glass of wine, and watched as he refilled the glass before she had the nerve to ask how he'd watched them.

"From the abandoned house," he said.

She'd tried not to look at that house as they'd crossed the lawn tonight, but had, and had been thinking about how that tunnel they'd been in last night went all the way to that house. She took a sip of her third glass of wine, before saying, "Patsy is with a friend of hers. I gave her permission."

He lifted a brow. "You gave her permission?"

"Yes, I'm the oldest, so I'm responsible for them." When it came to her sisters, she was not only responsible, she was willing to do whatever it took to keep them safe. That gave her the courage to lift her chin. Meet his gaze. "Which is why I am here, Mr. Randall. To hear how I can help you, so that you don't tell my father about them sneaking out."

"What about you?" he asked. "You are sneaking out, too."

"I can face the consequences—they can't." Her time of sneaking out was almost over. She only had a few months before marrying James. That was not something she liked to think about, nor did she like to think about what that would mean for her sisters.

He twirled his glass around on the table, as he looked at her and nodded. "Henry," he then said.

"Henry?" She knew his name.

"Yes. You called me Mr. Randall. I'd prefer you call me Henry."

"Oh, all right, Henry." She'd merely called him Mr. Randall in order to remind herself of the reason she was here. To help him in order for her sisters to continue experiencing a small amount of freedom. "Have you determined how I can help you?"

"I have." He glanced toward the bar. "I believe the person I'm looking for has started a bootlegging business and I need to be cautious as to who I question, in case someone recognizes me. I'm curious to know about the whiskey the Rooster's Nest serves." He lifted up his glass. "It appears to be a premium one."

A bit of relief filled her. "It is. It's Minnesota Thirteen. That's part of the reason this place has so many dockworkers as customers. They know where the good stuff is delivered to." She'd learned plenty during her first few weeks of sneaking out. "Murray gets deliveries every Sunday and Wednesday afternoon." She tilted her head slightly, toward the bar. "Murray also arranges deliveries for parties and special occasions."

"How do you know all that?"

She shrugged. "Listening. There was a man in here the other night, saying his whiskey was as good as Minnesota Thirteen, but Murray told him no, that he wasn't interested."

"You heard that?"

"Yes." She bit her tongue from adding that the man hadn't been happy or that her sister Patsy had danced with the man. She would help him, but she would protect her sisters at the same time.

Chapter Four

Could he be wrong about her? Henry wasn't quite ready to believe that. Nor was he ready to believe just how attracted he was to her. In more ways than just her looks. Her beauty took his breath away, but it was her, all of her, that made his pulse pound so hard it echoed in his ears. Something about her had the ability to turn everything that had been hard and cold inside him for years warm and soft. He didn't like it, had no idea what to do about it, either. This wasn't an ordinary assignment. None of the cases he worked on were ordinary, but this one needed his full attention; there were so many bits and pieces that didn't fit together.

Just like there were pieces of her that didn't seem to fit together.

She seemed so young and innocent, but mention her sisters and she was like a mother bear protecting her cubs. Or was she using that to protect herself? Protect the mole?

What she'd said about Murray and Minnesota Thirteen was true, and Vincent Burrows had tried to convince Murray to peddle his bootlegged whiskey, right before he'd danced with Betty's sister.

Coincidence again?

Couldn't be.

"I can give you a list of other joints that only serve Minnesota Thirteen," she said. "As well as those that don't."

Her smile, the way she blinked those eyes, heated up parts of him as if he was standing on a beach, soaking up every single ray the sun shone down upon the earth. He shifted in his seat, to ease the tightening of his body. The desire that kicked in every time he recalled kissing her had his heart beating faster and his adrenaline pumping harder than when he was about to make a bust.

He'd never experienced anything like this. Like her. And was having a hell of a time sorting out what to do about it. He'd considered not coming here to meet her tonight, but the idea of not seeing her played havoc on him. As much as he hated to admit it, he wanted to see her.

The piano player sat down, struck the keys, and instantly filled the room with a fast-beat ragtime tune, making sitting at the table too loud to talk. "Would you care to dance?"

She glanced over her shoulder, then looked at him, and shook her head. "We are here to talk, not dance."

The other sister was standing next to the piano, tapping her foot. He wondered if she was the reason Betty didn't want to dance. That, too, was curious. Was the other sister trying to hear what was said so she could report to someone?

He scanned the room, but just because he didn't recognize anyone, didn't mean that someone didn't recognize him.

Although he'd convinced himself that he was not going to take her into the tunnel again because restraining certain desires was becoming as hard as holding back a hound dog on the scent of an escapee; he had to do what he had to. "It's too loud to talk here," he said.

She nodded. "Yes, it is." She then waited for him to pull out her chair.

He took ahold of her hand, lightly, at first, then more firmly because a feather of a touch wasn't enough. His attraction to her grew in her absence as much as it did in her presence.

Without a spoken word, they slipped behind the curtain, through the storage room, and into the tunnel. He locked the door behind them and pulled out his flashlight. "Let's take a walk." Sitting beside her with the music filtering through would bring back memories of last night, of dancing and kissing, and he didn't need that. He needed to build his restraint back up.

"A walk? Where?"

"Down the tunnel."

"To the abandoned house?"

"No, we won't walk that far." He took her hand and led her down the steps. The walk would give him time to collect a bit more information.

He had spent a few hours investigating her father this morning. LeRoy confirmed William Dryer had indicated that his daughters were young, but Henry had soon discovered they weren't. They were indeed grown women. He'd discovered other information, too.

In fact, he probably now knew more about her father than she did.

The cabin in the hills that he was staying in, was where William Dryer was born. His mother had died shortly after his birth, and his grandmother long before then. William was raised by his father, Sylas, and his grandfather Edwin. Both Sylas and Edwin had been convinced there was gold in the Santa Monica Mountains, and laid claim to as many acres as possible each time land grants were available. They acquired thousands of acres, but never reported finding any gold. William had no formal education. He grew up searching for gold alongside his father and grandfather. After Edwin died, Sylas and William attempted farming the land, but it was too hilly and they couldn't afford the equipment that would be needed to make the land workable.

There was a falling-out between father and son and William had gone to work on a cargo ship, which was how he met Marlys, Betty's mother, up in Seattle. A short time later, Sylas had attempted to sell some land but couldn't because Edwin had put it all in William's name. William returned to California and sold off some small plots, but it was after Sylas had died that William received his major break, when movie studios started cropping up like weeds. They needed the one thing William had. Land. William ended up finding what his father and grandfather had been looking for, riches, but it hadn't come from gold. It had come out of the pockets of men looking to make it rich in the film industry, and William had made them pay far more than a pretty penny for every acre.

He still was. The list of requirements to purchase a single acre of Dryer's land was long—so long, only the rich could afford to meet his demands, and the rich men who thrived on being elite liked the exclusiveness that owning property in Hollywoodland provided.

Henry couldn't hold William's goals and ambition against the man. His shrewdness had made him a millionaire, something he'd dreamed of becoming since he was a young boy searching for gold with his father and grandfather. However, those same goals and ambitions, those dreams of becoming rich, were still all William cared about. Making money far unseated his family, his wife and daughters. Very few people were aware that Dryer had a family, and those that were had thought the girls were young, practically babies, until recently.

A few weeks ago, Dryer had put out the word that he was looking for husbands for his daughters, and the list of qualifications was as long as the ones needed in order to purchase property in Hollywoodland. Meaning only the rich would qualify. Even though he had money, plenty of it, he wasn't about to share it with anyone. Including his own family.

Everything Betty had said about her father, about his strict rules, had turned out to be true. The man practically kept them under lock and key. Prisoners. Henry could see why Betty and her sisters snuck out at night, because, like most prisoners, all they could think about was freedom.

He remembered feeling that way at the orphanage.

But there was more. William Dryer also seemed to be a recluse himself. Not in his house, though. He left early every morning and didn't return home until late afternoon, and he wasn't at building sites. He left most of the sale of land and home building to the man he was currently using to build his houses. James Bauer.

"Do you stay in the house at night?" Betty asked as they walked.

"No. I just use the tunnel to access places."

"Where do you stay?"

"I can't tell you that," he said. "For your own safety." He meant that in more ways than one. Not only for security against outsiders, but also in case her father was to learn that Henry was using the shack on his property.

"When you were in Seattle, do you remember a beach cottage on the bay?"

"No. I don't, but I only went to the bay that one day."

"Why?"

She sighed softly. "My grandmother was ill, had been for a long time. Tuberculosis. She came home with us and wanted clams one last time before leaving. That's why I was digging them that day. We left the following day."

"And you never went back to Seattle?" he asked for clarification. His mind still wanted to believe she was involved in this, somehow, some way, because if she wasn't, he wouldn't have a reason to see her again. That wasn't easy to admit, but he could no longer deny it. This wasn't about the case as much as it was about him. Which made it worse. He knew the trouble of getting mixed up with a woman.

"No. There was no reason to," she said. "My aunt came home with us, too."

"Where are they now? Your grandmother and your aunt?"

"My grandmother died, in the sanitorium, a few weeks after we arrived home, and my aunt entered the convent."

He stopped walking and took ahold of her hand. "I'm sorry for your loss."

"Thank you, that's kind of you to say—"

She let out a little squeak and jumped closer to him as the roof overhead started to rumble.

He folded an arm around her. "It's all right. There's a street above us. That was probably a truck—the cars aren't that loud."

Her thick lashes slowly lowered, covering those big blue eyes for a moment. "It frightened me."

"I should have warned you."

The tiny smile she offered was tentative, yet sincere. "I shouldn't be such a scaredy-cat."

He released her and stepped back, knowing if he didn't, there would be another kiss.

She rubbed her arms, looked down both sides of the dark tunnel.

The tunnel was cool, chilly even. He removed his jacket and draped it over her shoulders. "Let's walk back to the Rooster's Nest."

"But you haven't told me what you need me to help you with."

No, he hadn't, but what she'd said earlier would help the other agents that were working on finding Burrows. "That list you mentioned, of joints and the booze they serve, that would be really useful." He'd met with another agent working on the case, one of the three who he knew he could trust, and it seemed that every time they got a lead on where Burrows was, he had moved on as if he'd been tipped off. A list of joints serving Minnesota Thirteen would be helpful. Burrows was sure to show up at them sooner or later.

"I can bring it to you tomorrow night," she said.

"That would be good." Then, after receiving the list, he would be done seeing her. Her being here was nothing but a coincidence, and he had to remember what happened last time he'd allowed a woman to get mixed up in his life. He took her elbow, started walking back the way they'd come. "Thank you."

"How long will you be on this case? Using this tunnel?" she asked.

"Not long. A month at the most." He expected it to be less than that, needed to make it be less than that so he could move on.

"What will you do then?"

"That depends."

"On what?"

"Several things." The emotions filling him couldn't be ignored. She wasn't hard enough, cold enough to be working with the mole, but she was dangerous. To him. He hadn't let anyone get under his skin for years and years.

"What things?" she asked.

"I never know where I'll be assigned to next or what the job will be. Could be anything from counterfeiting to bank robbing."

"That has to be hard, never knowing where you'll be," she said. "It sounds dangerous, too."

"I'm used to it." He liked it, too.

With a soft half laugh, she said, "I don't think I could ever get used to it. The moving or the danger."

"I'm sure most people would agree with you," he said. "It's all I've ever known." He'd always liked that, moving, never getting attached to any one place, to any specific people. He thrived on being alone.

"You don't have a family? A home?"

He'd worked on making sure there were no emotions attached to his past. It simply was what it was. "I grew up in an orphanage, until I was fifteen. Then I was adopted, but I only lived with them for a couple of months." John and Esther had made him feel welcomed. They'd even given him a last name; up until then, he'd just been Henry, but they weren't his parents, and he knew they never would be. His real parents had left him, as a three-year-old child who only knew his first name, on the front steps of the orphanage. He'd wondered why, for years, but eventually decided it didn't matter if he was as unlovable as a child, or as an adult.

"Why did you live with them for only a couple of months?"

"Because I went to school, to a junior college, when I turned sixteen and lived in the dorms there for the next two years, and then I became an agent with the Bureau and started traveling. Moving from assignment to assignment." He'd never told anyone that before. No one. Other than his uncle Nate, no one in the agency knew he'd been adopted. There had been no reason for him to tell her, either. It had just come out, like he knew he could trust her.

She stopped walking and turned, faced him. "I'm sorry, Henry."

"Why? There's nothing for you to be sorry about."

"Yes, there is." Sadness filled her eyes as she looked up at him. "Everyone should have a family. No matter how strict or stern, family is everything. I would do anything for my sisters."

She was so sweet. So precious. The desire to kiss her, to hold her, was painful. He held strong and merely touched the tip of her nose with one finger. "I've already figured that out." He would do anything for one of his partners, but that was different to her reasons. She would do anything out of love. He did it out of duty.

Betty was certain she'd never felt so sorrowful for someone in her life. She might not agree with most of her father's harsh rules, but he was her father, and she had her mother and sisters. Her family. She couldn't imagine life without any of them. Her heart literally ached for Henry. For the loneliness he must have known his entire life. She wanted to take that all away for him. Stretching on her toes, she leaned forward and kissed his cheek.

After the kisses they'd shared, she wasn't sure why that one made her cheeks grow warm and tingle. Attempting to hide her the flush of her cheeks, she bowed her head, but then lifted it and looked at him. She could be truthful with him, and that felt good. "I'm going to miss you when you leave."

"You are?"

"Yes."

"Why?"

She huffed out a breath. "Because I like you and I like helping you. I know I haven't done much yet, but all you have to do is tell me what else you need." That was very true. She had a list of all the joints she and her sisters could visit and couldn't, and would share the entire list with him, going over each place and what she'd learned about each place. She wanted to do more, wanted to help him in any way she could.

He was looking at her, with a slightly odd expression. Like he couldn't believe what she'd said.

"It's true," she said.

He touched her cheek, softly. It nearly took her breath away. Then her heart skipped a beat as he leaned forward. Her eyes fluttered shut as she tilted her face upward, fully ready to meet his.

Disappointment washed over her as his lips touched her forehead. "I like having you help me."

In order to hide her reaction, she asked, "What other information, besides the list, do you need?"

Holding her elbow, he started walking again. "For now, the list will be good. It will help a lot."

Falling in step beside him, she began telling him about the places that were on the list, and any information she could remember off the top of her head. He asked questions about the joints and she answered them, and then because she truly wanted to know more, she asked him about his life at the orphanage.

She kept a smile on her face, but it was hard. His answers were matter-of-fact, but to her his childhood sounded so lonely. He sounded so lonely, she couldn't stop herself from holding his hand.

"Tell me some fun things about growing up there," she said quietly. "There had to have been something." Despite how she and her sisters complained, they did have fun together, especially with the sneaking in of material and sewing new outfits. He had to have had something like that.

He looked at her oddly, but then nodded, and grinned. "We, me and two other boys, used to sneak down into the kitchen at night and steal food. Not a lot, just enough for the younger ones who'd missed a meal for one reason or another. The kitchen workers would set traps to try to catch us, but we never got caught."

She laughed. "No wonder you became an intelligence agent. You'd been righting wrongs way back then."

He winked at her. "Or maybe we were just thieves. The other kids called us Robin Hoods, but they never ratted us out."

"You were Robin Hoods, and of course no one ratted on you. They would have gone hungry if not for you. You were their hero." He truly was in her eyes, and she wanted to know more. "What were their names? The other two boys?"

"Mick Lawrence and Darrin Wolf." He shook his head. "I haven't thought about them in years. I never saw them again after I was adopted. They said they'd keep making sure the younger kids got fed."

He grew quiet, and she squeezed his hand. "I'm sure they did."

"Yeah, me, too." He pulled his hand away from hers and shone the flashlight on his wrist. "It's time for you to meet your sisters."

Reluctantly, she nodded. It was time and she'd promised Jane she wouldn't be late again.

She climbed into bed that night thinking about Henry, about him being adopted, not having a family or home and traveling all the time, chasing criminals. He was the most interesting person she'd ever met, a true hero. A very handsome one, and though she shouldn't admit it, even to herself, she was sorely disappointed that he hadn't kissed her again tonight.

Sorely.

She'd wanted to fully kiss him. To feel his hands touching her. His body pressed up against hers. The ache for that, the ache for him, had been burning hot inside her since the dance-off, and had grown stronger every passing day.

She was contemplating that the following morning, when directly after breakfast, her father requested her presence again.

Without delay, she entered his office and sat on the edge of the sofa. This could be because he'd found dust on a lightbulb, and, no matter who had dusted, she was the oldest, so it was her fault, or any other small household matter. Or it could be about James Bauer. The one thing she was certain about was that it had nothing to do with Henry, or sneaking out. She'd believed him when he'd said he wouldn't tell anyone.

Father was a formidable-looking man. Tall, with short gray hair and a permanent frown etched in his face. "James Bauer has asked my permission for the two of you to get to know each other. Starting next month, you will attend one event with him per week."

She sucked in air and blew it out, working up the wherewithal to answer. It was Henry who helped her. The Henry who lived in her head. The one who used to make sure smaller children had food and the one that would only be here for another month. She had to hold in a smile when she thought of Henry as Robin Hood. "When next month?"

Her father frowned.

She kept her head up, her back straight. She'd never outright rebelled against her parents, and wasn't about to do that now, but did have pertinent questions that she would like the answers to. "Next month, by the calendar, is a week away, or do you mean next month, such as four weeks from now?"

Father slapped the top of his desk. "What difference does it make?"

She didn't flinch at the sound of his hand smacking the wood or at his bellow. Years of experiencing such actions also aided her in holding her gaze on him. That was just Father. How he acted, how he spoke. It was as if he was always frustrated at everything, everyone. "I would simply like to know."

If Henry still needed her assistance, she wanted to provide it. Actually, it went deeper than that. She had to provide it. Had to help him because that made her feel good, and she hadn't had much of that.

Father huffed out a half sigh, half grunt. "I will let you know."

"Thank you," she said, but didn't move because she hadn't been excused yet.

"I will also let you know the exact date of the wedding," Father said.

She didn't move, not even her head to nod in acknowledgment. Something inside her wouldn't let her because if she nodded, that meant she agreed with it, and she didn't.

"You can leave now," he said.

She rose and left the room.

Father left the house a short time later, and Betty completed her list of chores, counting the hours and minutes until she'd be able to sneak away and show Henry the list she'd compiled.

When that time finally came, he was once again sitting at the table near the piano when she entered the speakeasy, and though that instantly made her smile, by the time she arrived at the table, a raw sadness was welling inside her.

"Is something the matter?" he asked.

She shook her head and sat in the chair he held out for her. The meeting with her father hadn't totally struck her until this moment. She had a month, or less, before her life changed completely. She'd known it was coming, that she would marry James, but it suddenly was too real, too soon. She didn't expect Henry to save her like some prince on a white horse, but she wanted fun, a life, before it was too late.

Betty glanced over her shoulder, looking for Jane. Her sister was right where she expected her to be, talking to the piano player. Jane loved music and was telling the piano player what song he should play next.

Henry was still standing at her chair and Betty stood back up. "Can we go to the tunnel?"

"Why?"

"Privacy."

He took her hand, led her to the curtain and through

the storage room. Once they were in the tunnel with the door shut behind them, he asked, "What's the matter?"

She didn't know where to start. How to explain what she was feeling, what she wanted.

He shone the flashlight down the tunnel, then back at her. "Could you not find the list you said you had?"

She shook her head. "No, I have the list. I thought we could go over them, back here, where it's quiet."

"We went over most of them last night."

"I know, but I had more written down than I remembered."

He nodded. "All right. Shall we sit down?"

She walked down the short flight of steps. "Can we walk?"

He was still standing on the steps and looking at her with a slight frown.

"All the way to the house?" she asked. "I'd like to see it."

"There's not much to see. Some of the furniture is in the basement covered with dust sheets, but other than that, it's just a house."

"I know, but I want to see it." She shrugged. "Please?"

"All right." He stepped down the stairs and shone the flashlight ahead of them as they started walking along the tunnel.

She pulled a slip of paper out of her pocket and held it out to him. "Here's the list. We can go over it as we walk."

He shone the light on it. "Go ahead."

She began to read, and as she did, the time she'd spent at each place came to mind, and she told him anything that came to mind that wasn't written down. It was a long list, and about halfway through he stopped her.

"You've been to all these places?"

"No. Some are just on this list because of things I'd heard," she explained. "They are on the can't-visit list." She shook her head. "The list isn't the only reason I wanted to come down here."

"Oh?"

"No, I wanted to know more about you."

"What about me?"

"Everything," she said. "I've never met anyone like you. You've been to so many places, seen so many things. It's exciting. Thrilling. I've had more fun with you the past few nights than I've had my entire life, and…" She shook her head. "I just want to know more. Anything you want to tell me."

"I've already told you more than I've ever told anyone else, Betty."

His voice was low, nearly a whisper and it made her heart race.

"You have?"

"Yes, I have."

She stretched up on her toes and kissed his lips, softly, quickly. "I'm glad." She then looped her arm through his and leaned her head against his upper arm. "And I still want to know more. Tell me about some of the traps the kitchen workers set out to catch you."

He did. Stories about pots and pans tied together with trip strings and flour sprinkled on the floor that had her laughing, and then stories about sneaking extra blankets for cold children that had her confirming all over again that he'd been a real hero as a child.

She listened to all he said, but more than that, she listened to how he said it. She could hear the happiness in his voice when he spoke about certain things, and people. That made her feel so good. Knowing there had been some happiness in his childhood.

He'd just finished telling her a funny tale about a picture his friend Mick had drawn on a chalkboard that had them both laughing, when he shone the light ahead of them. "We're here."

There was a solid, curve-topped door ahead of them, with black hinges and a large handle. It excited her to open the door, see what was behind it. "I feel like I'm sneaking into the orphanage kitchen," she said with a giggle.

He laughed as he opened the door and motioned for her to walk inside. "There's no food here, and not much to see, either."

"Yes, there is," she said, taking in the white sheets draped over dressers, chairs, a couch, and kitchen table. "Look at all this."

"They are just dust sheets."

"I know, but it's still exciting." She couldn't begin to describe the yearning inside her. She'd never felt it before. This burning need. Knowing he would soon be gone and she'd be married to James filled her with something she couldn't describe. It was like she wanted to break every rule there was, now before she wouldn't be able to. She set the list on a wood shelf as she picked up a dusty old bottle and blew the dust off it before setting it back down. "To someone who wants more."

"More of what?"

She twirled around. That was it. More. Of everything. The next month, she wanted to live like she was never going to live again. Laughing, she walked over and pulled a sheet off the couch, tossed it aside, and plopped down.

"More of everything!"

"Like what?"

She jumped back up and grabbed his hands. "Everything we've done since I met you. You are only going to be here a month, and during that time, I—I want to help you with more than just a list." She released one hand, held their clasped ones up, and twirled beneath them. "And I want to dance and laugh."

This wasn't like her, but it felt so good. So right. She stepped closer to him. "And kiss." She stretched onto her tiptoes and whispered, "I need you, Henry. You make me feel alive."

He cupped her face with one hand and, looking at her with those early-morning-sky-blue eyes, shook his head. "You don't need me for that."

Her heart skipped a beat, because she did. She did need him. "Yes, I do." She grasped his hand and pulled him onto the sofa. "Tell me more about your life."

"There's no more to tell." Touching her cheek, he said, "Tell me about you instead."

"I've already told you…" She paused and bit her lips together at the happiness that rose up inside her. "I could tell you about my first kiss."

He lifted a brow and she giggled. "It was with the most handsome man I've ever seen. First he rescued me, saved me from downing." She leaned closer to him, so close their noses almost touched. "Then he kissed me." She tilted her head and brought her mouth closer to his. "Like this."

She pressed her lips against his, and then used her tongue to part his lips like he had hers the other night in the tunnel.

She felt a rumble, a groan, in the back of his throat as he pulled her so close against him that she could feel his heart beating inside his chest. Hers was pounding, and it felt glorious, alive.

When their mouths separated, she was gasping for breath, but also laughing.

Then they kissed again. And again.

She'd lost count of their kisses when he ended a kiss and stood up, breathing heavily.

She stood up, too, and wrapped her arms around his waist from behind.

His body felt so good pressed up against hers, she wiggled against him. He twisted around and wrapped his arms around her. She kissed his throat, his chin, and then tilted her head back, giggling as he kissed the side of her neck.

Her legs wobbled and his hold around her waist tightened.

Henry's mouth found hers again; her tongue met his and the teasing, the tasting, had her pulse hammering in her ears. She couldn't get close enough to him, no matter how hard she pressed herself against him.

He pulled his mouth off hers, and breathing hard, whispered, "We need to stop this."

Her heart was so full. Her world so right. But she still wanted more. She wanted all the desires, the wants and cravings, encompassing her to be fulfilled. She'd read the magazines that Jane had snuck into the house. The ones about flappers and movie stars, and about sex. That was what she wanted, had wanted since he'd left her standing on the beach craving more. So much more. "No, we don't."

"Yes, we do," he said.

Tossing her last inhibitions of the dutiful, rule-abiding Betty she'd always been, if she truly had any left, to the wind, she asked, "Why?"

He stepped back. "It could easily go too far."

She stepped out of one shoe, and then the other, kicking them aside. Then reached up and plucked the hat off her head, tossing it on a sheet-covered chair. "What would you consider too far?"

"This."

The shimmer in his eyes made her pulse beat even faster. "I don't want to stop, Henry. I want you."

He grasped her hand, pulled her close again. "I've wanted you since the day I left you standing on the beach."

She laughed, because that made her feel good, alive. "I've never forgotten that kiss. The way it made me feel. The things it made me want." She kissed the underside of his chin. "I want you, Henry."

He let out a tiny growl that sounded so husky she nearly got goose bumps. Wonderful ones. She snapped one of his suspenders as she stepped back this time, and then pushed one of the narrow straps holding up her loose-fitting butterscotch-colored dress off her shoulder.

"Betty," he said with that husky growling sound. "Are you sure about this? Because I can't take much more."

"If I wasn't sure. I wouldn't be here," she said, and pushed the other strap off her shoulder. The dress fell slowly, revealing the only thing beneath it was a pair of white tap pants.

Her nipples were hard, her breasts tingling, and when he reached forward, cupped one, the muscles deep inside her, at her very core where a swirling heat was growing, tightened.

He rubbed her nipple with his thumb, then kissed one, and the other. She tossed her head back at the pure delight rippling through her from head to toe.

When he lifted his head, she pushed the suspenders off his shoulders. "Fair is fair."

He removed his shirt, his pants, and stood before her in his undershorts. She planted her hands on the wide spans of his upper arms, her hands absorbing the heat, feeling the firmness, and kissed his chest, giggling as the black hair tickled her nose.

She stepped back and pushed down her tap pants.

His mouth was back on hers when he lifted her, carried her to the sofa, and laid her down. He started at her ankles, caressing the skin with the heel of his palm, the tips of his fingers, and worked his way upward.

"Your skin is so soft, so silky," he said, kissing her stomach.

She buried her hands in his thick, soft hair, inhaling the spicy, soap-clean scent that she still remembered from that day at the beach.

Her body was begging, needing more. Each kiss, each caress, made her want more and more. She was squeezing her thighs together at the fire, the craving, pulsing hard and fast. "Henry," she nearly gasped.

"I know you're ready," he whispered. "I am, too."

He removed his undershorts and perched above her then, in one swift plunge, they joined together. The snap of pain was of little consequence as she arched upward, pressing her hips firmly against his as an unimaginable pleasure followed, consumed her. All she could think about was him, and the incredible sensations overtaking her entire body. It was as if he was lifting her higher and higher, until everything spun out of control.

She had to gasp for air as the overwhelming pressure threading through her entire being hit a crescendo like the final notes of a song, and then clutched tighter to Henry as wave after wave of bliss spread throughout her system.

An incredible warmth was unfurling inside her,

when suddenly they were separated. Henry grabbed the sheet and pulled it over her stomach as the wonderful weight of his body was once again atop her. The waves of bliss retuned as he encompassed her in his arms, and they lay together, catching their breath and kissing. The joy inside her was massive, and she knew now what all the fuss was about in those magazines. Joining with Henry had been the epitome of pleasure.

The epitome of broken rules, too.

Chapter Five

Henry was thankful that even during the most intense pleasure of his life that his common sense prevailed, near the last moment, but it arrived, and he pulled out before spilling his seed. The sheet protected her as he'd held her close, relishing the aftermath of a world-rocking event.

It was there, while he was still basking in a satisfaction that he'd never experienced, when he felt her stiffen. His weight. He was crushing her.

He rose and bundled up the sheet he would have laundered and returned, then collected the clothes strewed about. His and hers. He helped her off the sofa, helped her dress. The flush of her face, the flush of her skin that had been so enticing, so exhilarating only moments ago, made the back of his throat burn when he caught the nervousness in her movement.

Tilting her chin upright, forcing her to look at him, a ball of regret formed in the pit of his stomach. She'd been a virgin, there was no mistaking that. No words would form, other than he thought she was the most beautiful, the most precious woman on earth. If he had been capable of love, it would be her that he loved. He couldn't tell her any of that because he wasn't capable of love. Neither receiving nor giving.

He kissed her instead, a gentle, slow kiss that he hoped eased her qualms.

The smile she wore on her lips quivered as the kiss ended and she looked at him. The way she'd gone from vibrant to meek, from determined to timid concerned him. Rightfully so. Guilt filled him from head to toe. All he'd been able to see was her. Betty. She'd been all he'd been able to hear, to feel, to want. Want like he'd never wanted anything ever before.

"What time is it?" she asked. "I can't be late. Jane can't wait on me tonight."

"You won't be late." He finished buttoning his shirt and, while slipping his suspenders over his shoulders, sat down to put on his shoes.

She shone the light for him, and as soon as his shoes were on, she spun around and shone the beam on the door.

"What else can I help you with?" she asked after they'd been walking along the tunnel for a length of time. "Besides the list."

Henry's gut was still churning with his own shame, and hearing her say that made it churn even harder. From the beginning there hadn't been anything he'd needed from her. He'd convinced himself her being here, in Los Angeles, was too much of a coincidence out of selfishness. He'd never forgotten about her on that beach and rather than admitting that was his problem, he'd turned it into something it wasn't. Why was beyond him, other than she'd touched something deep inside him.

Her questions about his past had made him remember things he hadn't for years and years. Mick and Darrin, and other kids that he'd completely forgotten about, and memories that had been fun to recall. He'd never told anyone about any of those things, but it had been as if she had opened a book inside his head. One that he'd locked tight and put away.

"There has to be more I can do," she said.

No, there wasn't, but he couldn't tell her that. He'd dug a hole here, and had to figure out a way to climb out. "I'll let you know," he said, whereas in truth, he wouldn't. This had to stop. Now. Before there was a repeat of tonight, which couldn't happen.

"All right," she said. "I'll be here tomorrow night."

He wouldn't. He was no good for her. She was fun, loving, while he was hard and cold. Unlovable. That wasn't something that could change. The headmistress at the orphanage had told John and Esther that when they were adopting him. That he was too old, too unemotional, and that they should adopt one of the younger children who would be more appreciative of having a family. Move lovable.

As they stepped onto the stairs leading into the storage room, he took ahold of her hand. The pain inside him went deeper than regret. To something he'd never known. "If there are any repercussions from this evening, I will provide for you."

She frowned and then blinked those long lashes while pinching her lips together. "There won't be," she barely whispered.

"There could be." That was a real possibility, and that scared him. A baby, a family, the thought made his insides go cold. He'd never have that. Wasn't capable of having that. "And I'll provide." He shrugged. "Money." He'd been raised in an orphanage, and money was what everyone had needed. Right now, he felt like a bumbling idiot because he had no idea what else she might need. "Just let me know."

She nodded.

He opened the door, walked her through the storage room and to the edge of the curtain. He watched as she signaled her sister and then walked out the door.

The regret inside him turned into disgust as he made his way back through the storage room and into the tunnel. His insides burned at how the memory of tonight would have been so sweet and cherished if he hadn't realized what he'd done. It had been his fault. He'd accused her, believed she'd been a part of something she clearly wasn't, because everyone was always guilty in his eyes. He'd never realized that until tonight.

She hadn't been guilty of anything, but he sure as hell was. He could have stopped it. Should have stopped it, but he hadn't.

He entered the basement, picked up the sheet, and walked upstairs, out the door, and across the road. There, he sat down in the bushes and waited, needing to know she had made it home.

It felt as if hours passed before she and her sisters got off the streetcar and walked through the yard, then took the road up to the row of trees.

He waited awhile longer, then stood and traversed his way up the hill and down the other side to the cabin. Still guilt-ridden. Still mad at himself. Still thinking about how profoundly amazing it had been.

The following morning, he followed the same trail back down to the house. He'd told himself he didn't need the list she'd written out for him; it was just the guilt growing like a poison inside him that said he did. A poison he'd created.

He entered the house, disgusted at himself again because he'd left it unlocked when he'd left last night. Telling himself that didn't matter, he forced his mind to not think about anything, especially what had occurred here last night as he found Betty's list in the basement and then left the house and trekked back up the hill.

Halfway up it, a shiver tickled his spine.

He blamed it on the guilt festering like a wood sliver too deep beneath the skin to dig out without a needle, until the shiver came again, then he slid behind a tree and peered around it to scan the hill.

Someone was following him. How had he let that happen? Because his mind hadn't been on this job since he'd met Betty. He had to change that. For both him and her.

He stayed where he was, watched as his followers grew closer. Two of them. Twisting about, he picked a trail along the underbrush, until reaching the top, and then paused to glance back down. They were still there, following him. The man looked like Lane Cox.

Henry heaved out a breath. Lane had lost his wife and daughter in the train robbery and had worked closely with the FBI during the capture and trial of Gaynor. Henry had known Lane would be on Gaynor's escape like a hound. Every agent knew Lane could be trusted and would do anything he could to see justice was served. Including not printing information that hadn't been released to the public. But until he knew who the mole was for sure, Henry couldn't contact Lane. Couldn't let him know the truth about Gaynor. There was just too much at stake.

As Henry made his way down the other side of the hill, something else occurred to him. The second person with Lane was a woman.

Betty's sister. The one who'd danced with Burrows.

The only way Lane could have known to look at the abandoned house for him was from Betty.

The guilt inside him turned to anger.

He'd been duped.

Duped by a woman again.

He huffed out a breath and cursed at his own thoughts. She wasn't like that. He wanted her to be so it would be easier for him to forget her. Lane had probably tracked him down all on his own. Betty had nothing to do with it. Nothing to do with any of it.

Which was all one more reason why he could never see her again. He had to stop pulling her into all this. He knew how dangerous that could get.

Once at the cabin, he left the door ajar as an open invitation for Lane to approach.

That was exactly what happened. Lane appeared, surprised to see it was him and not Rex Gaynor. That explained it all. Lane would have tracked Gaynor to the end of the earth for killing his wife and child.

Henry's mind kept going down side roads as he, Lane, and Patsy discussed Burrows and the shipment of old bills that had been stolen off the train. All he could think about was Betty, and what he'd done to her. Henry's thoughts were as jumbled as his insides, so when Lane offered to learn more about Vincent's whereabouts, Henry absently agreed to meet him the following night at the Rooster's Nest.

When this was all over, he'd tell Lane the truth, but he couldn't right now, because no matter how badly he'd messed up with Betty, he still had a job to do.

As soon as Lane left, Henry, with the piece of paper containing the list Betty had compiled burning his skin through the material of his pocket, set out down the hill to search out another agent. One he was certain was clean. Jacob Nielsen, who—along with Curtis Elkin and Bob Mayer—had been assigned to arrest Burrows. Jacob had only been with the Bureau three years, so couldn't be the mole, but Elkin and Mayer had been there seven years, and out of those two, Elkin was who Henry believed was the mole. It wasn't anything he could put his finger on, but Elkin was sly, shifty, and though he never said much, he always seemed to be thinking. None of that was odd for an agent, but Elkin made it seem odd.

It wasn't anything more than a gut feeling. What Henry needed was proof, and he didn't have that.

Yet.

He'd give the list Betty had compiled to Jacob. She'd put that list together for a reason, and Jacob had to know he could be entering a setup if he was planning on looking for Burrows at any of them.

The sky had opened up shortly after Lane and Patsy had left, a full-blown thunder-and-lightning storm. Henry tugged down his hat and flipped up his collar against the rain as he continued down the hill. This time, he hadn't taken the trail that led to the house, he'd taken what had once been a road to the cabin. It was overgrown from lack of use for most of the way, but came out on the road before the curve that led up to Hollywoodland. That was where he kept his car. Well hidden in the trees.

Guilt was still churning his insides. After meeting Patsy with Lane, Henry knew he needed to talk to Betty. Needed to apologize to her. All he'd offered her last night was money if there were any repercussions. She'd need more than that. He didn't know how he'd provide it, moving from case to case, but he'd have to find a way.

Rain was coming down in sheets by the time he

arrived at the car. He wrenched open the door and jumped in. As he removed his hat to shake aside the rain dripping off his hair, he noticed the windshield was fogged over.

From the inside.

He grabbed the door handle, but it was too late. Pain exploded in the back of his head.

Betty had never hosted the type of anger living inside her today. She was even furious with her sisters. Patsy, who had been missing all day, showed up late for supper, dripping wet and with Lane Cox in tow, who stayed for supper, and was then sequestered in a meeting with her father. Second, Jane refused to sneak out because of what was happening with Patsy and Lane.

Betty was concerned for Patsy, and Lane, and understood Jane's fears, but she'd told Henry she'd meet him, and she would. Last night had been amazing; she'd just gotten scared afterward at how she'd broken every rule and needed to tell him that. It hadn't been because she'd been worried about repercussions. He'd made sure there wouldn't be any. She had to let him know that.

She didn't know what it was that made her want to be someone else, but when she was with him, she wanted to be someone who took risks and chances, broke rules, and lived. The exact opposite of who she truly was. Who she had been her entire life.

She'd even fought with Father this morning, refused to be the one to take Mother shopping as scheduled. It had been foolish, but she'd been thinking about what happened with Henry last night, how she'd been brave enough to take what she'd wanted. She'd wanted to be brave enough to have that happen elsewhere, too.

It hadn't. She'd ended up driving Mother, which

made her angrier at how she'd given in, been forced to give in and follow orders like she had her entire life.

She'd just climbed down the trellis when she heard a faint whistle from above. It was Jane, holding a hand out the window, with a single finger raised.

Betty's insides shook from head to toe. That could mean wait a minute, or it could mean for her to stay right where she was because someone was coming. The light was still on in Father's office and she sincerely hoped that meant he was still in it.

Relief washed over her as Jane climbed out the window a short time later and then scurried down the trellis.

"This is dangerous," Jane hissed. "No one has gone to bed yet."

Betty pressed a finger to her lips and then ran across the yard to the trees.

Jane followed, and as soon as they were on the road, she said again, "This is crazy! What if Mother or Father goes upstairs?"

"If that happens, we'll deal with it tomorrow," Betty said, half walking and half running along the road.

"Horsefeathers," Jane said. "What's so important about going out tonight?"

Betty would love to tell her sister. Love to tell her everything. Including the tunnel they could take that would get them to the Rooster's Nest faster than the trolley. But she couldn't. She couldn't tell Jane anything.

"What if Patsy needs us?"

"To do what?" Betty asked. "There's nothing we can do." Another real fear was living in her mind. "Don't you realize this could be our last night? After what happened with Patsy today, bringing Lane home, we all could be locked in our rooms for the rest of our lives."

"I hadn't thought about that."

"I have," Betty answered as they entered the yard of the house. "I most certainly have." She tried not to look at the abandoned house, but couldn't keep from doing so, wondering if Henry was inside, watching them.

Whether he was or not, he'd be at the Rooster's Nest, waiting for her. She was late, by almost an hour, but he'd wait. She was sure of that.

That thought alone helped erase some of her anger and frustration.

For a short time.

Because Henry wasn't at the Rooster's Nest. She even snuck into the storage room and pulled the shelf away from the wall, but the door was locked, so she couldn't get to the tunnel.

She waited, sat at their table, until Jane insisted if they didn't leave, they'd miss the trolley. Fighting tears the entire way, she knew what she had to do even before she and Jane climbed the trellis.

It felt like an eternity before her sisters were finally in their beds, asleep. She then left her room and quickly hurried into the bathroom and out the window.

The front door of the abandoned house was unlocked. Her heart skipped a beat as she hoped that meant Henry was here. Using the light of the flashlight, she made her way into the basement.

It was empty.

She didn't know if that made her feel better or worse. Either way, her heart sat heavy in her chest as she made her way back home.

There, lying in bed, she cried, convinced something awful had to have happened to him.

She continued to worry for several days, but then she knew the truth.

Henry was gone. She'd searched for him every night,

taking chances at sneaking out earlier than usual and visiting places not on her list, but he wasn't to be found.

Reality happened almost two weeks later, the night Lane and Patsy came home and said that Vincent Burrows had been arrested. The case was solved.

Betty cried that night like she'd never cried before, her heart was completely broken, and she knew she had no one to blame but herself. She was the one who'd broken the rules. Rules that had been put in place for good reason.

She wanted to hate Henry, but she couldn't. He'd kept the only promise he'd ever made to her. He'd never told her father about them sneaking out. Furthermore, he'd given her the opportunity to be someone she wasn't, and that had made her understand who she had to be.

Betty Dryer. A person who obeys the rules, because not obeying them leads to hurt and pain and loss.

The following morning, when her father requested her presence in his office, and stated that James would be over that evening to take her out, Betty kept her head up and agreed, knowing this was her life, this was who she was.

"Horsefeathers!" Jane said that evening while pacing the floor of Betty's room. "You don't have to go out with him! The fact that Father is allowing Patsy to marry Lane means things could be different for us!"

"No, it doesn't," Betty said, draping a white shawl around her shoulders and over her ankle-length gray dress with its dropped waistline.

"Yes, it does!" Jane insisted, throwing her arms in the air. "What's gotten into you lately? You don't even want to sneak out with me anymore."

"I went out with you last night," Betty said, picking up her white purse.

Jane huffed out a breath. "Only to make sure I don't break any of your rules."

Betty held her tongue; she had been more watchful of Jane on their nightly excursions. Actually, that was the only reason she went out—to keep an eye on Jane. And to scan the occupants. There was a flicker of hope inside her that she just couldn't blow out, the thought that one day she might see a set of pale blue eyes again.

Henry slapped his palm against the rail of the ship. Seeing land, and not being able to go ashore filled him with a boiling anger. Well over a week ago, he'd awoken inside a barrel aboard a cargo ship bound for Hawaii. After breaking himself out of the barrel, he'd convinced the captain that he'd been shanghaied, but hadn't been able to make the man turn the ship around and return him to the port of Los Angeles. Now he was told he couldn't go ashore until the ship was docked for unloading. He could have swum the distance to shore if his shoulder hadn't been dislocated when they'd shoved him in that flour barrel.

They. His assailants.

It had been two men who'd attacked him in his car that raining afternoon. He'd not gotten a good look at either one of them before they knocked him out cold. He'd come to while they'd been shoving him in that barrel, and he'd fought, but...

Anger renewed.

Not only at his assailants, but at himself for not having his mind in the right place that day. He'd been so focused on Betty. On what he'd done to her, that he'd let his guard down.

He'd never let his guard down before. He'd never questioned himself like he had with her, and this was where it had gotten him. In the middle of the Pacific Ocean.

Still thinking about her. And all sorts of other things. Like fatherhood. That frightened him like nothing ever had. He knew nothing, nothing about being a father.

If it had done nothing else, his time at sea had given him the opportunity to get his mind back in order. To think straight.

He could now see things with a clear perspective. He saw everything he could never have in Betty. He'd been like a kid, wanting it so badly, he'd do anything to get it. Including stealing, which made eating the candy bittersweet, knowing he truly didn't deserve it. He'd long ago set his path in life, that of being an agent, and that was the path he needed to remain on, because it was the only one he'd ever have.

"We're scheduled to dock at midnight." Captain Cahill stepped up to the rail. "There's a passenger steamer heading back to LA next week."

"Next week?" Henry shook his head. "I need to head back right away. On the next ship."

Cahill's beard was as gray as the hair on his head, and his leathery skin showed the number of years he'd spent at sea. "They are all cargo ships. Don't take passengers."

"Doesn't matter."

"Yes, it does," Cahill said. "Cargo ships *can't* take passengers. I explained that to you already."

"I'm not a passenger," Henry reminded. "I was shanghaied." The hairs on his arms quivered as they stood. If he hadn't managed to break out of that barrel, a warehouse worker would have discovered his dead and decomposing body at some point. Probably when it would have started to stink.

"I know," Cahill said. "But there's nothing I can do about it."

Cahill had said that several times, and Henry had been thinking about how he was going to get back to California, and knew there was one quick way for it to happen. Uncle Nate. "Where am I going to be able to find a telephone?"

"A telephone?" Cahill shook his head. "Telephone calls from Hawaii to the States cost a fortune and you don't have any money."

That was true. His pockets had been stripped clean. Even his badge was gone. "I'll reverse the charges."

The captain let out a gruff laugh. "Good luck convincing someone that will happen."

Cahill walked away, and Henry would have slapped the rail again, but his injured shoulder was still aching from when he'd done that earlier. He reached up to rub at his shoulder. The pain had subsided a great deal after it had been put back in place, but it still hurt to the point he could barely use it. The captain was right about finding someone who would trust him enough to use their telephone.

Trust.

He'd never trusted anyone in his life. Certainly not his birth parents, not the people who'd run the orphanage, or his adoptive parents, who he'd always known had only adopted him as an experiment.

He'd thought he'd finally found trust within the Bureau, then within a year, the mole had started to play his games, and no one knew who they could trust. Scarlet had proven that, too.

He'd known all that, then why had he trusted Betty enough to tell her about his childhood? The good things?

Maybe it was him who couldn't be trusted. She had to be wondering what happened to him. Just like his adoptive parents. Every time he spoke to his uncle, Nate said as much. That John and Esther wondered about him. Wondered when they'd hear from him, see him.

He clamped his back teeth together. Betty had done something to him. Inside. For years he'd told himself that John and Esther were only his parents on paper.

Just like Nate was only his uncle on paper.

He'd been trying to make up for that for years. Henry shook his head at his own thought. It wasn't as if he'd been trying to make up for that as much as he'd been trying to prove his worth. To let all of them know he had been the right kid to choose out of the orphanage. The right man to choose for the FBI.

That, too, his very job, had been all part of his adoptive father's plan to prove how well the junior-college idea could work, could benefit those unable to attend a full-fledged university. Therefore, upon graduation, John had sought out a job for his adopted son, through his brother. Nathan Randall. Nate had been a federal agent then and willingly took on the challenge of bringing a kid straight out of school into the agency, with the expectation that Henry would follow every rule, exceed at every assignment and hold his loyalty to the agency above everything else.

He had.

Because he'd wanted them to trust in him, because then, maybe, he could trust in them.

He'd blown that now. By getting shanghaied.

The only saving grace he had was that the case wasn't over yet. He had to get back to California, find the mole, and then...

Then move on to another assignment. Maintain his loyalty to the agency, to his uncle and adoptive parents.

Continue on with the only life he'd ever known.

The only life he'd ever know.

Henry pushed away from the rail, and hours later, found himself back in the same spot, talking with Captain Cahill.

"Just have them dial that number," Henry said, gesturing toward the piece of paper he'd given the captain. "My name's on that paper. Have them say it's concerning me, Henry Randall. I guarantee all charges will be reversed and any ship here will be given permission to provide me passage back to California."

"You must think you're really someone special," Cahill said with a mixture of doubt and amusement.

Henry didn't want to reveal exactly who they would be calling, because that would make it sound too unbelievable, and they could refuse.

"Whose number is this?" Cahill asked. "A good lawyer?"

"Yes," Henry answered. "He's an attorney."

Cahill laughed but held up the slip of paper. "I'm only doing this because I like you, and am still mad that someone was able to load a barrel onto my ship without me knowing about it."

That was putting it mildly. Cahill had been more furious about the barrel being hauled aboard than about him being in it. "I'll wait here," Henry said, knowing the captain would have a better shot at convincing someone to call his uncle without him present. He'd considered going ashore, but was wearing borrowed clothes, hadn't had a bath in over a week, and, besides the bum shoulder, he had a gash on his forehead from a blow he'd taken from his assailants at some point that still hadn't completely healed. He certainly didn't look like a federal agent, or the nephew of a very powerful man. This way, staying on the ship, Cahill would know where to find him as soon as the call was over.

"All right," Cahill said. "I'll let you know as soon as I've gotten the cargo squared away."

"Thanks. I really do appreciate it."

Cahill flashed a grimace of sorrow as he tucked the paper into his pocket. "I hope you still do when I return with bad news."

"It'll be good news," Henry insisted.

Cahill left with a shrug and a shake of his head, and was gone for what felt like half the night. It was. They'd pulled into port at midnight.

The sky and the sea were still black as tar when Henry heard his name being shouted.

"Randall! Randall! Get your carcass down here!"

With the aid of the dock lights, Henry saw Cahill waving at him and quickly maneuvered his way through the men hauling cargo down the long, rough-hewn, planked loading ramp.

"The call went through?" Henry asked, running the last few steps to meet up with Cahill.

"Yes. He wants to talk to you." Cahill pointed to a tall building behind him. "That is one hell of an attorney you had them call."

Henry nodded as they hurried up the walkway toward the building.

"The attorney general of the United States of America?" Cahill asked.

Henry nodded again.

"Why didn't you tell me that?"

"Because I didn't think you'd believe me," Henry replied.

"I wouldn't have," Cahill said.

Full of optimism, knowing he'd soon be on his way back to California, Henry grinned. "Then you wouldn't have believed he's my uncle, either."

Cahill's eyes nearly popped out of his head. "Nephew? Hell, get a move on!" he shouted, and picked up the pace to a near run.

Chapter Six

⁓⁓⁓⁓⁓⁓

Life certainly was a fickle thing. Within a few short weeks, Betty had gone from being the happiest she'd ever been, to being the most despondent. She literally had no control over her emotions. None whatsoever. One minute she'd be happy, helping with the arrangements for Patsy's wedding, and the next minute she'd be crying her eyes out, feeling nothing but sorrow.

That wasn't like her. She'd never broken out in tears at the drop of a hat. It was Henry's fault, that was what she'd tell herself when the tears started to flow, but then, she'd have to admit it was all her fault.

He'd disappeared out of her life once before, so why had she expected this time to be different? That was who he was. A lonely man who liked traveling from place to place, case to case. He'd told her so. Not the lonely part, she'd figured that out from his upbringing. Furthermore, what had she truly expected would happen when she broke every rule imaginable?

Truth was, she should be happy. James wasn't nearly as awful as she'd expected. He wasn't nearly as handsome as Henry, or as tall, or as muscular. He didn't make her insides feel all warm and gooey, either, but he was sensible. He had a very nice home, not far away from her parents' house, so she'd be able to still keep a close watch on Jane, even after she and James got married.

There was nothing mysterious about James, either. They'd gone out three times, and Betty already knew everything there was to know about him. He was also submissive, and after years of living with her father, she told herself she needed to be thankful for that.

She also needed to be thankful that James was as opposite to Henry as humanly possible.

The case Henry had been working on was completely closed. Lane and Patsy had written all about it in the newspaper, and Betty had questioned Patsy more intently, on exactly what happened.

She'd never used Henry's name, partially because she didn't want anyone to ever know how she'd so foolishly tried to be someone she was not.

She still didn't blame him. She couldn't. Especially when it came to that night in the basement. It had been so wonderful, so earth-shattering.

Tears hit again.

"What's wrong?" Jane whispered.

"I'm just happy for Patsy," Betty answered, keeping her voice low as they set out the crystal punch bowl and cups—making sure all the handles faced in the same direction. The wedding would take place in less than an hour, and everything had to be perfect. Per Mother's instructions. Patsy didn't care if there even was punch. She hadn't cared about any of the arrangements. She was so happy, so ecstatic to be marrying Lane, that she'd have married him anywhere at any time.

Betty refused to compare herself to Patsy. There was no use.

"Perfect!" Mother exclaimed. "Absolutely perfect. I can't believe how much we managed in such a short time." Shaking her head, she insisted, "That won't happen again. We'll have more time when it comes to your weddings."

Betty made no comment, in fact, she pretended that she hadn't heard a word her mother had said.

Jane, on the other hand, heaved out a sigh and whispered, "I'll elope before I go through all this."

Betty shook her head at Jane's comment, but then frowned. Jane just might do that.

"Come now," Mother said. "Time to get in position. Betty, remember, you walk up to the altar first, and walk slow, dear."

Betty nodded and stepped into place.

"You, too, Jane," Mother said, shifting her gaze. "Nice and slow. It's not a race."

"I know," Jane said. "I know. No one in their right mind would race to the altar."

Betty knew Jane was referring to her, and not Patsy. Patsy was in love with Lane. She wasn't in love with James. Perhaps she would be by the time her wedding rolled around.

She managed to keep her tears at bay until she was standing at the altar watching her sister marry Lane. His hair was dark brown, the same brown as his eyes, the very ones that looked at Patsy with such love and devotion that Betty couldn't stop the tears from slipping out. She truly was happy for her sister.

Patsy looked so beautiful in her long white A-line dress. Her white netted veil covered the long ringlets that Betty had curled in Patsy's hair earlier. Jane had then curled Betty's hair, and Patsy had curled Jane's.

A pang struck Betty, knowing that wouldn't happen again. The three of them would no longer share the upstairs rooms at the house. Patsy had already moved most of her belongings to Lane's apartment near the newspaper building.

Betty twisted, just enough to get a quick glance at Jane, who was also crying. Their eyes met briefly, and Betty knew Jane was thinking the same thing that she was. Things were going to be very different now.

Betty then glanced down at her own dress, a long gown of powder blue. Mother had suggested pink for both her and Jane's dresses, but Patsy had said no pink, and that her sisters could choose whatever color they wanted. Betty had chosen blue of course. Jane had chosen green. Pale green.

Their dresses were identical, and pretty. Simple creations that hadn't needed any adornments, other than single short strings of pearls around their necks. They each wore a pearl barrette, holding back their hair, including Patsy.

Betty then glanced toward her parents sitting in the front row. Mother had a matching barrette, but it was holding her long blond hair in a bun near the nape of her neck. Both she and Father looked very nice in their dress clothes.

Seeing the person seated directly behind her father, Betty's breath stuck in her throat.

James.

He wasn't the homeliest of men, just boring. Short and stocky, he had thin brown hair and round green eyes that blinked often. Almost too often.

He smiled at her.

Her heart once again grew so heavy; it felt as if it was in her stomach rather than behind her breastbone.

The ceremony ended. She kept her head up and

forced a smile to form and remain on her lips as she followed the newly married couple down the aisle. Then, as people started to leave their seats, she and Jane scooted around Patsy and Lane.

"Bee's knees, but Patsy looks happy, doesn't she?" Jane said as they hurried down the steps so they could be ready to serve punch, coffee, and cake as the guests arrived in the gathering hall of the church.

"Yes, she does," Betty agreed.

"I hate to admit it," Jane said quietly, "but I'm jealous of her."

"For marrying a man she loves?" Betty asked.

"No, for escaping. There will be no sneaking out of the window and climbing down the trellis for her."

"No, there won't be," Betty agreed as she positioned herself behind the table holding the punch bowl and coffeepot.

"You won't be doing that much longer, either," Jane said.

Betty held her breath for a moment. She didn't care if she ever went to another speakeasy, but Jane did. "I won't be marrying James for months. Not until the end of the year."

"Then why are you acting like it's tomorrow?"

Betty began to fill cups using a glass dipper. "I'm not."

"Horsefeathers," Jane huffed as she began to cut slices of the cake. "You haven't wanted to sneak out in days."

"Because we've been so busy with the wedding," Betty replied.

"Banana oil!" Jane hissed. "That's only an excuse. When we have snuck out, you haven't danced with anyone. I've watched you. You haven't had any fun. Why?"

"Yes, I have. There just hasn't been anyone I wanted to dance with."

"You mean the Reuben you won the dance-off with."

Betty nearly dropped a cup, and was saved from having to reply as people entered the room and immediately came to the table for punch and cake.

She had to fill the punch bowl several times, and made several trips into the kitchen to wash cups. As she returned with several clean and dry cups, her hands began to shake when she noticed Father and James approaching the punch table from another direction.

"Betty," Father said in his booming voice as they arrived. "Now that Patsy's wedding is over, it's time to make your engagement to James official."

Holding her breath, she focused on setting down the cups.

"The wedding will be a month from now," Father continued. "I'll make the announcement."

Betty's mouth had gone dry. "A month?"

"Oops, I'm sorry!"

Betty glanced up at Jane's exclamation, and was alarmed to see cake and frosting stuck to the front of James's suit coat.

She then turned to Jane, who pushed the line whenever she thought she could get away with it. Hence the reason she was the one to come up with them sneaking out at night.

Holding an empty plate, Jane held up a linen napkin. "I didn't mean to bump into you."

James blinked several times, looking at the cake on his jacket as if not sure what to do about it. "That's all—all right," he said.

Jane smiled and shrugged. "I'll get you another piece."

"That's all right," James said. "I don't care for cake."

Betty grabbed the napkin and wiped the frosting off his jacket. "Father, I don't believe now is the time to make any announcements."

Jane waved a hand slightly. "Father, Mother is looking for you. It must be time for Patsy and Lane to leave."

Father flashed Jane a glare that said he'd speak with her later before he turned. James bobbed his head at both of them as he moved away, as well.

"I don't like him," Jane hissed.

"He's not that bad and I can't believe you threw cake on him," Betty whispered in return.

"He's about as exciting as an earthworm, and I didn't throw it on him," Jane said, with mirth sparkling in her eyes. "I just bumped into him and the plate accidently hit him in the chest." She set the plate on the table. "Come on—we need to get upstairs with the bowls of rice so people can grab a handful to throw at the bride and groom."

"I don't know if I can trust you with a bowl of rice," Betty said, picking up one of the large bowls that had been waiting on the floor under her table.

Jane laughed as she picked up the other bowl. "I won't dump it over his head. That would be a waste of rice."

"And that slice of cake wasn't?"

Jane shook her head. "No. He's a palooka, a goofus, if I ever saw one. You know it as well as I do. Life with him will be like watching grass grow."

"Sometimes boring is good," Betty said.

Jane laughed. "Be warned. I'm not going to let you do it. It's just you and me now. But it's still one for all and all for one."

Betty's stomach hiccupped. Jane was right; it was

just the two of them. They did need to stick together. Now more than ever. But she had to stop Jane before she did something really foolish. "Don't—"

"Let's get a wiggle on," Jane said, "or the bride and groom will beat us up the stairs."

They carried the rice to the front doors of the church, and stood there as people filed out, grabbing a handful, and then lined both sides of the sidewalk so they could throw the rice on the bride and groom as they hurried outside and ran to Lane's car.

The crowd dispersed shortly thereafter, and Betty readily took on the job of sweeping the rice off the steps and sidewalk.

She was kneeling down, holding the dustpan with one hand while sweeping rice into the pan with the broom in her other hand when an icy shiver rippled down her spine.

Straightening, she glanced around, and goose bumps rose up on her arms as she noticed a man sitting in a car across the street, staring at her. The sun prevented her from seeing his face, but something about him, the way he was looking at her, was scary. Frightening.

She spun around and ran up the steps.

Following LeRoy, Henry entered the hotel through the back door in the alley and took the service elevator up to a room on the fourth floor that his uncle had set up as a meeting place.

LeRoy had been at the dock when Henry, dressed as a navy sailor, had walked off the boat. LeRoy had ushered him into the backseat of a black sedan, which dropped them off at the hotel's back door. Just as Uncle Nate had said would happen on the phone before Henry had left Hawaii.

Henry was given supplies, including clothes, money, a new badge, firearm, and the keys to a black Packard in the hotel parking lot and filled in on the details of Burrows being captured by agents Bob Mayer and Jacob Nielsen, as well as the news that no one had seen or heard from Curtis Elkin in weeks. Since the time Henry had been shanghaied.

"Elkin wasn't on the ship with me," Henry said, fingering his old badge, and the one that had belonged to Elkin. They'd supposedly washed up onshore near the docks. "He's the mole. I'm sure of it."

"I am, too." LeRoy set his coffee cup down on the table in the hotel room that overlooked the bay. "But we need proof. Solid proof." He picked up the file folder. "I've gone over this so many times, I can read it with my eyes closed. There's nothing here. Nothing."

The folder contained all the information the Bureau had on Elkin. His personal information as well as every case the agent had worked on.

LeRoy let the folder fall back onto the table with a smack. "We've never had this before. A mole, but it's the only thing that explains the leaks."

"Things Elkin knew."

LeRoy nodded. "Yes, but others knew them, too."

"The others are all accounted for," Henry pointed out.

"Yes, but that doesn't mean they weren't the mole. Elkin could have been shanghaied just like you, or…" His gaze went out the window, to the ocean. "He could have met a worse fate." Turning, he said, "So could you have."

"I know," Henry admitted, "which is why I believe it's Elkin. And I believe it was Elkin that shanghaied me. He wanted us to believe it was Burrows that shanghaied both of us." He fingered the badges lying on the table. "He wanted us to believe he was dead so he could take over once Burrows was arrested. He knew that was imminent."

"He did," LeRoy said. "And no one's seen or heard from him since the day you went missing, too."

"No other agents." Henry laid his hand on the folder. "But I bet men in Burrows's organization know exactly where he's at.

"Elkin got scared when Rex Gaynor's case was reopened," Henry said. "I saw it on his face the day you mentioned the passenger manifesto from the train while briefing the rest of the team on this assignment. He thought the case was too old, that no one would care about Gaynor."

LeRoy nodded. "I agree. That's why I pulled you aside, and we came up with the plan of you pretending to be Gaynor."

Henry's mind was still whirling. "Or maybe it was exactly what he'd wanted. The case to be reopened so he could be here, fake his own death, and become a mob boss instead of an FBI agent. There's definitely more money in it." Henry shook his head, still not sure of Elkin's motive. "The question is why? Something had to have happened to make him start leaking information, and something had to have happened to make him decide it was time to fully switch sides."

LeRoy rubbed his gray handlebar mustache. "Sounds like you're on the right track."

"I need to talk to Lane Cox, find out if there were any major prohibition busts along the coast." Henry's mind instantly shot to Betty. Actually, she'd been there the whole time; it was the list she'd compiled and the night she'd given it to him that became front and center.

"Lane Cox," LeRoy said. "He was with Bob and Jacob, helped them arrest Burrows that night."

Henry nodded. He knew Lane wouldn't have stopped until that happened, and getting the information on prohibition busts this past year would be faster than going through the bureaucracy of interagency sharing.

"He also got married yesterday."

Shocked, Henry asked, "Lane did?"

"Yes, to one of William Dryer's daughters."

Henry's spine stiffened. "Patsy?"

"Yes. You've met her?"

He nodded. "I've met all three of Dryer's daughters."

"Good, then you already know who they are."

Henry had to swallow twice because of how dry his throat had gone. "Why?"

"Think about it, Henry. With you dead, Lane Cox is the only one who could identify Elkin and Elkin isn't going to let that happen."

Henry rubbed his forehead. "Damn."

"Lane knows Elkin worked on that case seven years ago."

Henry shook his head. "But he doesn't know I was after Elkin."

"No, but Elkin does, and he knows Lane helped Jacob and Bob bust Burrows. Lane's wife was there, too."

Images were flashing through Henry's mind of all three girls sneaking out, walking through dark yards, down quiet roads. "They are all in danger," he said. "The entire Dryer family."

LeRoy nodded.

"What's our plan?"

LeRoy stood and carried his coffee cup to where a silver pot was sitting atop a rolling tray. After refilling the cup, he took a drink of it while walking back to the table.

Henry's nerves were pounding, his mind swirling, and waiting for his supervisor's answer was torturing him.

"Your uncle wants me to pull you off this case."

"No!" Henry leaped to his feet. "No."

"I told him you'd say that."

"We need men," Henry said. "Need their house guarded."

LeRoy shook his head. "On a hunch? I can't do that. Not even your uncle can do that. Elkin could be dead. He could have been shanghaied like you. We need proof, Henry. Proof that he's the mole, then I can have men here."

Henry ran both hands through his hair. The images were still flashing through his head. "Then I'll get it. Find him." Henry wished he had more of a plan, but knew it would come. It had to.

"Well, you're the man to catch him." LeRoy slapped the envelope of cash he'd set on the table earlier. "If this isn't enough, let me know. I've been authorized to give you anything you need, and there's no limit. Time or money, but you're on your own, until you can give me proof. I wish it wasn't that way, but it is."

Henry nodded, and heaved out a long sigh. He'd taken pride in being a top agent for years, in being the one people knew they could count on, but right now, it gutted him to know the stakes of this case were the highest he'd ever known.

LeRoy stood and stretched his arms over his head. "I'm not looking forward to the train ride back to Texas. I swear those seats get harder and the trip gets longer every time I take it. There's no sleeping on those things."

"Why don't you spend the night, leave in the morning, so you get some sleep," Henry suggested, even though his mind was elsewhere. On Betty.

"Can't," LeRoy said. "I have to leave town before Elkin knows I was here. Besides that, I promised the wife I'd be home by tomorrow night." LeRoy put on his jacket.

"I'll give you a ride," Henry said.

"No. Can't chance you being seen with me," LeRoy said. "There's a car waiting for me. This room's paid as long as you need it—whether you decide to use it or not is up to you." As they shook hands, LeRoy added, "Good luck. I know it's not much, but I'm only a phone call away."

Chapter Seven

"Do you need any help in there?" Jane asked through the closed bathroom door.

"No," Betty replied. It was so soft Jane probably hadn't heard her.

"I could curl your hair for you," Jane said.

Betty didn't want her hair curled. She wanted— Her stomach erupted as she braced herself as everything she'd eaten that day forced its way up, out, and into the toilet, yet again.

The door opened, and she had no choice but to look at her sister as Jane knelt down beside her.

"It's not that bad," Jane said soothingly. "It's only a date."

Betty shook her head before she had to hang it over the toilet again. She'd been sick to her stomach for a couple of days now, cried at the blink of an eye, and was exhausted during the day, yet wide-awake at night. Yet she didn't feel sick. She didn't have a temperature or the chills or any other symptoms.

"Here." Jane handed her a cool washcloth.

Betty took it, wiped her mouth, and then held the cloth over her face. The eruption in her stomach had settled. That was how it had been. Once she vomited, she felt better.

"Do you want me to tell Father you're too ill to go out?" Jane asked.

"No." Betty heaved out a sigh and removed the cloth. "I'll be fine in a moment." She sat on the floor and leaned the back of her head against the edge of the sink. "James is excited to go to the restaurant."

Jane sat down on the floor. "So?"

Betty shook her head at Jane.

"Horsefeathers! The idea of going out with him makes you so sick you throw up, yet you—"

"He's not that bad," Betty insisted. "I've told you that, including yesterday when you threw cake on him."

"I didn't *throw* cake on him," Jane said. "And yes he is."

Betty closed her eyes and forced herself to not compare James to Henry because she cried when she did that.

"Do you really think you can spend the rest of your life with him?" Jane asked.

"Yes," Betty said. It would be boring, but she could do it because that was who she was. She'd tried being someone she wasn't, and that hadn't worked out. She'd broken every rule, and her heart. James would never do that to her.

"Piffle!" Jane leaned her head back against the bathtub and stared at the ceiling. "Think of your children! A room full of dull, boring slugs."

Betty had to swallow around the hard lump that formed in her throat. Children. Her body began to tremble. It hadn't even been four weeks since she'd seen Henry. And he'd... No. No. She pressed hand to her stomach. That couldn't have happened. It was not possible. She shot to her feet.

"Where are you going?" Jane asked.

Betty didn't answer as she ran for her room.

Before she arrived, Father's bellow echoed up the stairs, telling her James was downstairs, waiting on her.

Tears formed in her eyes.

Jane grabbed her arm. "I knew it. You don't like him."

Betty shook her head and tried to breathe.

"I'll tell him—"

"No!" Betty swallowed hard. "Tell him I need a minute."

Jane shook her head.

"Yes. Please, Jane." Her anxiety was reaching a boiling point. "Please! I just need a minute."

"Fine!" Jane stomped off.

Betty ran into her room and flipped the calendar hanging on the wall to the previous month. Stared at the date she'd put an *X* on. Her last monthly visit. She leaned her head against the wall. She'd thought she'd already broken every rule.

It took her far more than a minute to compose herself. Then she went back to the bathroom and quickly brushed her teeth, washed her face, and twisted her hair into a bun at the nape of her neck. She glanced in the mirror and instantly recalled an image of her and her sisters putting on makeup and getting ready to sneak out. That had been fun. Exciting to defy the rules. She'd pay for that for the rest of her life.

She willed herself to turn around and leave the room.

Mother and Jane met her at the bottom of the stairs. "You look lovely, darling. Although a little pale." Mother pinched her cheeks. "A woman should always want to look nice for her husband, before they are married and afterward. Otherwise he'll look elsewhere."

"If only she could be so lucky," Jane said dryly.

Mother's lips pursed as she looked at Jane. "Your father chose James because he is a very wealthy man. He can provide Betty with everything she'll ever want."

Betty fought to keep the tears at bay. A baby. That was what she'd always wanted, but there were rules about that, too. Marriage first and then a baby. Not the other way around.

James walked out of Father's office, and his expression upon seeing her was, well, dull. He smiled, but there was no shine in his eyes, no handsome glow on his face, nothing that even remotely sparked a hint of joy inside her.

Years of being seen and not heard played into her favor as James escorted her out of the house and into his car. She didn't say a word, merely nodded as he talked. And talked. In a dull monotone. Nothing like Henry's voice.

Her eyes filled with tears as she recalled their last conversation.

If there are any repercussions from this evening, I will provide for you.

That was fine and dandy but she had no idea where he was, how to find him, and even if she did, he didn't have a house, a home. Those were things she wanted. Things a baby needed.

Provide. Money. That was what he'd said because he'd never be home. He'd be going from one job to the next, chasing down criminals. She didn't need money. She needed a husband.

She took a handkerchief out of her purse and dried her eyes.

"Allergies?" James asked. "I have them, too. I was just at the new clinic—maybe you should go there."

A clinic was the last place she needed to go right now. She squeezed her temples, and nearly leaped out of the car as soon as he parked along the curb in front of the restaurant.

They were only a block away from the newspaper office, and she couldn't help but think about Patsy and Lane. They'd looked so in love yesterday. So happy.

So not pregnant and engaged to a worm.

Betty chided herself right then and there for calling him that. She was just at her wit's end, and James was not helping. He was talking about hives from a bee sting.

She rushed into the restaurant as soon as he opened the door, pretending to be enthralled with the lush, elegant surroundings. There were crystal chandeliers hanging from the ceiling, a trio of musicians playing music in a corner, and the waiters, dressed in black tuxedos, had white towels draped over one arm.

The maître d' invited them to follow him to a table, and as soon as he led them through a doorway, the smells assaulted her, made her stomach gurgle. No. Not here. Her stomach seemed to settle as she walked, but she felt oddly woozy.

"Betty?"

She twisted at the sound of her name. "Patsy?" Surprised because she'd helped Patsy, as had Jane and Mother, fix up a cabin in the woods for them to honeymoon in for a few days. "What are you doing here?"

Her sister stood up, so did Lane, and they looked at each other, smiling. "We got hungry," Patsy said.

Lane greeted James cordially as Patsy looked at her

with an alarmed expression as Betty gripped the back of a chair.

"Lane, they can join us at our table, can't they?" Patsy asked.

"Of course," Lane said.

"Oh, well, uh—" James started.

"I insist," Patsy said. "I haven't seen Betty since the wedding." She then grasped Betty's hand. "We are going to visit the powder room. We'll be right back."

"You just got married yesterday," Betty said as Patsy held her arm on the way to the powder room.

"I know, but you are as white as a sheet," Patsy replied.

Once inside the elegant powder room, which had a waiting area complete with red-felt-embossed wallpaper and a matching velvet fainting couch, Betty sat down and hung her head between her legs.

"You look awful," Patsy said. "Are you ill?"

Betty lifted her head, slowly. Thankful the spell had passed, she said, "Just a dizzy spell—I haven't eaten much today."

"Are you sure that's it? Or is it how Father is insisting you marry James?"

"James isn't as awful as we'd imagined. He's…"

"Dutiful?"

"Yes."

Patsy shook her head. "You've been dutiful your entire life—don't you want more? Some fun and excitement."

She'd had that, and it had gotten her… Pregnant, that was what it had gotten her, with a man she'd never see again. "No," Betty said. "I like dutiful."

"Betty—"

"Enough about me—tell me how you are," Betty interrupted. She needed to eat and get home, where she could do some serious, serious thinking.

Patsy took hold of her hands. "I am so happy, Betty. So, so very happy. It's amazing. Lane is so wonderful." She giggled. "I know we've only been married a day, but even before then, he... I don't even know how to say it. I can be who I want to be with him, not who someone else wants me to be and it's so wonderful."

"I'm happy for you."

"I want to be happy for you, too, and I don't see that happening with James."

James wouldn't force her to be anyone; he wouldn't force anyone to do anything. It was just not in him. "He'll provide..." She nearly choked on the word. "Well. He has a nice house. He drove me past it the other day."

"A nice house?" Patsy shook her head. "A house is just a house. Father has a nice house, too, but it didn't make us happy."

"It will make me happy," Betty insisted.

"I know that's what you always wanted. Your own home to keep neat and tidy, your own children to take care of and keep in line." Patsy giggled slightly. "If not for you, Jane and I would have been caught sneaking out months ago. We would have been in trouble over and over again throughout the years." Staring her straight in the eyes, Patsy asked, "But are you sure James is who you want to have those babies with?"

Betty couldn't answer that. She knew the answer, but couldn't say it. "Can I ask you a question?"

"Of course."

"It's about when you and Lane helped capture Vincent Burrows. The article in the newspaper didn't mention the FBI agents by name."

"No, they have a dangerous job, and it could be even more dangerous if their names were in the newspaper."

Betty laid a hand on her stomach. "Was one named Henry? Henry Randall?"

Patsy's face lit up. "Why? Do you know him? Have you seen him?"

"No, I haven't seen him."

Patsy huffed out a breath. "I was hoping you'd say yes. He was shanghaied—"

"Shanghaied?" Betty's heart leaped into her throat.

"Yes, almost a month ago and Lane and I are beginning to think the worst."

Thankfully, Betty was already sitting down when she put the fainting couch to good use.

Henry stood in the shadows of a tall tree, where he'd easily be able to stop any and all women who climbed down the trellis tonight. He could have tossed a coin to decide if he should find Lane first, or Betty, but he hadn't needed any help in making that decision. As soon as LeRoy had left, Henry changed out of the sailor's uniform and drove here.

What he'd had to make a decision on was to knock on the front door and talk to William Dryer, or to talk to Betty first.

It had only taken him a moment to decide. The bedroom lights were on upstairs, which meant they hadn't snuck out yet. So, he'd parked down the block and snuck into the backyard to wait.

He'd only been there a few minutes when the lights went out. First one and then the other. Next, a set of legs came out the bathroom window and started climbing down the trellis.

Jane. He recognized her as soon as she was completely out the window, which was where his gaze remained, watching for Betty.

She never emerged and Jane was already scampering across the yard, toward the tree he stood behind.

He waited until the exact moment and then stepped out and grabbed her arm.

She slapped a hand over her mouth, but removed it as the fear left her eyes.

"Well, if it isn't the dancing Reuben."

All three of the Dryer girls were pretty, but the younger two didn't hold a candle to Betty. "Hello, Jane."

She lifted a brow, but didn't appear overly surprised that he knew her name. "Weeks of fun were wasted on looking for you."

He released her arm. "By whom?"

"My sister."

"Where is Betty?" He glanced at the window. "Her light went out right after yours did."

"Because I shut it off," Jane said. "Betty had left it on when she was picked up for her date."

He clamped his back teeth together at the anger that rose up in him. A different level of anger that he didn't know what to relate it to because he'd never known anything quite like it.

"With the man she's going to marry," Jane said. "She's already engaged to him."

He breathed through his nose at the hard ball that formed beneath his rib cage. "Engaged?"

"Yes. To James Bauer."

"The man who builds houses for your father?"

"Yes."

He balled his hands into fists. Engaged. "Where are they?"

Jane tilted her head back farther so the floppy brim

of her yellow hat didn't cover her eyes. "Why? What are you doing here?"

"Do you know where they are?"

She looked at him for a long moment before nodding. "Yes."

He took her arm again, and they walked toward his car.

"Where are we going?" she asked.

"To find them."

"Ducky!"

Henry's insides were a colliding mixture of burning anger and icy clarification. Engaged. That certainly hadn't taken her long. Or had she known that when... She must have. He'd heard her father had put the word out for rich men to marry his daughters. That was why she'd wanted to have fun, to... His throat burned. She'd duped him all right, but it had had nothing to do with the case.

There was a burning pain in his chest, right where his heart was.

He didn't know it could hurt like this, but what he did know was that a woman engaged to one man and seducing another, didn't have a heart.

"The restaurant is near the newspaper office," Jane said once they were both in the car.

He flipped the car around and headed into town. He flipped his mind around, too. "Do you know where Lane is?"

"Why?" Jane asked. "Do you know Lane?"

"Yes, and I know he got married yesterday. Did they go out of town for a honeymoon?" He hoped that was the case.

"No. He and Patsy are spending a few days in a cabin in the woods."

"Where? What cabin?"

She leaned forward and stared at him. "Why?"

"I just need to know where the cabin is. It's important."

"Not far from here," Jane said. "It's on my father's property."

Henry cursed beneath his breath. It had to be the cabin that he'd stayed in, and that wasn't a safe spot. Elkin must know about it. Just down the hill from it was where they'd knocked him out.

"What's this all about?" Jane asked. "You aren't just looking for my sister because you like her, are you?"

"No, I'm not." He held his breath for a moment at how things could change hour to hour and minute to minute. He had liked Betty, still did if the truth must be known, but he'd never really known what to think about her. All the way from a coincidence to someone he needed to protect, she made him feel things he'd never felt before. "I'm an FBI agent, and believe your family may be in danger."

"Danger? What kind of danger?"

"Does the name Curtis Elkin mean anything to you?"

"No. Should it?"

"No one's ever mentioned it?"

"No! What kind of danger?"

The buildings had been rolling by for blocks, and he kept one eye on the rearview mirror and one on the road all the way, not knowing if Elkin was already watching him or not. "Serious danger." He glanced at the businesses lining the street. "Where's this restaurant?"

"Right over there." She pointed toward the left. "There's James's car, and…and that's Lane's car!"

He had no idea what Lane drove. "Are you sure?"

"Yes! Pull over. Pull over!"

Jane was already holding on to the door handle. "We have to talk before going in the restaurant," he said while pulling the car around the block. He couldn't go inside. There was no telling if Elkin was following Lane, either.

"About what?"

"James Bauer." He wanted to know more about that man, but would find that information out from sources other than Betty's family. "This is serious, could be very dangerous and only family can know about it."

"And you."

"And the Bureau," he clarified, while coming up with a plan of where they could meet. It couldn't be inside, or the hotel—they were both too public. His only option was the abandoned house. The Bureau hadn't been involved in the bust of the mob boss, Burrows's uncle, so Elkin may not know about the house. Even if he did, the tunnel would be safe.

The keys to the house and tunnel had been on his key ring, the one he'd dropped on the floor of his car when he'd gotten hit over the head. LeRoy had given them back to him with his other items from the cabin. He hoped that meant Elkin didn't know about the house or tunnel.

Huffing out a breath, he knew he didn't have an option in not trusting Jane, either. "All right, this is what you are going to do."

Jane listened as he told her to get rid of Bauer, however she had to, and to tell Lane to meet him at the abandoned house. Because he didn't want them all together, he also told her to bring Betty to his car.

As Jane climbed out of the car, and he thought of seeing Betty, Henry's emotions caught up with him, yet he was calm, accepting what had been, and what would be, which was exactly what he'd wanted.

No, it was what he needed. She was engaged. He was fine with that because that was not something he could ever have offered her. It shouldn't have angered him in the first place.

He was to blame in all that had happened. He should have walked away from her that first night. Would have had it been anyone else.

He braced himself when the door of the restaurant opened, and let out a sigh of relief when it wasn't her. The man walked to the car Jane had indicated as James Bauer's car. Henry huffed out a grunt. James was short, stout and his shoulders were slumped forward. The man climbed into the car and drove away.

The restaurant door opened again, and Henry wasn't quite as prepared as he'd thought. Betty, wearing a dark blue dress, frowned as she walked toward his car. Lost in a memory he shouldn't have let enter his mind, it was last-minute when he opened his door so he could walk around and open hers.

As he stood, locked eyes with her over the top of the car, he wished he could take pride in himself for not feeling anything. But he couldn't, because he did feel something.

She didn't say a word.

Neither did he.

She opened her door.

He sat back down in the driver's seat.

She climbed in and stared out the windshield. "Jane will ride with Lane and Patsy."

He let the air that had been locked in his lungs out and started the car.

* * *

"What are you doing here, Henry?"

"We need to talk."

The hands she had folded in her lap were trembling. "About what?"

Jane must have followed his orders. "Do you know a man named Curtis Elkin?"

"No."

"Did you tell anyone about the tunnel in the abandoned house?"

"No."

"Not even Lane?" He knew she hadn't, but was buying himself some time to get his feelings under control. Hidden, where they belonged.

"No. Why would I have told Lane about that?"

He drove several blocks toward town, keeping an eye out for followers. The light, sweet scent of her perfume was filling the air, and a battle of wills fought inside him over how badly he wanted to touch her. Even just her hand. Her arm.

"Patsy told me you were shanghaied," she said quietly.

"I was, and I returned as soon as possible." He turned a corner and attempted to keep his mind on driving, not on how much he'd thought about her during his absence. No one had ever made him as confused as she had. As she did.

"Why did you return? Your case is over. Burrows was arrested."

"Yes, Burrows was arrested, but my assignment isn't over." He turned a corner, still watching for followers. There hadn't been any so far, and he hoped there wouldn't be. He'd always preferred to be the follower, not the one being followed.

"Is that why Lane and Patsy and Jane are to meet us at the house?"

"Yes."

"Why? What do any of us have to do with it?"

"I'll explain all that when we get there." He took another corner, heading back toward the outskirts of town and the house. "I wanted to talk to you first."

"Why?"

There was another battle going on inside him, over how she was being so reserved, almost indifferent. That wasn't the Betty he knew. The one he'd come to know very, very well. What had he expected? For her to leap into his arms? He should be happy she was so aloof because what had happened before couldn't happen again. "Because I needed to ask you about the house, if you'd told anyone." It was an excuse. He was again buying time before asking her if there were any repercussions he should know about. He'd thought about that a lot during his absence.

"No, I haven't told anyone." She looked out the passenger window. "Anything."

He nodded. "Congratulations on your engagement."

"Thank you."

Her reply had been soft, and shaky. Embarrassed? For being engaged to someone else so shortly after their…encounter. That irritated him. No, it went deeper than irritation. To a place he didn't know existed. Nor did he want to know. He forced it all to go away, to bury itself deep inside him as he drove a few more blocks where the sound of her uneven breathing echoed in his ears. "Are you all right?"

"Yes, I'm fine." Her reply was much faster and her breathing quickened.

"In every way?" He hoped she understood what he meant.

"Yes."

"That's good." Guilt along with an odd disappointment wormed its way inside him. He wasn't sure why, nor was he going to investigate it. What he was going to do was focus on this case. "I also owe you an apology."

"For what?"

"When we met again, after three years, I questioned if meeting you was more than a coincidence. Questioned if you had been involved in the leaking of information that had happened in Seattle and here Los Angeles."

"Me? Leaking information?"

He was blundering this. He wasn't used to apologizing, and making it sound worse than it was. "Yes, I had to. That's what I do. Investigate crimes. Find criminals."

"Exactly what involvement did you need to investigate?"

She was looking at him now. Giving him a glare that could make men tremble in their boots.

Chapter Eight

Betty had been angry before, very angry, but the level that was rising inside her right now went beyond all she'd ever known. *Investigating her. Leaking information.* Did he think she was completely stupid? He was making up an excuse. An excuse as to why… She refused to even remember that moment. Any moments she'd spent with him.

"I'll explain it all at the house," he said. "When Lane and your sisters arrive."

"No, you'll explain it now. What information was I supposed to have leaked?"

"None. I just questioned if you had."

"Why?"

He huffed out a breath. "Because that's happened to me before. A woman using her charms to get information."

Her anger was growing. So was the hurt inside. Everything about him went back to his job. It was the only thing he ever thought about, ever cared about.

She didn't respond to his answer because she was never going to talk to him again. Ever. The shock of hearing he'd been shanghaied had devastated her, and then hearing he was in a car, waiting for her, had elated her, but then she'd seen him. His face. How cold and… like he'd never wanted to see her again. That had been in his voice, too, when he'd asked if she was all right, in every way. She was fine, in every way, except for being mad. So mad because nothing about him, about them, had been what she'd thought. She'd thought they'd been falling in love, but he'd been investigating her! That was just too much.

More than a coincidence?

She'd like to tell him about coincidences. For instance, was it a coincidence that when she saw him her body went out of control? Was it a coincidence that she turned into someone she was not? Someone who acted without thinking. Someone who broke every rule?

None of that had ever happened to her before, yet it had, in Seattle and here.

Well, it was not going to happen this time. She knew who she was, who she would always be. And she knew who he was. An FBI agent through and through. Well, that was fine because she knew what she wanted and how to get it, and he wasn't a part of any of that.

Except for being the father of her baby.

He'd probably have to investigate that, too. Her insides quivered. She couldn't have him doing that.

"I'm parking here because I don't want a car in the driveway of the house," he said.

Betty glanced out the window, recognizing the building as one of the studios. He'd parked in the back lot, so all they had to do was run across the street.

"I'm certain no one has followed us."

Why was he doing all this? The case was over. Burrows was caught. There couldn't be more to it than that.

Unless he was investigating... No, her sisters didn't know about the baby.

She stepped out of the car when he opened the door, but didn't take his hand, or look at him. Despite the anger still boiling inside her, she didn't trust herself. When it came to him, she was like a two-headed coin tossed in the air. No matter which side it landed on, she was the one who lost. Lost all her sensibility and everything else that went along with it.

She had to fight to breathe as they entered the house. She could hear her heart pounding, feel her pulse quickening. She'd thought the pain of him being gone, of having left without even saying goodbye had been bad, but this, being in the very house where she'd abandoned all she'd known to be right and just, in order to fulfill a need that he'd put inside her, was beyond painful.

It was reality. She'd given him her heart that night. All the love she'd ever have to give, and she would never get that back. She'd walk around empty for the rest of her life.

"We'll wait here for the others," he said.

Her stomach fluttered as he handed her a flashlight. No, she wouldn't walk around empty. He'd given her something for her heart. A baby. And it was hers. All hers.

She had been afraid that he might ask if there were any repercussion from that night, and was glad she'd said she was fine. Even though she knew that was wrong, against another rule. A baby wasn't a repercussion, and she didn't want his money.

The others arrived and Henry locked the door and then led everyone downstairs, where they could use the flashlights without worrying that someone driving past might notice a light.

Betty half listened, because in truth, she only half cared what he had to say. The other truth was that sitting on the sofa in the basement was bringing back memories.

Henry spoke about a man named Curtis Elkin, who was also an investigation agent, but had been leaking information, and whom Henry now believed had turned completely away from the agency because the man hadn't been seen or heard from in weeks.

Lane seemed very concerned, so did Patsy, and Jane appeared frightened.

"Besides me, you are the only other person who can identify Elkin, Lane," Henry said. "Other agents could identify him, but without proof, the Bureau can't assign any others to chase him down."

"You're right," Lane said. "And the news that I married Patsy has gone from one end of this town to the other." He looped his arm around Patsy's shoulders and pulled her closer to his side. "I can't have her in that kind of danger."

"I know," Henry said. "That's why I'm here. My supervisor also believes that Elkin is the mole and as soon as I prove it, the Bureau will send more agents."

"So it's just me and you," Lane said.

"Yes," Henry said. "And the cabin you're staying at isn't safe. That's where they found me, knocked me out, stuffed me in a barrel, and shipped me off to Hawaii."

Betty's spine stiffened. "They stuffed you in a barrel?"

Henry was leaning against the door to the tunnel, arms crossed. He nodded to her, but said to Lane, "I'm concerned Elkin may go after anyone connected to you, including Patsy's sisters."

"I'm thinking the same thing," Lane said.

"There's no more sneaking out at night," Henry said, looking at her.

Betty hadn't cared about sneaking out in weeks, but Jane had, and would continue to.

Everyone in the room must have been thinking the same thing because they all looked at Jane.

She held up her arms, bent at the elbows and palms outward. "I'm all for a good time, but I'm not into danger." Jane then asked Henry, "But you aren't going to tell our father, are you? If he hears about this, we'll never be able to sneak out again. Ever. Or worse. He'll send us all away."

When Henry looked at Betty, as if she needed to verify what Jane said, she nodded. Father would.

"I'll start looking for Elkin tonight," Henry said.

"I will, too," Lane said.

"No, I will let you know when I need you. For now, Elkin doesn't know I'm alive or—"

Betty nearly shot off the sofa. "Alive?"

Henry nodded, but finished what he'd been saying. "Or back in town, and I want to keep it that way. Lane, I need to know about any busts that happened in the past year or so, not of speakeasies, but of supply rings."

"I can get that," Lane said.

Henry nodded again. "Good, and—" He looked at her. "No one goes out alone. Not even to the grocery store."

He gave a few more instructions, but again, Betty barely heard what he was saying. She was still stuck on him being alive. She'd never thought otherwise, and that made her sick. Not throwing-up sick, but an all-consuming ache.

Henry walked her and Jane to their house, and he

took ahold of her hand while Jane was climbing the trellis.

"I won't let anything happen to any of you," he whispered, and then waited as she climbed the trellis, entered the bathroom, and shut the window.

By the time she crawled into bed, she was a pitiful mess. She couldn't get over that someone had stuffed him in a barrel. He could have died.

He could have been dead right now.

That was the most dreadful thought, the most dreadful reality, ever. She wished she could find the anger she'd had earlier, but she couldn't. He hadn't been looking for an excuse. She had been. She had been trying to forget him for over three years, ever since that first kiss, but couldn't. That kiss had opened something inside her. A part of her she hadn't known existed, and when she'd seen him again the night of the dance-off, she'd wanted that part of her to be opened again.

He had opened it, and it had felt so good, she'd been unable to stay away. It was as if she'd been wrapped in a cocoon like a caterpillar and he'd made her feel like a butterfly, free to spread her wings and fly.

Or like a moth, drawn to a light that blinded her, made her lose her way.

Either way, seeing him again tonight confirmed one thing. She'd never be able to forget him. A person couldn't forget about someone they cared about, and she cared about him. Cared far more than she should. Cared too much about him to be angry. Much like she'd always cared too much about her sisters to be angry with them. Even Jane and her sneaking-out plan.

She hadn't gotten angry. She'd found a way for Jane to get what she wanted, and Patsy, for them to have fun, because that was what she'd always done. That was what she needed to do with Henry, too.

Find a way so he could catch this Elkin man.

She'd been thrilled at the idea of helping him before, giving him the list of the speakeasies, but this time, she was scared, because now she realized that every time she saw Henry, she lost a little bit more of the person she'd always been.

Surprisingly, she slept well that night, and didn't feel queasy upon waking. After getting dressed, she checked her calendar again, counted the days. Five. Had she jumped to conclusions? She was late by five days. That could happen. And something she ate could have upset her stomach.

Oddly, those thoughts didn't elate her, which confused her even more.

As she sat at the quiet table, eating breakfast, she pondered if what she'd always thought she'd wanted was true. Patsy had wanted to be a reporter for years, and Jane, well, Jane had wanted to be a flapper. Fashion, music, independence. That was Jane.

Betty, sighed. Why didn't she have any dreams like that? Hers had always been to have her own family. Her own house. It would be different than this; there would be conversation and laughter.

From who? James wasn't an awful person, but his conversations weren't overly lively. They were boring and long.

Had she thought she wanted those things, to get married and have children, because she'd never allowed herself to think otherwise? Why? Because she'd known that was the only option she'd have, just like following Father's rules was the only option?

She didn't like being this confused, and as soon as

Father nodded the meal was over, she began to clear the table, but stopped when a knock sounded on the front door.

Visitors at their house were few and far between, and Father's frown said he wasn't expecting anyone.

He rose and walked down the hall to the front door.

A moment later, Betty froze in recognition of the voice that greeted her father.

The wide-eyed look on Jane's face said she'd recognized Henry's voice, too.

Before Betty made it out of the dining room, Henry was following her father into his office and nodded at her before he shut the door.

He was wearing a black suit, and carrying a black hat in his hands, which made him look official. Very official.

Her insides turned cold, icy, but her hands were hot, sweating, as a thousand thoughts rushed to be the first to assault her. But there were too many, they clambered together. She didn't know if she should run and hide, or—

"We're doomed," Jane whispered. "If he tells Father, we're doomed."

Betty couldn't let that happen. She handed Jane the plates she'd lifted off the table right before the knock had sounded and, head up, walked down the hallway.

She didn't knock, just opened the door and stepped in. She quivered slightly at how the look on her father's face indicated he wasn't impressed by her actions, but then instantly looked at Henry.

Henry gave her a slight grin while asking Father, "Is this your daughter?"

"Yes, yes, it is," Father replied.

Henry gave her a slight nod. "It's nice to make your

acquaintance, Miss Dryer. I was just informing your father that I work for the government and that we are interested in preparing a house we own for sale. It needs to be cleaned and I was informed that you clean the houses in this area prior to the new owners taking occupancy."

Confused, she shook her head.

Henry nodded. "I would like to hire you to clean the property we are interested in putting up for sale. An abandoned house just a short distance from here."

His nearness did what it always did, opened that part of her that was impossible for her to control. She took a deep breath and nodded, fully aware of the house he referred to and understanding this must be part of his plan to catch Elkin. "All right, when would you like me to start?"

"You have chores here at home," Father said.

"I can still complete them," she said, surprising herself, both by contradicting Father and by how easily she'd done it.

The tension in the air, coming from William Dryer, caused Henry to question if this was the best plan. It had been the only one he'd come up with, and because he was a man of action, always had been, he had to put it into play. He was already hot on Elkin's tail. As soon as he'd left her backyard last night, he'd gone to work. Elkin was still in town, but had changed his profession. It appeared he'd taken over for Burrows when it came to moonshine. Burrows had started up a still near the docks, but that was only for show; in reality, the man had been plotting to steal shipments of Minnesota Thirteen, the most sought-after whiskey in the nation. Each shipload was worth its weight in gold, and an entire shipment had gone missing right before Burrows had been arrested. Yet, none of the speakeasies were lacking in their supply. Including the Rooster's Nest, which was widely known as a major port in the supply chain of the brew.

It wasn't the proof he needed to call in other agents, but it was enough that he had to make sure that Betty understood the seriousness of this case. He hadn't been able to shake how distant she'd seemed last night, and knew he had to speak to her today. Shy of climbing the trellis and sneaking into her bedroom, this was the only plan he'd been able to compile.

"If you are available, I would like to show you what we'd like to have you do," he said to Betty. "Now."

There was still confusion in her eyes, but she nodded.

He'd expected confusion from her, even defiance, as well as disapproval from her father, but, to his surprise, within minutes, Betty was walking out the door with him.

In the short time he'd spent alone with William Dryer, both prior to Betty entering the office, and after she'd agreed to accompany him to the house and excused herself to collect her purse and hat, Henry got a distinct sense that William Dryer was hiding something. Henry also determined he'd find out exactly what.

Betty returned, and Henry guided her out the door and toward his car. "Thank you for agreeing so readily."

"Why are you doing this? I'm assuming you truly don't need the house cleaned."

He opened the passenger door for her. "No, I don't, but I did need to talk to you."

"About the case?"

He waited until she climbed in the car before he said,

"Yes." He closed the door, walked around the car, and climbed in.

"Have you found him?"

"No, but I have made progress in learning his activities." He started the car and backed out of the driveway. "Neither you nor your sister can go to the Rooster's Nest."

"You said that last night."

Her perfume, so subtle that some might not notice it, was already playing havoc on his senses. By not doing anything more than sitting in the seat beside him, she had his pulse throbbing beneath his skin. "I need to know you understand that Elkin is a dangerous man—he's not going to stop until he gets what he wants. He could be anywhere, watching, waiting."

"What does he look like?" she asked.

His nerves sizzled and snapped like a shorted-out electric line. "Why? Have you seen something? Someone?"

"I'm not sure, but after Patsy and Lane had left after their wedding, I was sweeping the rice off the church steps and noticed a man sitting in a car. I couldn't see his face because the sun was shining on the widows, but I could feel him watching me, and then he drove away."

"Do you remember what the car looked like?"

"No. It was black. That's all I remember."

Henry didn't need to know more in order to confirm it had been Elkin, and that he was after Lane and possibly Betty and her sister. It was a cat-and-mouse game. Elkin would pounce sooner or later, and Henry had to be prepared to be ready for it at any time, anyplace. That was his main focus, but in the interim, he'd had another line of investigation that he wanted Betty to be involved in with him.

"Do you know Blake Owens?"

"No," she answered. "I do know that he built a few houses for my father, before James."

"That's correct." He continued to drive, past the abandoned house and the studios.

"Why?"

"Does Owens know who you are?" he asked in response. This was personal. He was going to discover all there was to know about James Bauer, so she would know exactly who she was engaged to marry. Lane had told him a small amount, that Bauer was a nice enough guy, but spineless, and Dryer had him wrapped around his finger. Lane had suggested he talk to Owens to learn more.

She shook her head. "I'm sure he doesn't. I've never met him. Why?"

"I have a meeting with him this morning. Undercover, and it would be helpful for you to come with me."

"Why?"

"I'm going to pretend that I'm interested in having him build a house, and it would be more believable if I had a wife with me."

"A wife? What would any of that have to do with catching Elkin?"

It was a stretch, but he hoped she'd believe him. He had never done something like this before, just for his own sake, but despite how hard he'd tried, he couldn't not care about her marrying someone else. She deserved a man who loved her, not one who was simply doing her father's bidding. "I have to make sure that Elkin hasn't already gotten to your father."

"My father?"

"Yes. Your father is a rich man and we don't know what Elkin's ultimate goal is. We have to cover all avenues." Guilt gurgled in his stomach at taking things this far, but it was for her own good. "I've suggested to Blake Owens that I'm interested in buying a home in Hollywoodland and a married couple would be more apt to do that than a single man."

He glanced over at her, noticing how she had a hand over her mouth and was swallowing, hard, eyes closed. "Are you all right?"

She nodded.

Henry slowed the car in case that was what was making her sick, because that was what she looked like, as if she was getting sick, and then pulled into the closest parking lot. He shut off the car and twisted in his seat, brushed her hair away from the side of her face.

That had been a mistake.

The smell of her perfume had been playing havoc on him, but this, touching her, was like he'd just been zapped by lightning. He'd tried not care about her, even pretended that he didn't, pretended that he truly believed she'd somehow been involved with him being shanghaied, but it had all been a lie. The biggest lie he'd ever told himself.

He'd been so good at not caring before she came into his life. So very good. It had started at the orphanage, when other kids would talk about how their parents were going to come back for them someday. He knew his weren't and pretended that didn't matter to him. That he didn't care.

Then, when he was adopted and, within months, moved into the junior college, he'd pretended he didn't care. Didn't care that his adoptive parents didn't want him any more than his real parents had. Eventually, he'd gotten so good at pretending, that he had begun to truly not care.

He just couldn't seem to reach that level with her. In fact, it appeared as if that may very well be as impossible as swimming across the ocean.

"Can I get something for you?" He glanced at the stores sharing the parking area. "There's a grocer right over there."

She dropped her hand away from her mouth and took a long inhale, then let it out slowly. "No, thank you, I'm fine now."

"Did you have time to eat breakfast?" he asked. "Are you hungry?"

"No. I mean yes, I had breakfast. I'm not hungry." She managed a tentative smile. "I'm fine now, really."

She was still pale, but no longer looked as pasty as she had a short time ago. "Are you sure?"

"Yes, I'm sure. What time is your meeting with Mr. Owens?"

He glanced at his watch. "In about ten minutes, but I can go later. I'll take you home."

"No. I'll go with you. I'm fine. We need to find out all we can so you can catch Elkin."

There was color in her face again. He tucked her hair behind her ear.

She grasped his wrist and pulled his hand away from her. "Truly, Henry, I'm fine. You need to start driving so we aren't late."

He settled back in his seat and started the car. As he drove, he had to wonder if he'd be able to salvage any of his old self once this case was over. Caring about her was so easy, and nothing had ever come easy to him before.

"I told Mr. Owens that my name was Donald Knight and that I'm moving to Los Angeles from Virginia."

She nodded. "Is that who you told my father you are? Donald Knight?"

"No, I told him my name was John Smith."

She grinned. "You are going to confuse yourself using so many names."

He'd already confused himself, not by using aliases, but by meeting her. Forgetting her would be something else that would be impossible. She was too beautiful, too special. "I'm used to being two people at the same time," he said. "You are, too, Lacy."

She made a little humph sound. "You are right about that."

Out of the side of his eye, he saw her remove the burgundy cloche hat and flip her head down. She then gathered her long hair together, wrapped it tightly, and then tied a white scarf high on her forehead before putting the hat back on.

He had a hard time concentrating on driving, and barely managed to make the corner in the nick of time onto the street that would take them to the address that Blake Owens had given him.

She opened her purse and, using a small compact mirror, applied lipstick, and then other makeup as he continued to drive. She also pulled out a pair of elbow-length white gloves, and put them on, as well as a pair of earbobs and a string of pearls.

By the time he'd parked the car and got a good look at her, he was amazed by how much she'd changed her appearance while he'd been driving. She'd looked pretty before, in her white-and-burgundy-striped dress, but now, with a few small changes, looked as if she could be in a fashion magazine.

Taking a second look, he shook his head. "Is that some kind of a magical purse?"

Smoothing the gloves over her wrists, up her arms, she giggled. "No."

He nodded. If there was a chance that Blake Owens knew her, the man wouldn't recognize her. If Henry hadn't witnessed the transformation, he might not have recognized her himself. She looked older, more sophisticated, and, as much as he didn't want to think about it, sexier, than she had earlier.

"Let's go." He opened his door. "We are already a few minutes late."

"My name is Lucy," she said as she grabbed the door handle. "Lucy Knight."

"Sit tight, Lucy Knight," he said. "I'll get your door for you."

While walking around the car, he took a moment to focus on his undercover role, Donald Knight, whose wife was Lucy. An amazingly beautiful woman.

He placed a hand on the small of her back as they walked into the office of Owens Construction Company, and took great pride in introducing his undercover wife, Lucy Knight.

Once settled in a chair inside Blake's office, Henry explained that he and his wife would be moving to California within a few months and were interested in having a home built for them, in Hollywoodland.

Lifting a brow as dark as the black hair on his head, Blake asked, "Would you be interested in a different location?"

In an attempt to make their ploy look legitimate, Henry glanced at Betty. She smiled at him and shook her head.

"As you can see, we aren't," Henry said to Blake while reaching over and taking ahold of Betty's hand. "Why do you ask?"

Blake ran a hand over the thin mustache covering his upper lip. "Because I can't build a house in Hollywoodland."

"Can't?" Henry asked.

"Well, I'm perfectly capable of building a house anywhere, but I *won't* build another one in Hollywoodland. I refuse to."

Henry knew the man was capable of building anything, anywhere. He was the most sought-after builder in the city and Henry had only been able to acquire this meeting because he'd said he'd been referred by Lane. "Why?"

Blake leaned back in his seat. "Have you checked into the specifications of building a home in Hollywoodland?"

"We meet the financial qualifications," Henry replied.

Blake shook his head as a flash of disgust crossed his face. "Dryer puts those right in his advertisements. William Dryer. He owns hundreds of acres that extend up into the mountains. What he doesn't put in those ads is how he doesn't care about building codes or safety regulations. Dryer has the builder he has working with him right now convinced those codes don't apply to them."

"Who is that?" Henry asked.

"James Bauer."

Betty didn't make a sound, but he felt her hand tremble beneath his.

Henry tightened his hold on her hand. "Is his work not up to par?"

"I'm going to be perfectly honest with you, Mr. Knight." Blake leaned forward and set his elbows on his desk. "I agreed to meet with you because Lane Cox asked me to. I've known Lane for years, and out of respect of our friendship, I didn't attend his wedding because I knew William Dryer would make a point of asking me to leave."

Henry threaded his fingers through Betty's as her hand trembled harder.

Keeping up with the premise of being out-of-towners, Henry asked, "Oh? Dryer was at Lane's wedding?"

Blake let out a huff. "Lane married one of Dryer's daughters. That Dryer had grown-up daughters shocked the entire community because those of us who knew Dryer had children didn't realize they were adults. The way Dryer talked about them led everyone to believe they were still young children."

"How?" Henry wanted to know.

"Just different things he'd say. When I worked there, he claimed he couldn't put any money toward roads or utilities because it took all he had to keep his children fed and clothed. He was always complaining about money, as if he'll never have enough. Other than comments now and again, he never really said anything specific about his family."

"When did you build houses for Dryer?"

"Three years ago." Blake shrugged. "I did build a house out there last year, for Jack McCarney, but I built it for Jack directly. He bought the land from Dryer first."

"Can you do that for us?"

"No, Dryer didn't like that, and put an end to it," Blake answered. "He won't sell just the land. It has to be a package deal. People pick out the lot they want and the house they want. Bauer builds the house and it's sold as one, house and land. If you ask me, Dryer is tying his own noose." He shrugged then. "Not that too many people care." He leaned back in his seat. "They both will when the lawsuits start hitting him."

Betty gasped at that.

Henry gave her hand a reassuring squeeze before asking, "What lawsuits?"

"The city council has adopted many specific ordinances over the past decade, from who can keep a cow on their property to where cemeteries can be built, and everything in between. They've also laid down specific building requirements, of which a builder can be fined for and made to replace or repair. Bauer is building those houses with two-by-four frames. They aren't strong enough to support houses of that size, but with over twenty thousand homes being built each year, the city can't keep up with inspecting every build, so he's getting away with it. The first rumble of any sizable earthquake and those houses Bauer is building are going to rattle apart, and mark my words, the people buying those houses will expect that the work is all warranted."

The phone on Blake's desk rang. "Sorry," he said and picked up the phone. "Give me five minutes," he said into the speaker. "My apologies, again," he said to them as he hooked the phone back on its stand. "I have another appointment, but I'd highly recommend you folks look elsewhere to build a house. There is plenty of property just as nice as Hollywoodland and a different builder will build you one that will last a lifetime." He slid a piece of paper across his desk. "These are some of the houses I've built, and some lots that are for sale at reasonable prices. If you care to take a look at them, we can talk again."

Henry picked up the paper. "Thanks. This will be helpful."

Blake stood up as Henry rose and then assisted Betty out of her chair.

"I hope I didn't dissuade you from moving here,"

Blake said. "It's a good place to live, and, well, I just believe people should get what they pay for."

Henry held out his hand and shook Blake's. "We appreciate your honesty, and we'll take a look at these properties."

Blake held his hand out to Betty. "It was nice meeting you, Mrs. Knight."

She took ahold of his hand, shook it. "You, too, Mr. Owens. Good day."

"Good day," Blake repeated to her, and then added, "Just give me a call when you're ready to talk again."

"We will," Henry replied, guiding Betty to the door with a hand on her back. He'd be calling Blake Owens soon. Very soon. He had more questions about Bauer and held no doubt that Owens could answer them.

Chapter Nine

"That didn't tell us very much," Betty said once they were driving away from Blake Owens's construction company.

Henry didn't agree. Their meeting with Owens had told him a lot. "Do you know which houses Bauer has built for your father?"

"Yes, I can show you if you'd like."

"How many are there?"

"Four, but I could only show you three. Father and James will most likely be at the fourth one, because it's still being built."

"Is it close to the others?"

"I'm not sure. I know where the three are because my sisters and I cleaned them after the construction was done. They are farther up the hill, past the one Mr. Owens built for Jack McCarney."

"Does your father help James build the houses?"

She let out a sigh so long he had to glance her way.

Shrugging, she said, "I'm not sure what my father does. I believe he helps when they dig basements, because at times his clothes are very dirty."

Henry didn't know what to think of that. From

what he understood, William Dryer didn't seem like a physical-labor type of man, but Dryer did like money, and probably was willing to do whatever he needed to in order to make more—including using substandard supplies. It irked him that Dryer cared more about making money than he did his daughters. No father should be like that.

"Let's take a drive up there."

She nodded in agreement.

"How long have you been engaged to James?"

"Not long," she answered, glancing out the side window.

Lane had told him that William had chosen James to marry Betty, for the pure fact that Bauer had money. James had inherited the building company from his father, but had also been working at it since he was a young man himself. Henry didn't want anything about Bauer to be likable, which wasn't like him. He wasn't the type to be jealous of anyone, but whether he wanted to admit it or not, the hard ball that had formed under his ribs was jealousy. Pure and simple. He was going to have to get over that. Even if she didn't marry James Bauer, she would get married someday, and it wouldn't be to him. "You don't mind that your father chose your husband?"

"I've always known that would happen. Father told us that when we were little."

"And you agree with it?" He shook his head. "That doesn't sound like you."

"Maybe you don't know me."

"Maybe I don't." Tension was building in his neck and he knew why. She was so meek and timid right now, nothing like the Betty he'd gotten to know during their nights together. It was as if she was two completely different people. That at the mention of her father, the vibrant, fun-loving Betty was instantly overshadowed by a shy, timorous girl who was afraid to even speak loud enough to be heard. He hated the idea that someone had that much power over her. It reminded him of the orphanage, how children had been forced into submission until they were like a regiment of well-trained soldiers who never questioned the orders they were given.

"You'll have to give me directions once we get to the abandoned house," he said.

"All right," she said. "You'll just keep driving on that road for a couple of miles, then there is another road we'll take. People live in two of the houses James built, but the third one is still empty, I believe."

"From what Blake said, I assumed the houses were sold before they were built."

She shrugged.

"Your father doesn't talk much about his business?"

She shook her head.

"Not even to your mother?"

"I don't know. She wouldn't tell us if he did because…" Once again, she turned to stare out the window.

"Because why?"

"Because we are to be seen and not heard, nor are we allowed to listen. That's why we are able to sneak out at night. We are sent to bed by seven thirty each night and not allowed back downstairs until breakfast."

It sounded as if her life was stricter than his had been at the orphanage and school. "What about weekends?"

"What about them?"

"Isn't your father home then?"

"No. Other than church Sunday mornings, he goes to work as always."

Henry's instincts earlier had been right. There was something very strange about William Dryer and his activities. He didn't believe William was involved with Elkin, but for Betty's sake, he was going to find out more.

Following her directions, he drove past three houses built by Bauer. From the outside, there was nothing shoddy looking about them. They were big, elaborate, from the looks of them, and sure to cost a pretty penny. Two were occupied and one was vacant, just as she'd thought.

He didn't stop to investigate further; he'd do that alone, and continued to follow the road. She didn't question him, so he continued to drive as the road made a large loop and eventually came out on the paved highway that eventually ran along the coastline.

"Wow," she whispered as the Pacific came into view. "I haven't seen the ocean in years."

Surprised, he asked, "Why? You live within miles of it."

She didn't answer, and he knew why. She hadn't lied about her father and his strict rules. Flustered at himself and all that she was deprived of, he pulled off the highway on the next road that would take them down to the beach.

"Where are we going?" she asked.

"To see the ocean."

Her eyes lit up, even as she shook her head. "I should get home."

But she didn't want to. He could tell. "You will. We'll only stay a few minutes."

"All right." She grinned then and pulled off her gloves while he found a place to park.

Still smiling, she held his hand as they climbed down

a short, rocky, and weedy hill that led to the sandy beach.

She drew in a deep breath as they stepped into the soft sand. "I can smell the beach at our house some days."

He laughed. "The smell of dead fish does carry in the air."

She slapped at his arm. "I don't smell dead fish."

"What do you smell?"

Closing her eyes, she lifted her chin, smelled the air. "I don't know. Faraway places. Freedom. Fun." She plopped down on the sand and pulled off her socks and shoes.

He sat down beside her and took off his, as well. She'd already jumped back up and was halfway to the water by the time he'd rolled up his pant legs and stood. "Wait up!"

She laughed and waved an arm in the air. "Hurry up, slowpoke!"

He ran and caught up with her near the water's edge and then walked beside her, making footprints in the wet sand.

She held her hands out at her sides and spun around so she was walking backward while facing him. "Isn't this wonderful?"

It clearly was to her, and that was enough to make him agree. "Yes." Seeing the transformation on her face was far more wonderful. The shine was back in her eyes, and on her face. So was a smile.

"I wish I could do this every day."

He couldn't tell her that she could right now, but that was only because of Elkin. When the case was closed, she could. "Why do you let your father hold such control over you?"

She frowned.

"That's what he's doing with his rules," he told her. He knew all about being controlled by rules. The rules of order at the orphanage had been strict and the punishment for disobeying them had been harsh. Junior college had had another set of rules, and the Bureau another, but they were for different reasons. Not just for control.

"It's his house, his rules."

"You're an adult. A grown woman." The dreams, the memories of the night they'd made love, would forever live inside him, and right now, they were reminding him of just how perfect a woman she was, in every way. "Maybe it's time to show your father that." He'd done that, shown his adoptive parents that he was a grown man. One they didn't need to provide for, or even care about. He would forever be grateful for what they had done, because his life would have been very different if they hadn't adopted him, but he also had released them from being responsible for him in any way by keeping his distance.

She dropped her hands to her sides. Frowning, she shook her head, but didn't say anything; it was almost as if she was shaking her head at herself, at whatever thoughts were floating around in that beautiful head of hers.

A gust of wind whipped around them and tugged at her hat.

He reached up, pulled it off her head, and caught the scarf as the wind untwisted it from around her forehead.

The wind then caught her hair, making it twist and tangle as it fell upon her shoulders, down her back.

He couldn't help himself and drew her to him. Her arms looped around his neck and her body pressed up against his. Gazing into her eyes, he did the one thing he'd sworn that he wouldn't do.

He kissed her.

Betty didn't have time to think about anything before her body responded. Just like it always did when it came to him.

She was instantly alive inside. She'd missed that feeling almost as much as she'd missed him. When their lips separated, she sucked in air, laughed, and kissed him again.

She could have gone on kissing him forever, and might have, if he hadn't pulled his lips off hers. His arms were still around her, and he held her there, tight up against him.

He was right, she was grown-up, and if she hadn't had that bout of queasiness while in the car, she might have taken what he'd said into consideration. She couldn't, though, because she was pregnant. Whether it was only five days, or ten, or twenty, she didn't need the calendar to confirm that. She just knew it. What she didn't know was what to do about it.

If she told him, he would *provide for her.* She had no idea what that might mean; it could be wonderful. It could be the exact opposite of wonderful, and she wasn't sure she could take that chance. Life with James would never be wonderful, but it wouldn't be dangerous. She was certain of that.

She didn't like this. This balancing of right and wrong along with safety and danger, but that was what she had to do because it wasn't just her. There was a tiny baby that she needed to think about. A little life she was now responsible for.

That was scary.

"I need to get home," she said, releasing her hold on him and stepping back.

His chest rose and fell as he let out a long sigh. "Yes, you do." He touched the side of her head, smoothed back her hair.

His touch made her nearly as breathless as when they'd been kissing. She hated herself for not being able to tell him about the baby, but she couldn't. Just couldn't.

He took ahold of her hand, held it as they walked back to where they'd left their shoes.

He took her hand again to help her stand up after they'd put on their socks and shoes, and continued to hold it as they climbed the hill. Every step was making her hate herself more and more, but she couldn't tell him, because if she did, and he left, left her alone, her baby would be taken away. Forever.

Once in the car, and fighting hard to keep her emotions in check, she asked, "Are you going to look for Elkin now?"

"Yes."

"You said last night that he is another FBI agent."

"He is. Or was."

"Does that happen often? An agent who flips sides." That was how he'd put it when telling them about Elkin.

"No. It's never happened before, not on this level. He's been leaking information for years. But he's been slick, a real mole—it wasn't until Rex Gaynor was offed that he started to worry he might be found out."

"A mole?"

"Yes, that's what he's referred to as. He's gone underground, sneaking around, leaking secrets. Tipping off criminals."

"Do they know he's an FBI agent? The criminals?"

He'd pulled onto the road, and she couldn't help but look over her shoulder, at the spot on the beach where they had kissed. It was so bittersweet. Everything about her life right now was bittersweet. A baby. That should be such a joyous event, but she couldn't share the joy that she did feel when she thought of having a baby. Couldn't share that with anyone. She felt like a mole herself.

"Yes, I believe they do, but they won't turn in someone who is keeping them from going to prison."

"I suppose they wouldn't." She gathered her gloves and scarf and tucked them in her purse. "The FBI doesn't bust speakeasies, that's prohibition agents, so who do you bust?" She wasn't exactly sure what she was trying to do, other than convince herself what she knew was true. That his job was extremely dangerous.

"Anyone committing a federal crime," he said. "We were involved in the Burrows case because when the train was robbed seven years ago, a shipment of old currency that had been being transported in order for it to be destroyed was stolen off the train. No one was supposed to know about that money being on that train. Rex Gaynor claimed upon his arrest that Billy Phillips, his partner, is who had known about the shipment. Billy had died at the scene, so there was no way to discover who had told him about it. Until Rex was poisoned in prison. The case was seven years old, so for Rex to be poisoned didn't make sense, until we discovered a piece of evidence that had been overlooked. That Vincent Burrows had been on the train."

Dangerous, yes, but she also found it interesting. "You think Burrows had him poisoned?"

"Yes."

"Why?"

"Because Rex knew Elkin had worked on the case back then. I think Elkin had told Burrows they had to get rid of anyone who knew about the case. I believe Elkin thought the case was so old, that no one would care about a convict dying in prison. I know he was surprised when the review of the passenger list was brought up."

"Do you think he'd told Burrows about the money seven years ago?"

"Yes, and I believe he was the reason a counterfeiting ring left that beach cottage, on the cove where you were digging clams, hours before we were about to bust them, and how a train robber in Kansas got the slip on us and is still on the loose."

She'd removed her hat and was brushing the snarls from her hair, but stopped midstroke. "The beach cottage? That's why you asked me…"

"Yes, it seemed too coincidental."

A tiny tingle coiled its way up her spine. "You never knew about us sneaking out. You thought right from the beginning that I—"

"I'm sorry for that. You're right. I never knew about you sneaking out, not until you told me. In my line of business, you question coincidences."

She nodded. Not wanting to think how she felt about that right now, she asked, "Why do you think Elkin did it?"

"I don't know. People always have a reason, though, one they've justified in their own mind, right, wrong, or indifferent."

"What will you do when you find him?"

"Take him to Washington, DC, where he'll stand trial, just like everyone else."

The brush stalled in her hand. "Washington, DC?"

"Yes, to the agency headquarters."

"And then you'll be assigned to another case."

"Yes, I will."

She dropped the brush into her purse and picked up her hat. "Do you know where?"

"No, I never know." He glanced her way. "That's why everything I own fits in a single suitcase. It could be Washington State, Montana, Maine, Texas." He shrugged. "Anywhere within the forty-eight states of the United States of America."

Her stomach sank, and churned, for no reason. He'd just corroborated what she'd already known. "Do you ever see your family?"

He didn't look her way as he said, "Haven't seen them in over four years." In the next breath, he said, "We're here."

She glanced out the windshield, saw a grocery store. "What are we doing here?"

"I told your father that I was taking you to buy supplies." He gave her a wink. "Let's go shopping."

She waited until he opened her car door, then as he held out a hand to help her out, she asked, "You really like your job, don't you?"

He nodded. "Yes, yes, I do. It's the only part of my life that has worked out."

"What do you mean?"

He shrugged. "My childhood prepared me for this. Of going through life alone, chasing down criminals fits into that perfectly. I don't have to worry about anything except for getting the job done."

"And moving on to the next one."

"Exactly."

She climbed out of the car with as much composure as she could muster. Her legs felt weak at the knowledge she was going to have to keep the most wonderful part of her life a secret forever.

They bought a variety of cleaning supplies, which they delivered to the abandoned house. There, he insisted she didn't need to do any cleaning, now or later, and then he walked her home.

As soon as he left, it was as if the light went out inside her. It was like a switch that he could turn on and off. Even with sadness over what she knew had to be, while being with him today, she'd still felt whole, alive.

Although the tears were there, she didn't cry that afternoon while baking, or when her father returned home with James in tow. She most certainly didn't cry while eating the evening meal with James sitting next to her.

After the meal, while Mother and Jane cleaned the kitchen, she and James sat on the sofa in the front room. He was asking her about the wedding, the honeymoon, and it was making her head hurt, her heart hurt.

"I have no preferences," she said, thinking about how Patsy hadn't cared about her wedding for a very different reason. Patsy hadn't cared because she'd been so in love with Lane, all she cared about was marrying him, not where or when or even what she wore.

"But you must have preferences," he said. "It is to be the happiest day of your life." His smile increased. "And night."

Betty nearly shot off the sofa, but she didn't. Instead, she changed the subject, "How long have you been building houses?"

"My entire life." He sighed slightly. "But I'd never ran the company before, and when I inherited it, I—I, well, it was harder than I thought. I owe your father a great deal for helping me."

That didn't sound like her father. He never helped anyone. "Helping you how?"

"By partnering with me. I can design homes and oversee their building, but I wasn't very good at negotiating costs of supplies and labor. Your father has helped with that a great deal."

She could imagine that her father had. He believed he should get everything for as close to free as possible. Another thought entered her mind. "Is that why you've agreed to marry me, James? It was part of the negotiations, the partnership between you and my father?"

His face turned beet red. "I—I do want to marry you, B-Betty. I—I think you're very pretty, and I think you'll make a wonderful wife."

He was being forced into this as much as she was. Father was the only one getting what he truly wanted. A partner who he could fully control. Just like he did her and her sisters. She was about to ask more, but Father appeared and told James it was time he left.

She almost felt bad for James at how he jumped to obey Father.

As she made her way upstairs, she wondered about that, and what it meant. Marrying James wouldn't release her from her father's rules. It would mean that she and her husband were both under his hand.

Jane knocked on her door shortly after she'd entered her room. Betty frowned as Jane walked in and shut the door. She was wearing a shimmering bronze dress and matching hat.

Betty shook her head. "We can't go out. You heard what Henry said."

"Yes, I did, and I saw the light out the window," Jane said as she walked to the closet and opened the door.

"What light? What window?"

"The bathroom window." She opened the closet door and then the lid of the cedar chest.

The chest was actually a hope chest. Instead of holding flapper attire, it was supposed to hold all the things she'd need for when she got married. They each had received a trunk upon graduation from high school, and gifts for their birthdays and holidays to put inside them ever since. Those gifts, sheets, dishes, and other household items were under her bed so her flapper attire was readily available.

More thoughts of weddings, of marriage, made Betty's head hurt.

Jane held up a green dress with several layers of long fringe.

Betty shook her head. "What light?"

Jane dropped the dress and held up a black one.

Betty shook her head again and repeated, "What light?"

Jane dropped the black dress and picked the green one up again. "The one Henry is holding." She carried the dress to the bed. "He's standing out by the tree in the backyard." Walking back to the closet, she added, "Waiting for us."

Betty's heart lurched. "He's what?"

"Waiting for us," Jane said, and knelt down, digging in the chest for the mate to the black shoe she held in one hand. "Now, hurry up—he's been out there for half an hour already."

Betty pulled off her dress. "Why do we have to change clothes?"

"Because Henry decided that we have to keep the same schedule as before. If we don't, Elkin might think we are onto him." Jane tossed the shoe toward her and then dug out a long string of black pearls. "I for one agree with him."

"When did he tell you that?" Betty pulled the green dress over her head.

"While you were sitting on the sofa with the worm." Jane dropped the pearls over Betty's head.

Betty considered saying James wasn't a worm and that he was being forced into this marriage just like she was, as she twisted her hair up and applied a quick brush of lipstick to her lips and mascara to her eyes, but knew Jane would argue the point.

Jane handed her a black hat that hosted an ostrich feather, and Betty stepped into her black shoes on her way to the door.

It had all happened so fast, that as her feet touched the ground, Betty had to hold on to the trellis to keep from swooning.

"Come on," Jane whispered.

"Give me a moment," Betty said. "I'm dizzy."

"Again?"

Betty shook her head. "From getting dressed so fast."

"Patsy said that happened last night," Jane said. "That you almost fainted dead away."

Betty pushed off the trellis. "Because I'd just heard Henry had been shanghaied!"

"Well, come on," Jane hissed. "Before he gets shanghaied again waiting on you!"

Her light-headedness dissolved the moment she saw Henry at the tree, in one way. It increased in another because somehow, sneaking away tonight, with him at her side was more exciting than it had ever been. Everything was more exciting with him. The exact opposite of how things would be with James.

They took the tunnel to the Rooster's Nest and as

they walked, Betty thought how this was the first time she and her sisters would actually acknowledge they even knew one another while visiting a speakeasy. Other than the few slight warnings she'd had to give Jane or Patsy over the past several months, when it had appeared as if one or the other was about to go against one of the rules they'd put down, they'd rarely spoken to each other inside a tavern.

Jane was giddy at sneaking through the storage room, despite the number of warnings Betty gave her.

As soon as they, one by one, stepped out from behind the curtain, Jane nodded toward a table near the bar. "There they are." With a giggle, she added, "And Rodney is playing the piano. He's the best!"

Betty looked at Henry. He grinned as they made their way over to the table where Patsy and Lane sat.

"Ostrich ears, but this is so darb!" Jane said as the three of them sat down. "All of us out together."

"That's what I told Lane earlier," Patsy said.

Betty smiled in agreement, even though there were parts of this she hated. Specifically, the reason they were all here. It wasn't for fun. It was to catch a criminal.

As soon as a cigarette girl had placed two cocktails on the table, neither of which held alcohol, Jane took a sip of hers and then set it down. "So, where is he?"

Betty looked at Henry over the rim of her glass. He was still wearing the black suit and hat from this morning. It made him look official, but also handsome. Because he was so very handsome. The light, the warm and gooey feelings, he created inside her were all there, and she wondered how that could be. They should be gone, or at least hidden, because once that criminal they were hoping to catch was caught, Henry would be gone.

"It doesn't work that fast," Lane said.

"Horsefeathers." Jane looked at Henry. "Do we have to sit here all night, or can we dance?"

"You can dance," Henry said.

"Ducky." Jane pushed away from the table. "Hate to have good music go to waste. I'm gonna find me an Oliver Twist."

She was gone within a flash and, laughing, Patsy stood.

So did Lane.

"Excuse us," Patsy said. "But I have my very own Oliver to dance with."

They walked onto the dance floor hand in hand, and gracefully slid into a loving embrace. Betty couldn't contain the sigh that pressed hard to be released inside her.

"Do you want to dance?" Henry asked.

"No, that's all right."

"No." He stood. "It's not all right." He took her hand. "I can tell you do."

Chapter Ten

It took every ounce of Henry's willpower to keep from pulling Betty close as they slowly danced their way around the dance floor. Keeping her at a distance, instead of within a loving embrace like the one that Lane held his wife in, was supposed to keep his body from reacting to Betty's nearness. Supposed to because that was what he'd told himself, but it appeared, that just like not caring for her, keeping his body from reacting was impossible. Everything about him craved her even when she was nowhere near. Up close, within inches, his desires were so strong, his pulse pounded so hard it echoed in his ears.

"Did you complete your baking today?" he asked.

"Yes. Did you learn more about Elkin?"

Her eyes looked even bluer beneath the black hat with one long feather stuck in the side of it. And her face. It was so lovely. He never got tired of looking at her. "I did," he said, trying to keep his wits about him. He'd never felt like this before and now, to add to his confusion, he also felt guilty over what had happened between them. She'd do anything to protect her sisters, see that they were happy, and he'd used that for his own gain. There was no pride in that. There was no pride in wanting something he could never have, either.

"Will what you learned be helpful?" she asked.

"Yes."

She kept glancing at her sisters. Both of whom were on the dance floor. Patsy's head was on Lane's shoulder, and Jane was flirting so heavily with the man she was dancing with, the batting of her eyelashes could have caused a windstorm inside the tavern.

Her sisters were both attractive, but Betty, she was beyond beautiful. Henry's insides roiled, because he knew if he gave himself an inch of slack, his tenacity would dissolve and he'd end up doing more than pulling Betty close. He'd kiss her. Like he had this morning. Despite his best efforts, he hadn't been able to control himself then, and may not be able to now. He should have told Lane the women couldn't join them tonight. But Lane was right, anything out of the ordinary could make Elkin question if they were onto him, and Lane being anywhere without Patsy right now was out of the ordinary.

Lane had been so crushed when his wife and baby daughter had died during the train robbery that Henry had been shocked to learn he'd gotten married again. Until he'd seen Lane and Patsy together. They were in love. Deeply in love.

That a man who'd never experienced love could recognize it in others also amazed him, and made him wonder what that meant.

"Do you think he'll come here tonight?" she asked.

Henry gladly let his thoughts shift. "No," he said, mainly so she wouldn't worry. This whole thing with Elkin didn't make any sense. It was all so random. He'd scoured through all the records of past cases, but hadn't been able to find a solid thread between the cases where information had been slipped. The crimes hadn't even been committed within the same crime families, and in several different states. The only thing that did make sense was that a major bust of a supply ring had happened last year, and within weeks, Burrows had arrived in California. He must have planned on taking over for that supplier, and Elkin had to have known about it and wanted in on it.

"Then why are we here?" she asked.

"Because Lane said Patsy was afraid Jane would sneak out anyway."

She nodded. "That's true. I was worried about that myself."

"Why do you take on so much responsibility for them?"

"Because they are my responsibility. I'm the oldest."

A shiver rippled down Henry's spine, not from anything she'd said. It was the two men entering the speak-easy.

"Henry?"

Catching her attempting to twist far enough to glance in the direction he was looking, Henry pulled her unresisting body close. He couldn't let Elkin see him, recognize him. Not until the time was right.

He kept their heads close together, almost as if they were kissing, while cutting through the center of the dance floor, making a beeline for Lane.

Once beside them, he pulled her close again while tapping Lane on the shoulder. "He's here. At the bar."

Betty's head snapped up. "Who's here?"

Henry had no choice but to answer. "Elkin."

She didn't move her head, but her eyes shot to the bar. "The short one with glasses?"

Henry's spine stiffened. "Is he looking this way?"

"No, I just see the side of his face," she said. "Is he looking for Lane?"

"No. He's peddling Minnesota Thirteen from the stolen shipment."

"How do you know that?"

"Because it fits everything I've been piecing together," he said. "I just need the proof."

The music ended and he released her waist as she let her arms fall away from his shoulders. Before he realized what was happening, she shot around him. He reached to grab her arm, but missed, and then spun around to follow her.

Lane grabbed his arm. "Elkin doesn't know you're alive, and from what you've told me, it needs to stay that way."

Betty was already on the other side of the dance floor, approaching the bar.

Lane pulled on his arm. "Turn around. I'll keep an eye on her."

Henry's jaw was clamped so tight, his back teeth stung.

"He can't do anything to her here," Lane said. "And, if we are right, and he knows who she is, he's going to try to draw me into it. It's exactly what we want."

No, it wasn't what Henry wanted. He didn't want her involved at all.

"Come on," Lane said. "We need to step off the dance floor. If she's anything like her sister, she'll get the information out of Elkin faster than anyone else, including an undercover FBI agent."

Henry turned around so his back was to the bar, and stepped off the floor beside Lane and Patsy.

"She'll get the information," Patsy said. "Betty

knows more about Minnesota Thirteen than most of the men in this room. She'd researched every kind of alcohol at the joints when we started sneaking out, and set down rules as to what we could and couldn't drink."

"She did?" Lane asked.

Henry knew the answer. She'd given him a copy of the list.

"Yes. One of us going blind was a sure way to get caught," Patsy answered. "Minnesota Thirteen was the only hard alcohol Betty deemed safe, but none of us liked the taste of whiskey. We didn't like the taste of beer, either, so all we ever drank were fruit drinks or an occasional glass of wine or champagne." She shrugged. "Most of the speakeasies we visited didn't serve wine or champagne."

"No, they don't," Jane said as she stepped up beside him. "What's Betty doing talking to the guy wearing a pair of cheaters?"

"That's Elkin," Patsy said. "Betty's going to see if he's selling stolen whiskey."

Henry looked at Lane, who grimaced and shrugged, and then settled his gaze on the bar again. This had not been a good idea and he hadn't imagined he'd agreed with it.

"Ducky," Jane said.

Henry didn't comment. For someone who'd never had siblings, he had to admit that he found the way these three girls had stuck together, in everything, pretty amazing.

"I was just telling Henry about how Betty researched all sorts of alcohol when we started sneaking out," Patsy said. "How she knows all about it."

"She did," Jane said. "And she researched all the joints we could go to, and the ones we couldn't. If they had extra rooms, for—" She cleared her throat. "You know, we weren't allowed to set foot in them. Or any that had recently been raided, because if they'd been raided, that means they are run by the mob," Jane continued. "Those are the only ones that get busted, and that's because there are other things going on at those joints than just people having a good time."

Henry had known all that from Betty, but he was more impressed by how she'd laid down the law to her sisters. In his opinion, Jane and Patsy could be a handful, and Betty must have had her work cut out keeping them in line anywhere they went. "What's happening?" he asked Lane. "What's she doing?"

"Talking," Lane replied. "Elkin is answering, whatever she's asking. He's nodding and smiling."

Henry twisted slightly, just enough to get a quick glimpse of Betty, and Elkin. They were indeed talking. Smiling.

Jane stepped closer and plopped a hand on his shoulder. "I'll stand right here, so it looks like the four of us are sharing chin music." Tilting her head, she asked, "You can see beneath the rim of my hat, can't you?"

"Yes," he answered. He appreciated her insight. She'd positioned herself just right, so he could see Betty, but to anyone looking their way, it would look like he was whispering to Jane.

"So, what are they doing?" Jane asked.

"Still talking," he, Lane, and Patsy answered at the same time.

"Well, ducky. I'm the odd man out," Jane said. "Keep telling me what's happening."

"He's writing something down," Patsy whispered. "Now he gave it to Betty."

Elkin had given her a slip of paper, and Henry's

hand balled into a fist as he watched Elkin touch her wrist. She didn't pull her hand away, nor did the way she smiled up at him waver.

"What's happening now?" Jane asked.

"They are still talking," Patsy answered.

Henry's last nerve was about to snap when Elkin released her wrist. Betty then stepped around him, to his side, so if he did look this way, she blocked his view, and then walked beside him, toward the door. The other man followed. Henry's entire body was tight with tension. He was fully prepared to clear the entire dance floor while crossing the room if she stepped out the door with Elkin.

She didn't, but remained standing there, beside the door, with one hand discreetly held up at her side.

"She's telling us to stay put until the coast is clear," Patsy said.

Henry bit his lip to keep from saying he'd figured that out. Her sisters were trying to be helpful. Not trying. They had been helpful. If they hadn't been here, he would have stopped her before she'd made it to the bar, and Elkin would know he was alive, and after him.

The seconds dragged on like a sea snail trying to slime its way across the sand, back into the water. Henry had to force himself to remain still.

When Betty finally dropped her hand and started walking toward them, he shot forward, right through the dancing couples crowding the dance floor.

He grasped her arm. "What were you thinking?"

She looked at him and grinned. "I was thinking that you needed proof, and that I could get it." She waved a slip of paper near his face. "And I did."

He cared more about her than he did any information. "I didn't ask for your help." He wasn't mad at her for helping; he'd just been scared that something could have happened to her.

"Yes, you did." She flashed him a smile. "Oh, wait, that was when you thought I was more than a coincidence."

He bit his tongue at the sassy grin she flashed him, as well as the wink.

"So, spill!" Jane hissed as they all sat down. "What happened? What did he say?"

Henry's neck muscles tightened as he glanced at the excitement shining on the faces around the table. This was the most unorthodox team he'd ever worked with. Three flappers, a newspaper reporter, and him, an FBI agent. No one in the agency would believe this. No one in the agency had better learn about this. He'd be fired for bringing so many civilians in on an undercover case.

"I told the bartender that my sister and brother-in-law had just gotten married, and that I want to throw a party in their honor, but that I only want Minnesota Thirteen and have been having a hard time finding it," Betty said, leaning over the table. "I made sure the mole heard me."

"Oh, I like that name," Jane whispered. "The mole."

Henry pressed a hand to his temple and the sting of pain at how she'd exaggerated the word *mole* to sound like a monster in a story told to a child. "What did he say?"

"He asked me how much I wanted. I told him ten cases." Betty shrugged as she looked at him. "I wasn't sure how much you'd need for evidence, but assumed that would be sufficient."

She'd assumed right. One or two cases could be picked up here or there, but not ten. Only a supplier

could provide that many. "Ten cases would be sufficient, and expensive," Henry answered.

"That's what he said," Betty replied. "I told him
money was of no concern, and that I might be having
another party soon, and would need more then."

She was good, making Elkin think she had no idea
who he was, or that he knew Lane.

Handing him the slip of paper, she said, "Here's the
address. I'm to meet him there night after tomorrow.
Nine o'clock, with six hundred dollars."

"Six hundred dollars!" Jane exclaimed. "Baloney!"

"That's what he said," Betty replied, biting on her lip
as she looked at him. "Six hundred dollars."

"I have the money." Henry picked up the slip of
paper. "But you aren't meeting him."

"I have to," Betty argued. "When I told him that I'd
have someone with me to help me load it in my car, he
said no, that he'd help me load it."

She would not be meeting Elkin, but Henry wasn't
going to argue that point right now. He examined the
address on the paper, then handed it to Lane. "Do you
know this place?"

"That's the railroad district. I know the general area,
but not this exact address," Lane said. "It's north of the
warehouse district by a few miles, but along the shore-
line. You can't miss it. There are trains and trucks everywhere. There are some docks there, too."

Made sense. The rail yard would be the perfect place
to unload and hide an entire shipload of whiskey. Henry
took the slip of paper back and put it in his pocket.
He'd check out the area tomorrow and have a full plan
in place by the next night, including who would take
Betty's place.

"Are you going to be able to arrest him?" Betty asked.

"Why wouldn't he?" Jane asked her sister.

"Because the FBI doesn't arrest bootleggers," Betty explained.

"She's right," Henry said. "Normally, we don't." It was confusing for those who didn't know the specific departments under the justice system. "Bureau of Investigation agents are assigned to gather facts and evidence for the Department of Justice in what are considered federal crimes. Fraud, treason, espionage. Over the past few years, with the increase of criminal gangs expanding across state lines, there have been a large number of racketeering cases that we've, the Bureau, become involved in because of multiple jurisdictions."

"What's racketeering?" Betty asked.

"Various activities most often conducted by the mobs. Smuggling, counterfeiting, and certain aspects of bootlegging. Prohibition laws have numerous loopholes. It's not illegal to consume alcohol, but it is illegal to sell, manufacture, or transport it. Mobs are making millions of dollars by being middlemen. They purchase the supplies needed to manufacture the alcohol, then give it to someone who actually makes the brew, private citizens, whole blocks of them. These people will make and bottle the moonshine. The mob will then distribute it to the speakeasies, under the pretense that no funds were exchanged for the alcohol. That any monies paid by the tavern to the establishment, meaning the mob, were for the protection of their business. The speakeasy is who actually sells the product. The mob, the middlemen, the establishment, as they often call themselves, actually broke no laws."

Betty nodded, yet frowned. "What about Elkin? If he

sells me the whiskey, then you can arrest him because he's not a middleman, he's the seller?"

It was a complex system, but everything within the government was complex. "Yes, I have the authority to arrest him, but for selling ten cases of whiskey, he'd merely get a slap on the wrist. A local judge could release him the next day. The intel, or information that I need to gather on him, is his part in obtaining the whiskey he's peddling. If he's smuggling it, transporting it, that is a federal offense and I then could detain him, arrest him, and transport him to Washington, DC, for the attorney general's office to press federal charges against him."

"So we need to find out where he got the whiskey he's selling," she said, rubbing her chin.

He could imagine that the thoughtfulness he saw on her expression right now was how serious she'd looked when searching out safe alcohol and speakeasies for them all to visit.

"Yes," he answered. They might as well know the rest. It was no longer a secret. "Vincent Burrows was trying his hand at racketeering when he was arrested. Rather than having people brew whiskey for them to distribute, mobs out east, where Burrows was from, steal shipments of alcohol from Europe, from the Caribbean, from wherever a ship is sailing in from. It's cheaper to steal it than to make it, and for the most part, it's better quality, so they make more money." He'd been working on one of those cases when he'd been duped by Scarlet. He looked at Betty, with her eyes so big and bright and shining. He couldn't believe he'd ever compared the two. "Minnesota Thirteen is the most sought-after whiskey in America right now because it's twice distilled, which is why it's safe to drink."

She nodded. "I know. And I know it's shipped by rail, up through Canada and then down the West Coast by ship, and to ports beyond. It is known worldwide. Some call it Canadian Whiskey, but it's not. It's made in Central Minnesota, and called thirteen because that is a variety of corn that has a short growing season and is used to make the whiskey."

Henry nodded. She had done her research. "Burrows had gotten his hands on a few cases of it and started peddling it around town. Then, for some reason he decided to cut it, half and half with his own brew."

"We saw his still," Patsy said. "At the docks. Both Lane and I."

"He might have been thinking he could make even more money that way," Henry said. "By filling bottles of half Thirteen and half his own brew."

"Except that it tasted so awful, no one would buy a second supply from him," Lane added.

"Or," Henry said, which was what he thought happened, "he only had a few cases. Not a full shipment. And was trying to make it stretch until he got more."

"You think Elkin has that full shipment, don't you?" Betty asked.

Henry nodded. "I think he was behind stealing it, and undercut Burrows." Some of the things that had never made sense were starting to click. Elkin wasn't just a mole to the FBI, he was double-crossing the mobs, too. Playing things from both ends.

Betty shook her head. "What I don't understand is, if Minnesota Thirteen is made in Minnesota and shipped everywhere, why aren't prohibition agents stopping that? The trains and the ships?"

With his mind circling, Henry answered her question, "They are, and confiscating it, but who do they arrest? The train engineers? They don't know every item that's been loaded onto the cars. Neither do ships. The captain of the cargo ship I was put on didn't know I was in one of those barrels marked as flour. There were hundreds of them, most of them full of flour. There aren't enough agents to be at every train depot and ship dock in America, checking every box, barrel, and crate."

"This is all very interesting," Jane said. "But ultimately, what's our next step?"

Henry knew what his next step was—making sure Betty did not meet Elkin as she'd arranged. If Elkin was double-crossing both the FBI and the mob, he would try to get rid of anyone who knew him, so he couldn't be ratted out on either side. That was why he'd talked to her tonight, and had given her an address—it was a trap.

Betty couldn't believe how exciting this was. How thrilling. Being with him always had been, but this, actually helping him. It was… Well, she could fully understand why Patsy had been so adamant about becoming a reporter.

Being a reporter didn't appeal to Betty; she didn't even know how to type, but helping Henry solve his case did appeal to her. She'd always liked learning about things, places, people. When she and her sisters first started sneaking out, and she'd spent those first few weeks on bar stools, talking to the bartenders about the different beverages they served, and the local joints, she'd enjoyed it. It had been out of necessity. She didn't want either of her sisters to end up blind from drinking widow-maker juice or end up in jail because the joint they were at had been raided.

Safety first had been the first item in her plan when

they'd embarked on their nighttime adventures. She had made sure that the rules, the plans, she put in place for her and her sisters kept them all safe.

Now Henry's safety was what she was concerned about. So, the first thing she had to do was get a good look at that address, before it was time to be there.

"It's getting late," Henry said. "We better call it a night."

They all agreed and Jane chattered nearly the entire way to the abandoned house.

Betty didn't mind. Having her sister there kept her from thinking about other times she'd walked down this tunnel with him.

Henry walked them all the way to their backyard, to the trellis.

As Jane entered the window, and Betty grasped ahold of the wood to start her climb, Henry stopped her. "I'll see you in the morning."

Warmth filled her. "At the house?"

"Yes," he said.

"All right." She couldn't pull her eyes off his, and her lips tingled as if waiting for his to touch them.

He released her hand and stepped back. "Good night."

She swallowed at the wave of disappointment that washed through her, but nodded. "Good night."

As soon as she entered her room, Betty wrote down the address that Elkin had written on the paper she'd given Henry.

Twirling the pencil between her fingers, she glanced at the calendar on the wall, then lifted it down. She stared at the little mark she'd made when she'd had her last monthly, and counted forty weeks. May. The second week. That was when her baby would arrive.

May. It seemed so far away and right around the corner at the same time. So far away before she'd be able to hold her baby in her arms, the one thing she had wanted since she was a little girl dreaming about being a grown-up.

There wasn't much time before everyone would know she was pregnant and everyone would be able to count. Her father would be enraged if she, her baby, created a scandal.

When she was here, in her bedroom, alone, she believed marrying James was her best option, her only option, but when Henry was near, she couldn't even consider marrying James because Henry... Henry was who she loved.

It was time she admitted that. Her heart had decided that she would love him for the rest of her life, and no matter how hard she tried, her heart wouldn't let her change that.

Henry was also who made her want more—in so many ways. Ways that didn't fit with her. When she was with him, she was impulsive and risky. That wasn't her. It was thrilling and exciting, but that wasn't her. It was like he turned her into someone she was not.

James wouldn't do that. He didn't do that. He would let her be who she was. He would provide her with a home, near her family where she could continue to look out for her sisters and help her mother, while obeying Father's rules.

Was that truly what she wanted? Obeying Father's rules until the end of time?

It would be safe. Orderly.

Babies needed that.

Tears burned her eyes as she replaced the calendar, hung it on the nail, and dressed for bed. Another wave of sadness washed over her as she tucked the green dress in her hope chest. That would soon be over, forever. Nights out. James had never gone to a speakeasy, never gone dancing. He'd told her that. Her life with him wouldn't be exciting, but it would be predictable. No surprises. No rule breaking.

She crawled into bed and cried herself to sleep, and awoke in the aftermath of dreams that had made her heart race. They'd been about Henry.

She tried to erase them as she dressed and prepared to see him again, at the house she would clean. Once again, that reminded her of how different she was from her sisters. Both Jane and Patsy despised chores. She didn't. There was satisfaction in having things clean, neat, and tidy.

She'd had another dream last night. Or maybe it had been a memory.

Because she did remember it. How she'd cried when Aunt Joan had been forced to go to the convent. She had been pregnant, and Betty would forever remember hearing her parents talk, about how the baby would be taken away as soon as it was born and given up for adoption.

She and her sisters hadn't even been able to say goodbye to their aunt. She'd just been gone one morning when they woke up, and they'd never heard from her again. Weren't allowed to even ask about her.

The tears fell faster as she thought about her mother, and how that had to have hurt, to never see her sister again.

Tears fell for herself, too, how she had to marry James. It was her only answer.

Her stomach revolted, and she ran for the bathroom.

Chapter Eleven

Betty, leaning over the sink, sucking in air after, stiffened at the sound of the door opening, and let out a sigh at seeing Jane in the reflection of the mirror over the sink.

"Are you sick?" Jane asked.

Betty cupped water in her hand, used it to rinse out her mouth, and spat in the sink. "It must have been something I ate."

"You haven't eaten yet. Mother sent me up here to see where you were. Breakfast is almost ready."

The mention of food made her stomach erupt all over again. She dropped down next to the toilet, but there was nothing left to come up. It was worse this morning than it had been. Probably because the baby was revolting against her marrying James.

No, the baby wouldn't know the difference. No one would ever know the difference.

"I'll tell Mother you're sick," Jane said.

"No." Betty pushed off the stool and stood. "I'm fine."

"No, you aren't."

"Yes, I am." She shook her head. "Really, I'm fine now."

"You're awfully pale."

Betty lifted the washcloth off the edge of the sink and used it to scrub her face, giving her cheeks some color. She then fluffed her hair, so it hung closer to her face. "There. How's that?"

"Better." Jane nodded. "Somewhat."

"Then let's go," Betty said, and followed Jane out of the bathroom.

Breakfast was ready, and she and Jane had to hurry to get the table set before things grew cold. Betty ate cautiously, just some toast, which made her feel much better, and the cleaning up went quickly.

She hurried upstairs, to put her hair up and put on an apron for cleaning, and was just about to leave for the abandoned house when Jane entered her room.

"Sit down," Jane said, closing the door behind her.

"Why?"

Jane huffed out a breath and, holding a magazine against her chest, she paced the floor.

"Why?" Betty repeated. "I need to—"

"*I need to* read you something," Jane said.

Betty sat, but said, "I don't have time to hear about actresses today." Jane was forever sneaking popular magazines into the house, mainly those about actors, actresses, and singers, and always had something to share out of them.

"It's not about actresses. It's about you."

"Me?"

Jane nodded.

"What are you talking about? I'm not in any magazine."

Jane huffed out another breath and held up the magazine. "This is a woman's journal."

Betty shook her head. Jane snuck those into the house, too.

"It's all about women and…" Jane shrugged. "Sex."

"Sex?" Betty's heart began to pound. Jane couldn't know about what she and Henry had done that one night. That was impossible. She also couldn't know the outcome. No one, not even her sisters could know about that.

"Yes, and more."

"More of what?"

"Articles. I just pulled it out from under my bed to read until it's time to start chores, and flipped it open, and started to read." Jane turned the magazine around. "This is the article."

"'Pregnancy: What to Expect.'"

Betty's insides turned to ice, but she kept her head up, prepared to deny everything. She had to.

"You've been throwing up every morning," Jane said. "And you've been dizzy, light-headed, faint."

Betty's mouth was dry; as much as she wanted to deny those symptoms, to lie to her sister, she couldn't.

Jane threw her hands in the air, and the magazine. As it fluttered to the floor, she said, "You're pregnant."

Betty gnawed on her bottom lip, knowing if she opened her mouth the truth would come out.

"When did you have sex?" Jane asked. "And why didn't you tell me? Who did you have sex with?" She pressed her hands to the sides of her face. "Please don't say it was James."

Betty's stupor disappeared. "Of course it wasn't James." She jumped off the bed and started pacing the floor, feeling frantic.

Jane grabbed the magazine off the floor. "Let's see, morning sickness. Dizziness. Feeling faint. Are your boobs tender?" Jane asked.

Betty grabbed for the magazine, but Jane twisted out of her reach. "I don't need a magazine to tell me anything."

Still reading, Jane continued, "'Overemotional. Crying for no reason. Exhausted. Confused. Mood changes.'"

Betty snagged the magazine this time and tossed it on the bed.

"What about your nipples?" Jane asked. "Are they dark? You can compare them to mine, if you need to." Jane had pulled out the front of her yellow-and-white-striped dress and was peering down.

"I don't need to compare anything." Betty plopped down on the bed.

"How long have you known?" Jane asked softly.

"Not long," Betty answered, placing a hand on her stomach.

Jane sat down beside her. "Why didn't you tell me?"

Betty's entire body was trembling. "Because there's nothing you can do. There's nothing any of us can do."

"Henry is the father, isn't he?"

"Yes." Fully despondent, Betty closed her eyes against the tears already trickling out. "Oh, Jane, what am I going to do?"

"You're going to tell me about it," Jane said. "Every sordid detail!"

Betty wasn't about to do that; some parts were too private, too special, but she did tell Jane the things she'd wished she'd been able to before. About how she and Henry had met up in Seattle three years ago and how they'd met again at the Rooster's Nest the night they won the dance-off. About their nights in the tunnel.

She stopped there, not sure how to explain anything else.

"At least you don't have to marry James," Jane said.

Betty's tears flowed faster as she pressed both hands to her stomach, wanting to protect the baby inside her. "That is the one thing I have to do."

"No. You can't."

"I have to—if Father finds out—"

"He won't. Because you'll marry Henry." Jane leaped off the bed. "You've told him, right?"

Betty shook her head.

Jane grabbed her hand. "Come on—you have to get over to the house and tell him. You can't be having a baby six months after you get married. Everyone will know you were pregnant when you got married."

"I know that," Betty said. She wanted to tell Jane more, about why she had to marry James and not Henry, about how she couldn't be someone she wasn't, but Jane wouldn't understand. No one would understand.

Henry sat back on his haunches, and glanced at Betty, who had spread apart the tree branches to get a better view of the man and the creek in the small valley below.

"What's he doing?" she asked.

"Sluicing for gold," Henry answered. William Dryer was dumping shovelful after shovelful of dirt into the sluicing box set in the middle of the creek. As rich as he already was, Dryer still wanted more, and must still be convinced there was gold in the Santa Monica Mountains.

Henry had to wonder why a man who had everything—money, a family, a beautiful home, successful business—could still want more. That was how it was for some people. Enough was never enough.

Dryer had put time and money into wanting more, too. The dump truck parked near the large pile of dirt was brand new. The sluice box looked modern, too. It was a large one, and made of metal. He was seriously looking for gold.

From the looks of it, Dryer spent plenty of time out here. The road was well used, and hosted a large gate, complete with a chain and lock, so no one else could drive all the way to the creek. There was also a small cabin, which looked old, but well maintained.

"This must be where he goes every day," Betty said.

Henry had parked down the road from the Dryer house this morning, and had followed William, far enough behind that the man had never noticed him. All the way to the road that led to the creek. Then he'd gone back to the Dryer house, and when Betty had walked out the door, to go to the abandoned house, he'd brought her to the car, and then they'd driven up here together.

He'd parked his car in the cover of some trees and they'd walked in. He hadn't been sure what he'd find, but it hadn't been this.

She let go of the branches slowly, so they eased back into place.

"Ready to go?" he asked.

She nodded.

They made their way back down the hill and he double-checked the backseat before letting either of them climb in.

"I remember the only time I heard my parents argue," she said as he got in and closed his door. "I was about ten, we'd just moved into the house we live in now and Father had sold a couple of other lots for people to build homes. My mother was angry. Very angry. I'd never heard her raise her voice, but she did that day. She was telling my father that if he didn't quit searching the hills for gold, she was taking us girls and leaving him. She said something about how they had almost starved because of his gold searching and she wouldn't go through that again."

"It doesn't look like he quit." Henry started the car and backed out of the trees.

"No, it doesn't. That's about the same time us girls were told we weren't allowed to leave the yard. Father said it was because of the traffic, of people coming to look at land, but I think it was because we used to go exploring in the hills. He didn't want us to see what he was doing. And tell Mother."

To Henry, it appeared that the money William made selling land and houses was simply a way to fund his gold searching. "Did your father tell you that his grandfather bought up all this land because he was convinced there was gold in the hills?"

"No. We always believed Grandpa had bought it for farming, but that it was too hilly. Father never talks about his family." She shook her head. "This explains why his clothes are so dirty some days. He must change his clothes up here, and brings them home only once a month or so to wash. Mother would tell us he must have been helping dig basements on those days."

"Do you think she knows?" Henry asked.

"No. I'm sure she doesn't. And I'm sure she'd be very angry if she did find out."

"I guess that explains, in part, why he's so strict." Not only with his family, but within the elite houses he insisted on building. The fences he wanted people to build around their property were to keep people in their own yards, and out of his hills. Henry wasn't sure if Dryer was just selfish, or that obsessed with gold.

"And so grumpy," Betty said. "He's afraid. Afraid someone will learn his secret." Frowning, she asked, "Did you know? Is that why you followed him this morning?"

A mixture of shame, guilt, and what he'd come to assume was jealousy rolled around in his stomach at how he had been searching for a reason for her not to marry Bauer. Until he realized that this wasn't about what he wanted, it was about what she wanted. Therefore, he'd give her the information she needed to make up her own mind, and a bit of power. How she used it would be up to her. "No, I didn't know, but I thought you should know whatever I'd found."

She frowned slightly, then nodded.

"There's one more thing I want to show you."

The house Bauer was building was about five miles away from where they'd seen Dryer sluicing for gold, and just like it had been yesterday, the site was void of any workers. A skeleton frame of the exterior had been built, and lumber was piled in stacks. Two-by-fours, just as Owens had said.

He pulled in and parked.

"This is the house James is building," she said.

"Yes, it is."

The basement was made of concrete blocks, and the tracks surrounding the remnants of what must have been the dirt dug out for the basement told Henry something else. William Dryer had hauled the dirt that had been dug up for the basement up the mountainside to his sluice box. That was why he had a dump truck. He must do that with every home built up here. That was commitment if nothing else.

More commitment than it appeared that Bauer had. There were no fresh footprints or tire tracks around the build site.

"It looks as if no one has been here for some time," she said. "And those are two-by-fours, aren't they? Like Blake Owens said."

"Yes, they are." He started the car and drove out of the building site.

"I'll talk to my father about the building codes," she said. "Rules are rules and they all should be followed."

She was looking out the passenger window and the level of guilt inside him was high enough he should be drowning. He'd found every excuse he could to be with her since the beginning. He had to get over this deep-down draw he had toward her like some sort of lifeline that he was afraid to break. Why? Because for the first time in his life he'd wanted someone to care about him? No. He'd wanted that before, but had known it wasn't possible. It wasn't possible this time, either. That was why being an FBI agent fit him. Because when he stood, facing a criminal, guns drawn, he didn't worry about getting shot, about his life ending, because there was no one waiting for him to return.

She, however, deserved a wonderful life, and he hoped she would find it. Even if it meant that was with James Bauer.

"I was fooled by someone once," he said. "They used me to get what they needed."

She frowned. "The woman you mentioned—the one who charmed information out of you?"

"Yes." If this was what it took for her to understand why he'd taken her to the building site, so be it. "Her name was Scarlet, and she was warning rumrunners where blockades were being set up to catch them. I didn't want to believe it at first, but the proof was there, so I had to."

"What happened to her?"

"I arrested her," he answered, emotionless. He didn't feel anything toward Scarlet or what had happened. "She's still in prison."

"She got what she deserved." She let out a long sigh. "James isn't trying to fool me. I know what I'm getting." She grinned slightly. "Because of you. I appreciate what you showed me today. Both my father and the building site. I have to think about all of that."

He hoped she did.

As they pulled up next to her house, she asked, "Where are you going now?"

"I have a few more leads I want to check out," he answered. "Stay here. You don't have to clean anything at the abandoned house." That, too, had been an excuse. He'd been justifying his actions in his own mind since meeting her that first night. He'd been doing that in other aspects of his life, too.

"Yes, I do," she said. "My father may want to inspect my work."

"So? Tell him he doesn't need to inspect anything. It's your work, not his." He didn't want to say more, about staying home due to Elkin because he didn't want to scare her. "I'll see you later."

She opened her door and stepped out. "All right, but you be careful. I worry about you with such a dangerous job." She shut the door.

He didn't want her to worry. Not about him or anything else. He'd been after Elkin as an agent, still was, but it now was also personal.

* * *

Whether the house needed to be cleaned or not, that was where she went after Henry drove away, because it would give her time alone. Usually, she did some of her best thinking while cleaning, but hadn't come to any conclusions, other than she would talk to her father about the building codes. She'd thought a lot about his gold mining, how he'd kept that from Mother for all these years.

It seemed so wrong, and she was truly trying to justify it, because it was too close. Too close to her own thoughts about lying to James about the baby. That was what it would amount to. A lifelong lie. She also realized what she would have to do in order to perpetuate that lie. Being here, in the house where the baby was conceived, made such thought nearly inconceivable.

She'd wanted to be with Henry. Still did. She doubted the desires she had for him would ever wane. Married or not, doing that same act with James made her sick to her stomach. One that wouldn't go away by throwing up. It was an ugly, dark feeling that encompassed more than her stomach. It made her heart ache. Just like thinking about living a lie for the rest of her life did.

She couldn't do it.

She would have to tell Henry.

Face whatever consequences that came about.

She'd stand her ground, too. With her father.

After all, she now had ammunition.

That didn't make her feel any better, but she had to find a way to make this work.

Her heart jolted as the door flew open.

"Come on—we have to go!" Jane said.

"Go where?" Betty asked, with a hand pressed to her breastbone as she caught her breath.

Patsy stepped in the door behind Jane. "Henry called. Said we needed to meet him at the address."

"Called who?"

"Me," Patsy said. "At the newspaper office."

Betty shook her head, tried to make sense of what she was being told. "Why would Henry call you?"

"He sure couldn't call you," Jane said, untying the back of Betty's apron.

Accepting that answer for what it was, Betty removed the apron and set it on the floor by the mop and bucket. "Why? Why do we need to meet him there?"

"You know the address, don't you?" Jane asked.

"Yes." She had memorized it last night.

"Then let's go," Jane said, pushing her toward the door.

Reluctant because that was who she was, only Henry made her impulsive, she pointed at the car. "Whose car is that?"

"Mine," Patsy said. "The one Lane gave me before we were married so I could drive back and forth to the newspaper office."

Betty did recall that, but it had been during the time Henry had been missing, while he'd been shanghaied, so she hadn't paid much attention to anything else.

"He didn't like the idea of me sneaking out and taking the red line all the way to the newspaper office."

"You took the red line all that way?" Betty asked. "When?"

Jane and Patsy shared a knowing look.

"Never mind," Betty said. She obviously hadn't been paying close attention at all during that time. Thank goodness nothing had happened to Patsy. She would never have forgiven herself.

Once they were in the car, driving away from the

house, Betty's concerns shifted. "Tell me what Henry said when he called."

"I didn't talk to him," Patsy said. "The front secretary took the call, and she said that Henry called and told me to bring my sisters to the address."

"He didn't tell me he was going there," Betty said aloud, while thinking that he had said he wanted to check out some leads.

"Did you tell him everything?" Jane asked pointedly.

Betty shot a glare into the backseat. "No."

Jane shrugged and looked out the window.

"Where's Lane?" Betty asked.

"He's interviewing a new city councilman," Patsy answered. "I left him a message. And I told Mother that I need the two of you to help me measure curtains."

"Measure curtains?"

"Yes," Patsy answered. "I needed an excuse, so I said I needed help measuring the windows in our apartment for new curtains. She knows how good you are at that. Jane and I can barely sew a seam without your help." Patsy took the corner that would lead them to the main throughway. "What's the address?"

Los Angeles had over a million people living within the city limits, and Henry swore nearly every one of them was on the roads near the railroad district this morning. Every corner he made, traffic was stopped. Horns were honking and people shouting.

There were every size, shape, and model of truck trying to back into places or trying to pull back out onto the roads. The shrill of train whistles was constant; so was the screeching of metal wheels grinding on the metal tracks.

Trains had the right-of-way, but more than one daring trucker shot across one of the many sets of tracks a moment before a train barreled past, blowing its horn.

Henry steered his way through the spiderweb of train tracks and dirt roads, searching for the street written on the slip of paper Betty had given him last night.

He found the street and began to follow it, searching for the addresses on the occasional buildings he drove past. Which was easy because traffic was as backed up on this street as it had been everywhere else.

From his calculations, he had about ten more blocks to go before the address he was looking for would be found. At the pace he was driving, it would be dark by the time he got there. It wasn't like anyone was waiting on him, he just wanted to scope out the place. After dropping off Betty, he'd gone to the hotel and called LeRoy. Something had crossed his mind while watching Dryer sluice for gold this morning. Greed. For some men, the more they had, the more they wanted. It made men do many things. That had to be what was driving Elkin, and LeRoy confirmed something else. Elkin had applied for a supervisory position, which he hadn't gotten, and within a few months, the leaks had started to happen.

He let out a long sigh; all this driving, all this wasted time, was giving him far too much time to think. About all sorts of things. Including Betty. He didn't want her worrying. Did not. Worry didn't do anyone any good. It was a waste of time.

So was all the denying he'd been doing. He'd been trying to fool himself into believing that he'd never cared about anyone or anything. It had worked for years. But not any longer. Betty had opened something inside him that had been hidden away, as if he'd had a trunk inside him as solid as the one on the back of his car, as dark and big, too, and unopenable without the key.

Betty had the key.

She'd used it, too.

Damn it.

He'd liked the delusion he'd had for years. It had served him well. His belief that caring about anyone didn't fit into his lifestyle.

He cared about her. There was no doubt about that. He couldn't even say how it happened. It just had. Like a shooting star. No one knew where or why, but suddenly it was there, shooting across the sky, leaving a fizzling light in its trail, for a moment so brief, unless you were watching, you wouldn't see it. Could only be told about it.

That was what had happened. Had been happening for a while, but he hadn't been listening, or had been pretending he was deaf. It wasn't just the way she made him feel; it was things she made him remember. The other kids at the orphanage, how he'd stolen food for them, because he'd cared about them.

Whether he now accepted that, knew it all to be true, it didn't change anything. He still had to walk away, move on to his next assignment because there was nothing else he could do. Because if he didn't, he'd have to look at other aspects of his life that he'd been fooling himself about for years.

He'd spent too long convincing himself that he didn't care about anyone or anything, not even about being an experiment. He couldn't accept that had been false, because if he did, his entire life was false.

Ultimately, that would mean, he was not who he was. A loner. A rolling stone. Someone who didn't want a home, a family.

The traffic had dissipated substantially as he'd driven the last few blocks. Though there was still a massive amount of railroad tracks, there were no more large loading docks for trucks to pull in and out of. There were mainly long lines of empty railcars and old buildings. Dilapidated and abandoned from the looks of most of them.

It appeared the road he was on also came in from the north, and he was in the midst of telling himself that was what he should have done, come in along the coastline, when a car caught his eye. A Chevrolet. Exactly like the one Lane drove.

The car was driving toward him, but turned quickly, and drove past a long line of old delivery trucks.

Henry's instincts flashed a signal. A familiar one, like a lighthouse beacon, flashing out of sync in order to warn ships to be cautious of pending weather. He stepped on the gas and turned where the Chevrolet had turned, scanning for where it had gone.

He found it stopped on the far side of the trucks, and hit the gas again when he noticed Lane stepping out of the driver's door.

His tires skidded on the gravel, spewing dust as he hit his brakes next to Lane's car.

"I'm glad to see you," Lane said.

Henry threw open his door. "What are you doing here?"

"Looking for my wife, and her sisters," Lane said, slamming his car door.

Henry stepped out of his car as a thousand curses raced through his mind, as did images. "What are they doing here?" That was a stupid question. He knew the answer, so he changed his request to "Tell me what you know."

"Patsy's car is parked next to the old depot I just drove past," Lane said. "No one's in it."

Henry reached in his car and pulled his service pistol out from beneath the seat. Tucking it in the front of his pants, he said, "Let's go find them."

Chapter Twelve

"I don't think we should go down there," Betty whispered to her sisters while looking down the steep set of stone steps that led to a dark space beneath the depot. The dank, musky smell gave her a sinking feeling in her stomach and made the hair on her arms stand on end.

"This could be it," Jane said. "Where the mole is hiding the goods. Maybe that's why Henry called us."

"I know," Betty said, with both hands on her stomach. The address she'd been given last night was for this, an old depot building. She hadn't even wanted to get out of the car, but as Jane had said, Henry had called them. "But I don't think he'd want us going down there. We should just leave."

Jane sighed. "Quit being such a mother hen." She slapped four fingers against her lips, then shrugged, and pulled them away. "You've always been a mother hen. Making sure everyone is safe and following the rules."

Her sister was right, but that was her role. As the oldest she had to watch over them, set a good example. "I've had to with you two." She pressed a hand more firmly against her stomach. She would be that way with her baby, too. Watch over them, keep them safe. Betty looked at Patsy, hoping she would agree. "Let's leave. We can wait in the car for Henry."

Patsy nodded. "Yes, let's wait in the car."

Jane huffed out another sigh, so loud it echoed off the brick walls. "All right. This place is a little creepy."

"A little?" Betty walked past Jane and entered the hallway that would take them back to the large central room with the large open archways that they'd first entered. She'd only taken a few steps when a muffled thud stopped her. She twisted, looked at her sisters. "Did you hear that?"

They both nodded.

"It was probably a train," Jane said.

There were train cars lined up on the numerous tracks surrounding the depot, but Betty shook her head. "The sound came from inside the building," she whispered.

Patsy nodded. "Someone else is here."

"Henry," Jane said. "He called us."

"No." Betty's heart crawled into her throat, pounding so hard she could barely breathe. "If Henry was here, he'd say so. The sound came from up there." She pointed down the long hallway that led to the central room. "The way we came in." Twisting, she glanced down the hallway behind them. She hadn't wanted to explore the building, but upon entering it, with its high, domed ceiling and brick pillars, it had seemed safe enough to look around for Henry. But they hadn't found him, because he wasn't here. She was sure of that.

"There has to be another way out," she said. The hall was dim, but not dark; light was shining in from a room near the end. "This way."

They tiptoed quickly, like they did while sneaking out at night, so their heels wouldn't click against the wood floor. Hurrying past the basement steps, they stayed near the wall, single file. Betty hoped beyond hope that the room providing the light into the hall would have a door leading outside.

She slowed her steps as she neared the room, and held up her hand, so her sisters would stop behind her for a moment, then peered around the corner, into the room.

It was huge, ran nearly the length of the hall, and empty, but there were windows, and a door.

She rushed into the room, ran across it to the door, and grabbed the big brass knob.

It didn't move. She tried to twist the knob harder, with both hands, but it barely moved no matter which way she twisted. "It's locked!" she whispered, trying to shake the door with the knob, but that didn't budge it, either.

"Let me try," Jane said, grasping the knob.

Betty stepped aside, doubting, yet also hoping that Jane would have more luck than she had. As her sister tried making the knob work, Betty scanned the room. The windows were near the ceiling, far too high to reach, let alone climb out if they could somehow manage to climb up there and open one.

"Maybe the noise we heard was just a bird or something," Patsy whispered.

Betty doubted that as much as she did Jane getting the door open.

Jane kicked the door. "Why would they lock this door when the entire front is wide-open?"

"Shhh!" Betty said the same time as Patsy.

"I'd say because they don't want people trespassing."

Betty's insides leaped, at the same time a wave of relief washed over her. She didn't need to see him to know it was Henry. His voice made her heart race, even when she wasn't scared, but it was the unique warmth filling her that confirmed it was him.

Jane let out a groan and leaned her head against the door.

Patsy had already turned around, and let out a tiny gasp right before saying, "Oh, Lane, am I glad to see you."

"Glad?" Jane spun around. "They just scared us to death."

Betty still hadn't turned to face the men, because she was afraid that when she did, she was going to latch on to Henry and never let go. This place had scared her like she'd never been scared before.

"You should be scared to death," Henry said. "All three of you."

Betty's heart thudded harder, and she couldn't stop herself from spinning around. He was right there, grasped her arms and pulled her up against his chest. The comfort of his body touching hers was so great, she gasped and then wrapped her arms around his waist. "Why did you ask us to meet you here?"

"I didn't," he whispered and kissed the top of her head.

She leaned back, looked up at him. There was strain on his face, lines on his forehead and around his eyes that she'd never seen before. "You didn't call Patsy?"

"No." His hold tightened even as he said, "It's time to go."

He kept one arm around her as she turned around and began walking toward the door.

Lane peeked out the door, and then led Patsy into the hallway, followed by Jane, and then Henry and her, but they all stopped at nearly the same time, when a man stepped into the hallway from the basement steps.

Betty's lungs locked tight. It was him. Elkin.

Wearing a brown tweed suit, and with his brown hair combed flat down to his eyebrows, and a menacing glare enhanced by his thick round glasses, he looked far more evil than a mole.

Henry pulled her backward, behind him as he stepped forward. He also pulled Jane back, too, behind Betty.

"I knew those cute billboards would lead you here, Randall." Elkin let out a bitter laugh. "You could have knocked me over with a feather when I saw you last night, at that joint, dancing with a doll. You, the supreme agent, mixing pleasure with work. Didn't think you'd ever cross that line."

Betty saw how hard and stiff Henry's entire body grew, and her mind frantically searched for something she could do, other than grasp ahold of Jane's hand as her sister wrapped an arm around her waist from behind.

Patsy was behind Lane, who was standing next to Henry, and she shot a quivering look at Betty.

Betty reached over and took ahold of Patsy's hand with her free hand. She had to get them to safety. They were her responsibility. Slowly, cautiously, she took a step back, forcing Jane to back up and tugging Patsy with them.

"Did you really think you'd get away with it, Elkin?" Henry asked. "Being a mole? Selling out?"

"I already did," the man said.

Henry shook his head while asking, "Why'd you do it?"

"Because I was sick of putting my life on the line for

seven bucks a week!" Elkin shouted. "I'm worth more than a buck a day. Others believe that, too. One little piece of information brought me more money than I made in a year working for the Bureau."

"That's called bribery," Henry said. "And it's illegal."

Elkin laughed. "Dough is dough."

"The dough you took was dirty money, but you still wanted more." Henry said. "Your greed is going to make you rot in jail, Curtis."

Elkin's eyes narrowed behind his glasses, grew beady. "I should have tossed that barrel in the ocean."

"Why didn't you?" Henry asked.

Betty couldn't believe how calm Henry sounded. Her entire body was trembling. She was scared stiff. For Henry. For herself, and her sisters, yet she knew she had to get her sisters out of here and took another step backward, forcing Patsy and Jane to do the same, slowly, quietly.

"Because you didn't want my body to be found too soon?" Henry asked. "Because you had to fake your own death, too? Hoped the badges would be enough for people to believe we were both dead?" Henry shook his head. "You didn't think that one through, did you? Didn't think I'd survive?"

The mole shifted his stance, lifted his head as if that made him taller. "That bimbo helping me said you weren't breathing when we stuffed you in that barrel."

"The bimbo you killed?" Henry asked.

Elkin shook his head. "You don't know that! No one does!"

"Because his body hasn't been recovered? The one you were hoping people would believe is your body?" Henry shook his head. "You failed, Elkin."

An evil smile formed on Elkin's face. "No, I haven't."

Betty couldn't hold back a gasp as the man lifted his hand and pointed a gun at Henry. She'd never felt so scared, or helpless. There was nothing she could do.

"You have," Elkin said, waving his gun.

"What do you think you are doing?" Henry asked.

"I'm going to get rid of you for good." He laughed. "And your friends. Including your doll."

Betty had been about to step forward and grab Henry, pull him back into the room, but froze, because he suddenly had a gun in his hand, too.

"I don't think so," Henry growled. "You've seen me shoot. You might get a shot off, but mine will be a kill shot. You know that. Dead center. You call it, your chest, or your head."

Betty's knees nearly buckled at how harsh and grim Henry sounded. The other man sounded serious, too, but Henry sounded far more believable. Like he was going to kill this man.

"What's it going to be, Elkin?" Henry asked, taking a step forward. "Head or chest?"

"You don't scare me, Randall."

"I'm not trying to scare you. I'm telling you how this will play out if you pull that trigger." Henry took another step toward the man.

Betty was torn between reaching forward, grabbing him, and pulling her sisters backward. She didn't want anyone to die and pinched her lips together to hold a sob in.

He shook his head. "I don't think you want to be dead, Elkin, and I know I don't want to kill you, but I will." He took another step. "I will, right here. Right now."

Betty squeezed her eyes shut against the tears now

blinding her. This couldn't be happening. Henry talking about killing a man.

She wasn't sure what happened next, because when a loud grunt and thud made her open her eyes, Henry and Elkin were on the floor near the basement steps, fighting.

A gun went off.

Screaming, Betty shoved both of her sisters through the doorway behind them.

More furious than he'd ever been, Henry leveled a blow that knocked Elkin's glasses off his face. Then he flipped Elkin over onto his stomach and planted his knee in the man's back. As he grabbed both of Elkin's wrists, he shouted to Lane, "Get the women out of here."

"You aren't going to win this, Randall!" Elkin yelled. "I have backup. Here and everywhere else."

Henry knew that was a real possibility and dug his knee deeper into Elkin's back as Lane led the women down the hall.

He felt Betty's eyes, but kept his eyes averted. Unable to look at her. He might have just captured the man he'd been searching for, but he wasn't proud of the way it went down, at gunpoint, with him threatening to shoot a man and her watching. Her in danger!

That was the worst part. If Elkin's finger had touched that trigger, he would have shot the mole. Dead. Because he couldn't have taken the chance that a bullet would have hit her. The Bureau should never have issued Elkin a gun. The man couldn't hit a target three feet away.

Henry exhaled the hot air burning his lungs. That was what had scared him to death. Elkin's aim. They'd been five feet apart. Elkin's bullet would have struck one of them, and there was no telling who that might have been.

Holding Elkin's wrists with one hand, he reached down and picked up his gun, shoved it in his waistband, and then picked up Elkin's.

He'd grabbed Elkin's wrist when he'd tackled him, and had twisted the man's hand upright, diverted the gun, so the bullet that had been fired had hit the ceiling. The fact it could have struck someone still nearly gutted him. And still infuriated him.

The hallway was empty. Betty and the others were gone. Henry jumped to his feet, and then pulled Elkin off the floor. Rage had his blood boiling and he fought to keep from spinning Elkin around and slamming his fist in the man's face for putting Betty in such danger. But the truth of it was, he'd put her in danger just as much as Elkin had. More so, she was here because she'd wanted to help him.

Elkin started spouting off again, about how other people knew he was here.

"No, they don't," Henry said. "You don't want them knowing you screwed up. That you hadn't killed me. That's why you gave out this address, knowing I'd come. Thought you'd get a jump on me." He gave Elkin a hard shove, forced him to move down the hallway, quickly, all the while glancing behind them, toward the basement stairway. Others could be coming, but he doubted it. "You've double-crossed too many people, Elkin."

As they entered the main room of the depot, Lane appeared in one of the open archways.

"They're gone." Lane jogged toward them. "I told them to go to our apartment."

"Good," Henry said, breathing out a sigh of relief that

Betty was safe. Tightening his hold on Elkin's wrists, he said, "Take his belt off. My cuffs are in my car."

It would use precious time, but he had to make sure Elkin was secure if someone else did enter the building. He'd need both hands to respond and keep ahold on Elkin.

Lane pulled off Elkin's belt, and Henry used it to bind the mole's wrists together behind his back, and then nearly dragged Elkin as he ran through the depot, to get where he and Lane had parked their cars as fast as possible.

He had the mole, and should be happy, but wasn't. This wasn't over. He didn't have the evidence he'd hoped to have upon capturing the man. Elkin wasn't going to give a full confession. He could bet on that.

Once at his car, he pulled his cuffs out from beneath his seat and clamped them on Elkin's wrists.

"The central precinct?" Lane asked.

Henry nodded. "Yes." That was the only police precinct he could trust. Like most other cities, the mob bosses had bought off police departments from beat cops to captains in charge, but the chief at the central precinct had let it be known no one was immune to arrest within his jurisdiction. Henry had already met with Chief Miller several times over the past few weeks and knew Elkin wouldn't stand a chance of escaping detention under Miller's care.

"I'll follow you," Lane said.

"No," Henry answered while shoving Elkin into his car. "You go check on Bet—the women." She'd been frightened; he'd heard her gasps and sobs as she'd stood behind him and he wished he could go comfort her, but duty called. Took precedence. He hated that, but had no choice.

"All right, I'll meet you at the precinct afterward."

Henry shook his head. He had a lot of work to do before he could make sure Betty was all right. He rubbed his forehead. She may never be all right after what she'd just been through. "No, I need you to see that Betty and her sister get back to their house. Once I get Elkin behind bars, I'll round up some prohibition officers to scour this place, see what we can uncover."

"Will do," Lane said. "I'll go to the precinct after that, give them my statement of what happened. How Elkin confessed to shanghaiing you and taking bribes."

Henry nodded, but didn't tell Lane that a statement of hearing Elkin's minor confessions wasn't worth more than the paper it was written on when it came to putting the man away for good. Federal crimes were never that easy. He needed a lot more evidence to hand over to the Justice Department in order for Elkin to get what he deserved.

He did have one hope left. Vincent Burrows.

Upon arrival at the precinct, he informed Chief Miller that prohibition agents and police officers needed to be dispatched to the old depot, and then requested the opportunity to interrogate Burrows.

He'd wanted to interview Burrows since the man's arrest, but knew Burrows wouldn't sing until he was backed into a corner.

"Tell the deputy to walk Burrows past Elkin's jail cell," Henry told the chief. "Make sure they see each other."

With a barrel chest and bald head, the chief looked as no-nonsense as he was, yet, right now, he grinned. "We could clean up this city if we had a man like you around here on a regular basis."

Henry knew it would take more than one man to

clean up this city, but was glad to be ridding it of both Elkin and Burrows.

As soon as Burrows entered the room, Henry said, "You should have taken the bait, Vincent. Your future would be looking a whole lot brighter if you had."

Wide-eyed and turning whiter by the second, Burrows smoothed his thick black mustache with a trembling hand.

"You thought I was dead?" Henry asked.

Burrows shot a nervous glance around the room, then back at him.

Shrugging, Henry said, "Elkin tried, but he failed."

Burrows half sat, half dropped into the chair on the other side of the metal table. "Don't know anyone by that name."

"Yes, you do. You know Curtis Elkin. And you know that I was pretending to be Rex Gaynor." Henry leaned across the table, looked the criminal straight in the eye. "That was for your benefit, you know. If you'd taken the bait, came to me, you'd be where Curtis Elkin is right now."

Burrows shook his head even as sweat beaded across his forehead. "I said I don't know anyone by that name."

"I know you do," Henry said. "You just walked past his jail cell. His glasses broke during his arrest, but you still recognized him. The federal agent you've been paying off for years." Although he didn't have the proof, he had his instincts and went with them. "You and your family. He's been spilling since I handcuffed him. How you paid him to tell you about the money on that train seven years ago, and for that shipment of Minnesota Thirteen you hijacked, and that counterfeiting ring up in Seattle, that train robbery in Kansas."

Sweat poured down the man's face as he shook his

head nonstop. "I ain't never had nothing to do with counterfeiting, never robbed no train."

"That's not what Elkin says," Henry lied.

"He's trying to pin them on me," Burrows insisted. "It wasn't me."

It was amazing what a mobster would say to save their own neck. Henry shrugged. "Looks like you're the one left holding the bag."

"No! No!" Burrows shoved his hands below the table to hide how they trembled. "I'm not taking the fall for someone else." He pulled out his hands, waved them in the air. "Jimmy Tribbiani, he's the counterfeiter, and Tony, Tony, his cousin, he's the train robber."

The dots of Elkin's trail started connecting in Henry's head. The leaks had been so random, and so far away from New Jersey, which was where Burrows's family operated their bootlegging business, that Henry had never made the connection before. It made sense, though, that the family started sending members west, and explained why they weren't caught for their crimes. They'd been new to the areas. Unknown to locals. They'd also thought that they were untouchable with a dirty agent informing them of anyone on their tail. They practically had been.

"He's the reason you were busted," Henry said. "So he could take over the West Coast operation that you were setting up." Taking it one step further, even though he had no proof of the correlation, he added, "Your uncle Leonardo, the one who built the house here in Los Angeles." He paused for a moment, to make the image of Betty and him in the basement of that house fade. "Didn't your family question why his operation was raided?"

"That rotten stool pigeon! He's been double-crossing

my family from the beginning." Burrows slammed a hand on the table. "He double-crossed me on that shipment of hooch! Gave me ten cases. I couldn't make any money on ten cases. Had to borrow money from that old dame so I could start a still and cut it so I had enough to distribute to the joints to even get things rolling."

If there was one thing a mobster hated, it was being double-crossed. That was the surest way to get bumped off. Elkin should have known that. Probably did, but had gotten away with so much over the years, being a federal agent, he'd thought he was untouchable.

That was no longer the case. Henry leaned back in his chair and folded his arms over his chest. "How much time do you want to serve, Vincent?"

Burrows attempted to cover up the way his jaw dropped by rubbing his thick mustache before he said, "None."

That wasn't about to happen, but there was no sense in telling Burrows that now. He'd find out soon enough. "I know you killed Billy during the robbery. Why'd you have Gaynor knocked off?"

"It was Elkin's idea when he heard that I was coming out here. He said Gaynor was talking, that he'd identified me. Gaynor had shown Elkin where he'd pitched his share of the money. Elkin took mine, too. That's how we paid him to give us tips on busts. He knew where it could be spent."

That was what he needed. As an agent, Elkin knew where the money could be pawned off on innocent folks not knowing it had been taken out of circulation. He also knew why, after seven years, Elkin had decided it was time to completely switch sides, and Vincent moving to California, to expand the business out here, was Elkin's chance. Henry was happy. He was more than ready to be done with this interview. He needed to get to a phone, call Lane, and make sure Betty was all right. "Let me tell you how this is going to go down, Vincent."

Chapter Thirteen

It was after ten at night, and not a single light shone in any of the windows of the Dryer house. That could mean Betty was sleeping, or it could mean she was out with her sister, visiting a joint. Lane had said she was fine, that they were all fine, but Henry needed to see for himself. Now. Tonight, and had already concluded this was where he'd start. Her house.

If she wasn't here, he'd have two choices. To wait or start searching speakeasies. He had a feeling that after the harrowing event with Elkin, she wouldn't want to go out, but Jane would, and Betty was committed to her younger sisters.

He also knew which room was hers.

The trellis creaked, but held beneath his weight, and the bathroom window was open, which could mean they were gone and he'd be waiting for two hours, or that she was home, and he had to be careful to not startle a scream out of her upon entering her room.

He'd never thought he'd be doing this, sneaking into her bedroom, but he'd never thought many of the things that had happened since meeting her would ever have happened to him.

He wished things could be different, but today had proven they never could be. His job, his life, was too dangerous. He'd never been so afraid, so worried, that someone would be injured as he had been today.

He'd walk away a different man than when he'd arrived, that was a given. He hadn't had any defense to prevent that from happening. He hadn't known it had been happening. Due in part to denial, and the other part, her. She'd changed him with little more than a smile and a twinkle in her eyes.

A smile and a twinkle he'd never forget.

Without making a sound, he snuck out of the bathroom and into the hall, where he paused briefly, listening. As the silence echoed in his ears, he made his way to her bedroom door and tried the knob.

It turned, and the moment the door opened, he knew she was in the room. Every part of his body came to life like a match struck on a shoe bottom. That was another thing he'd never experienced. That instant feeling of completion. Of being whole. It was hard to describe, even to himself, how he didn't feel as if something was missing in his life when she was nearby.

He closed the door and crossed the room, to her bed. Moonlight shone through the window, highlighting her hair as she lay on one side, her cheek upon the pillow.

Asleep, she was as enchanting as she was while awake and he could stand here, simply staring at her for hours.

"Hello, Henry."

"Hello," he whispered in return, amazed at how happy the simple sound of her voice made him.

She rolled onto her back, then sat up, pulling the blankets up beneath her chin. "What are you doing here?"

He sat on the edge of the bed. "Checking on you." He touched her hand. "How are you?"

"Fine. Did you get all the evidence you need on Elkin?"

"Yes. He'll be in jail for many, many years."

She smiled. "That's good."

"I'm sorry for what happened. I would never have called Patsy, never have—"

She pressed a finger to his lips. "I know. Lane told us that it was Elkin who called the newspaper and left that message." She removed her finger and touched his cheek before letting her hand fall. "When are you leaving?"

His stomach clenched. Despite knowing what had to happen, it hurt. Leaving hurt worse than anything he'd known. "In a few days." It just wasn't his job, the oath he'd taken, or how he owed John Randall for giving him an education and career, it was him. He didn't know how to love the way she deserved to be loved and was too old to learn.

She nodded and pinched her lips together.

The tears glistening in her eyes saddened him. "I'll see you—"

"No." She shook her head. "I can't see you again, Henry. I wish I could, but I can't." She sniffled. "Saying goodbye to you is so hard, but that's what I'm doing, saying goodbye." She lifted her chin. It trembled. "You need to go take Elkin to Washington, DC, and then go on to your next assignment. Keep being an FBI agent, because you are a very, very good one. You saved all our lives today, without blinking an eye. The Bureau needs you. Our country needs you."

It felt as if his heart was being torn out of his chest and there wasn't a thing he could do about it because he couldn't change the truth, couldn't change what was. His eyes hadn't stung like they were right now since he'd been a small, small child.

Tears streamed down her face. He wiped one of her cheeks with his thumb. "Betty, maybe—"

"No, Henry, this is goodbye," she whispered. "It has to be."

Anger, frustration, and more sorrow than he'd ever known filled him, forced him to blink harder, faster, and look away from her. He had to do that in order to remember, to admit, she was right.

The pain inside him grew. Got darker. Uglier. He didn't bother to work out how it was all directed at him.

Didn't need to.

Betty had thought about this all day, what she was going to do, and knew the conclusion she'd come to was the right one. She couldn't think about herself, her heart; she had to think about the life growing inside her and how everything she did, from this moment on, was for the baby. If it was just her, she'd live out of a single suitcase for the rest of her life if that was what it took to be with Henry. But it wasn't just her, she had the baby to think about. That was her main concern now. Had to be.

She swallowed the sob filling her throat. "Will you kiss me one last time? Hug me one last time?"

His arms were around her so fast, held her so tight, she nearly cried out at the pain of knowing she'd never know such splendor again. He kissed her then, and she kissed him in return. One final time.

She would have gone on kissing him, but knew it would only prolong the inevitable, so she broke the kiss and pushed him away. "Goodbye, Henry." Then, because she was afraid that she wouldn't be able to keep from stopping him, she flipped onto her side and pulled the covers over her head.

Just as she had known the moment he'd entered her room, she knew the moment he left it. Silently. The exact same way he'd entered her heart that day on the beach in Seattle. He wasn't to blame for that. She wasn't either. She hadn't had any control over how her heart had fallen in love with him that day. How it would forever love him because she didn't have any control over changing it. Her heart had a mind of its own, and once it had fallen in love with him, there had been nothing she could do about it.

The tears fell faster, harder, and she curled into a ball at the pain consuming her. The very pain she would have to learn to live with the rest of her life.

The pain was still there when she crawled out of bed the next morning, got dressed, and went downstairs.

Father was sitting at the table, reading the paper, as usual. Henry had been right about so many things. Her father was strict, stern, so he could get what he wanted while deceiving all of them.

It was time for him to know he'd taught her well. "Good morning, Father," she said, calm and matter-of-fact. That was how her life would be from now on. Matter-of-fact. "Please tell James to meet me at the courthouse at nine o'clock this morning. Both persons must be present to apply for a marriage license."

The sounds of breaking china reverberated into the room. Betty kept her chin up as she looked toward the doorway. Jane stood there, mouth agape and a pile of broken dishes at her feet.

Father had lowered his newspaper at the sound of

dishes breaking and glowered toward the kitchen. "I'm not scheduled to see James this morning."

Betty held in the emotions rippling her insides. "Is he building a house or not?"

"Yes," Father barked. "He's waiting on materials." He snapped his paper back up before his face. "We'll discuss this after breakfast. Go help your sister and mother."

"No." It hurt to be so cold, so uncaring, but that was who she had to be. "They don't need my help, and we will discuss this now. You are the one who wants me to marry James as soon as possible, so I will. There is a five-day waiting period. Then there will be a wedding."

Father slapped his newspaper onto the table as Mother rushed into the room.

"Five days!" Mother exclaimed, clearly flustered. "Darling, that's not possible. We don't even have your dress yet."

"I'll wear one I already own," Betty replied.

"No, you won't, and there's more than that. There's the guests and—"

"Guests?" Betty huffed out a half chuckle, half sob. "I don't have any friends."

"That's not true," Mother said. "The church was full for Patsy's wedding."

"Because she married Lane. The church was full of his friends." Betty shrugged. "If James has friends, he can invite them. Or not. I don't care."

"Betty Louise!" Mother exclaimed. "What has gotten into you?"

The truth. The blatant truth. "Nothing has gotten into me," she answered. "This is merely my life."

"Now, see here!" Father shouted. "You will not talk to your mother like that!"

She looked him straight in the eye. "Should I lie to her instead? Lock myself behind a gate?"

His eyes widened.

She didn't so much as blink. "Like father, like daughter."

He squirmed, slightly, but she saw it. Maybe she'd been wrong. She could break a rule when Henry wasn't near.

"One more thing, those materials James is waiting on, I do hope they will be up to the building code standard."

"Betty?" Mother had her hands pressed to her breastbone. "What are you talking about?"

"Father knows." She'd said all she was going to say. Holding her composure, she turned and walked away, down the hallway and up the stairs.

She'd barely closed the door, when it flew back open and slammed shut.

"What are you thinking?" Jane asked. "Mother is sobbing. Father is yelling."

Betty shrugged.

"Stop it!" Jane stomped a foot. "This isn't you!" She planted her hands on her hips. "You can't marry James!" Glancing at the door, she hissed, "You're pregnant with Henry's baby, remember?"

"Of course, I remember!" She'd always remember that. Always remember her baby's father. "You heard Lane yesterday. Henry will take Elkin to Washington, DC, and be there for months while the trial is happening."

"So?"

Betty sucked in air to fuel her resolve. "You said I can't have a baby six months after I get married."

Jane stared at her, mouth open and shaking her head. "You never told Henry, did you?"

Betty's throat burned, so did her stomach full of guilt. That was another thing she'd have to learn to live with. "No. And I'm not going to."

"You have to."

"No, I don't." Her resolve was fading, fast. "I can't. I can't do that to him. You saw him yesterday. He's an FBI agent. That's his life." She plopped down on the bed, and tried hard not to cry, but failed. "He doesn't want a wife, or family. Everything he owns fits in one suitcase so he can go wherever, whenever. Chasing mobsters and villains."

Jane sat down on the bed beside her, held her hand. "That could change, when he knows the truth."

"That's the problem," Betty whispered. "I don't want him to have to change. He's never been loved and doesn't ever want to be." She didn't know how to explain it, but felt it in her heart. "You saw him yesterday, with Elkin."

"Yes, I did. Elkin was holding a gun on him," Jane said. "What did you expect him to do?"

She'd gone over this a thousand times in her mind. "To do to exactly what he did," she admitted. "And I have a baby to think about."

Jane squeezed her hand harder and leaned her head against hers. "Yes, you do. What if James treats you and the baby terribly? What if he—"

"Is like Father?" She shrugged. "I've lived with that my whole life."

Jane sat up straight and shook her head. "You can't do this. I won't let you."

"It's not your choice—it's mine."

"No." Jane stood up. "If you won't tell Henry, then I will."

Betty stood, faced her sister, and laid down the ultimatum. "Then I'll tell Father about us sneaking out. For months."

Disbelief filled Jane's face. "You wouldn't."

"Yes, I would. Because this isn't about me, or you, or even Henry. It's about my baby, and I won't take the chance, take any chance, that this baby will be taken away from me like Aunt Joan's was, because we both know Father will do that before he'd let me marry Henry." Determined, she continued, "Marrying James is the only way that's not going to happen."

"There has to be—"

"No, there's not." She was breaking, inside and out. Sitting on the bed, she wiped at the tears rolling down her cheeks. "You said it a moment ago. This isn't me. And that's why I have to do this. Henry… Marrying him…" She shook her head. "It would be as if I was trying to be someone I'm not."

Jane knelt down in front of her, cupped her cheeks. "What if marrying him would be your chance to be who you are?"

The Dryer home grew even more solemn than usual over the course of the next two days. Betty didn't care. James had met her at the courthouse, they had their marriage license, and would get married in three days. That scared her, mainly the wedding night. To the point she was so sick to her stomach she could barely keep anything down. She kept eating, trying to keep food down, for the baby's sake.

The rest of her, her emotions, her ability to feel, was

numb, as if her insides were wrapped in a quilt to keep anything else from breaking.

She was in the back porch, doing laundry, when Mother opened the door. "Betty, there's someone at the front door. They want to speak to you."

Betty plucked a sheet out of the washer to run through the wringer. No one ever came to the house to see her. "Who is it?"

Mother wrung her hands together. "The man you cleaned the house for—he's here to pay you."

Henry. Her mouth went dry, but her insides, still shrouded in that heavy quilt, helped her maintain the unequivocal calm she'd mastered the past couple of days. He shouldn't even be in town. Betty shot a glare toward Jane. They'd barely spoken the past few days.

Jane shrugged and shook her head.

"Betty?" Mother asked.

Betty dropped the sheet back in the water. "I'll talk to him."

"I wish I knew where your father was working today," Mother said to Jane as Betty walked past her.

Betty sucked in air and breathed it out, several times while walking through the house, telling herself she could do this. She could see Henry. She could do anything she set her mind to. Even face him. The man she'd forever dream about.

She grasped ahold of the doorknob on the front door, and stood there for a moment, knowing he was on the other side of it. Her body knew it, too. Despite that invisible quilt she'd come to depend on, parts of her were growing warm, tingling.

Pulling open the door, she asked, "What are you doing here?"

He was leaning against one of the tall white pillars

on the front porch, wearing a white shirt with black suspenders and pants, and looked even more handsome than any memory. Any dream. That made her tremble harder. Her knees threatened to buckle, as if forgetting she needed them to stand straight.

"I came to talk to you," he said, pushing off the pillar.

This—doing what she knew she had to do—would be so much easier when he was gone. "I thought you'd already be in Washington, DC, by now."

"No, I still had some work to do here." His eyes never left hers. "Lane just told me you're marrying James on Saturday. Why?"

She did her best to make a shrug look natural. "It's as good of a day as any."

Something, anger perhaps, flashed in his eyes. "Don't make light of this, Betty."

"I'm not." She squared her shoulders. "I'm telling you the truth."

"The truth?"

She nodded, even as her entire body flinched inside.

Henry was fighting hard to maintain his anger. Harder than he'd ever fought before. He'd been dumbfounded, shocked, and furious when he'd hung up from Lane this morning, after learning that Betty was marrying James in three days.

Three, damn, days.

He grabbed her hand. "I'll show you the truth."

She pulled her hand away. "I'm not going anywhere with you. I can't. I'm—"

He glared at her. "You can't? You can get married in three days, but you can't leave the house without permission? What are you? A woman or a child?"

Her eyes narrowed. "Fine." She followed him to his car and climbed in. "Show me."

This was not going as he'd planned, as he'd imagined, but that was typical when it came to having anything to do with her. He should have walked away before she'd opened the door. Should never have come here in the first place. It was as if he was a glutton for punishment.

Or he was trying his damnedest not to feel. Not to care.

He shut her door and walked around the car, got in the driver's side.

She was staring straight ahead.

He started the car, backed out of the driveway, and drove up the hill, toward Bauer's building site. He'd show her just what kind of a man she was marrying. He'd cursed her father a hundred times over when Lane said that on the phone, and had made Lane repeat what he'd said because he'd been sure he'd misunderstood.

According to Lane, he hadn't misunderstood anything. William Dryer wasn't forcing her to marry Bauer on Saturday. It had been her idea. She was the one pushing for the quick wedding.

The silence was more than he could take. "Why, Betty? Why are you pushing to marry him so quickly?"

"It's what my father wants."

"But it's not what you want."

"How do you know what I want?" she snapped. "You don't. No one does except me."

"And this is what you want? Marrying James?"

"Yes, it is." She looked out the passenger window. "Now, what did you want to show me?"

"We're almost there," he said, fully prepared to let her see the type of man she was pushing to marry.

They drove the rest of the way in silence. He shouldn't be excited to show her that Bauer was a lazy bum, but as he turned onto the road leading up to the building site, a mean streak of enjoyment formed inside. She was about to see Bauer's continued disregard for the law herself. Then she could decide to not marry him.

However, as the site came into view, he was the one who couldn't believe his eyes. There were men everywhere. Sawing boards, pounding nails, putting up walls, a roof. What the hell? He'd been here yesterday and the site looked exactly like it had last week. Nothing but a two-by-four frame.

"Is that what you wanted me to see?" she asked. "The house that James is building?"

Hell no. He didn't pull off the road. Continued right past the building site swarming with men. That shot his investigative work all to hell.

"Take me home, Henry."

Huffing out a breath, he said, "No one was working on that house yesterday."

"Because James was waiting on materials," she said. "And if you noticed, they are now using two-by-sixes. Fully up to code. I've spoken to both my father and James about that. Every house built by James will be up to code."

He clamped his jaw tight.

"Take me home, Henry. Now. I'm marrying James because that's what I want to do, and you are going to DC because that is what you want to do."

"Have to!" He pulled the car to the side of the road. "I'm going because I have to go. It's my job."

"I know it's your job," she said. "Now, please take me home."

She sounded despondent. He certainly was. He

pulled back onto the road and spun a U-turn, taking her back toward her house. Keeping his eyes on the road, he told her the truth. The absolute truth. "I'm leaving tomorrow. Transporting Elkin and Burrows to Washington, DC, because that's my job. I don't have a choice." His throat was on fire, and he had to swallow before saying, "You do."

She didn't respond.

His insides were an inferno of his darkest emotions. What had he expected? For her to say she wouldn't marry Bauer? That she'd be here waiting for him for whenever, if ever, he returned? What kind of satisfaction would that have been? None. Not for her or him.

He drove down the road and parked in the driveway of the abandoned house. The moment he'd seen her, he'd forgotten about the money that was in his shirt pocket. He took it out. Handed it to her.

"What's that?" She didn't take it.

"Money for cleaning the house."

"I don't want any money from you."

"Your father will expect—"

"I don't care what he expects." She opened the door and climbed out.

He opened his, too. Met her at the front of the car. Touched her arm. "I don't want to part like this."

She drew in a deep breath and glanced around. "Will you be transporting Elkin and Burrows by yourself?" she asked.

"No, two other agents will be with me, and we'll meet our supervisor in Texas—he'll travel the rest of the way with us."

"That's nice. I wouldn't want you to be alone, all that way."

He didn't want her to be alone, either, now or ever. "Why are you marrying Bauer? The truth."

She stood silent, staring out at the house with its boarded-up windows for so long, he was about to repeat his question, when she turned, looked at him.

She licked her lips, bit down on the bottom one, and then, shaking her head, said, "Because I'm pregnant, Henry."

Chapter Fourteen

Henry knew the loud swishing noise was blood rushing to his head, muffling his hearing, but it hadn't been there until she'd spoken. "Why didn't you tell me?"

"I just did."

"I told you that night—"

"I know what you told me that night." She moved away from his touch. "That if there were any repercussions, you would provide."

"And I will. We'll get married. I will—"

"No," she interrupted. "We won't get married, because I won't marry you."

"You are pregnant with my child." His insides nearly buckled at that. His child. He didn't know anything about being a father. He'd have to learn, though. Fast.

"No, Henry, I'm pregnant with my child." There were tears in her eyes, but she sounded cold, aloof. "A child that I will love and cherish the rest of my life."

The air he breathed in felt as if it was grains of sand, pitting his throat, filling his lungs, his heart, burying anything he might have felt there. "It's my child, too."

"And what will you do with a child? Love them? Cherish them? Haul them around from town to town,

"The other thing I can tell you is that Esther had become quite frustrated with the headmistress. The woman had one excuse after the other as to why we shouldn't adopt you, everything from you were too old and would never adjust, to that they thought you'd been stealing food, but couldn't prove it." John chuckled. "I'd never seen your mother so angry as when she told that woman if she said one more bad word against you, that she would be removed from her position. I of course agreed with Esther, wholeheartedly. It wasn't until after we adopted you that we discovered why that woman hadn't wanted you to leave."

Confused, or still just numb, Henry asked, "Why?"

"Because you were practically running the place. You'd already completed all the courses they had and were teaching several classes of younger children. They all looked up to you, and you were so worried about them when you left there."

He didn't remember that. "I was?"

"Yes, you never admitted it—that wasn't your way. It's also why we enrolled you in junior college right away—you were at a loss with nothing to do."

Faint memories were filtering into his mind, of teaching classes to the younger children.

"We continue to contribute to the orphanage every year," John said. "In your name, for specific needs, new books and beds, blankets, and clothes. We remain very thankful that they provided for you until we'd adopted you."

After a short pause, John asked, "Are you all right, son?"

"Yes," Henry answered immediately. "I'm fine. I was just curious is all. Had some time on my hands and was just thinking."

assignment to assignment? Let them play with your gun and handcuffs? Let them sleep in your suitcase?"

"Hell no!"

She closed her eyes, took a deep breath. "You're an FBI agent and—"

"I'll—I'll quit and—"

"No, you won't, and I don't want you to. That's the only thing you've ever loved. The only thing you've ever cared about. That's why you thought I was a coincidence—"

"I apologized for that! I was wrong!"

"I was wrong, too, Henry. About what I thought was happening when we met again. It wasn't. I know that now. And I know you don't want to marry me. I also know that my father would never let me marry you, and—"

"I'll—"

"No!" She stopped his protest. "There's more."

Arms folded across his chest, holding back the anger building inside, it took every ounce of his will to stand there, listen to her.

"I have to marry James. He's stable. Kind and generous. James will provide everything that both the baby and I need. He'll make a wonderful father."

He'd heard, but his mind was going in several directions at once. None of them nice thoughts. She was saying he wouldn't make a wonderful father. That was what he heard. "That's why you moved up the wedding date. So you can pawn my child off as his."

"Yes. I have to, because if I don't, and my father finds out I'm pregnant, he will send me to the convent and have the baby put up for adoption. I don't want that, and I don't believe you do, either."

He let out a growl that included a curse. "Hell no!"

"But you know I'm right, don't you? That I don't have any other choice."

He wanted to grab her, hug her, shake some sense into her, but he couldn't, because she was right. He didn't want his child raised in an orphanage, but he... Damn it. He didn't know anything about being a father.

"Fine, marry him. With my blessing." He turned, walked around the car. His legs shook, but his heart turned as hard and cold as he'd remembered it being as a child. If she were to ask, beg him to wait, to stay, he wouldn't. He'd climb in the car and drive away.

Which was what he did, because she didn't ask, or beg him to wait. To stay.

Henry couldn't remember driving to the hotel; he didn't know how long he'd been sitting there, either, staring out the window, not seeing anything. He thought he'd seen the sun set, and that it was now rising.

Not that it mattered. The pain inside him was so strong, so raw, it consumed him, his mind, his heart, his soul.

His thoughts had gone down alleyways that he'd to- tally forgotten, and ventured along lines that were noth- ing but wishful thinking. He'd never been in a place like this, and didn't know what to do.

He'd picked up the phone several times, but this time, when the operator came on the line, he gave her a num- ber.

Two rings later, the sound of the man's voice nearly made his eyes sting.

"It's Henry," he said into the speaker.

"Henry! It's good to hear your voice! How are you, son?" John asked.

He swallowed the lump in his throat. "Goo are you? And Esther? How is she?"

"We are doing fine, just fine," John replied. your case going? Nate told us about you being haied. Nearly scared us to death."

"I'm sure he made it sound worse than it was. answered. "The case is solved. I'll be transpor detainees to Washington soon."

"Will you have time to stop and say hello? V to see you."

"I'll try," he answered, and for the first tim ally would try. He wanted to see them. "Can I a question?"

"Of course, son, what is it?"

"It's about my adoption."

"I'll answer anything I can."

"Do you know what happened to my birth Although he'd convinced himself otherwise that mattered to him right now. A lot.

"We always wondered if you knew, bec never asked," John said. "The headmistress s the note that was tucked in your pocket the r father left you there. It said that your name v and that he was your father, and that your m died. It also said that he was very ill. He v that you were going to get sick and didn't The note said that he would be back to get yo as he was better. There was no name, and wh ever returned to claim you, it was assumed

Henry wasn't sure what he'd expected t there wasn't much there. Probably because already taken all he'd had to give.

"That's all I know," John said. "I'm sorry

"No, that's what I wanted to know," Hen

John laughed, "Well, if you ever find yourself with time on your hands, your mother and I would like to see you. It's been a long time."

"I'll make it home, soon," Henry answered.

"We do understand how busy you are," John said. "But we still miss you."

Henry's insides clenched. "I miss you, too, and Esther, tell her I said hello."

"I will," John answered. "We love you, Henry."

Henry hung up without responding, and instantly felt so guilty, he almost called John back, but didn't.

Why? And why hadn't he remembered teaching classes to the children? Just like he hadn't remembered Mick Lawrence and Darrin Wolf until Betty asked? Because he'd convinced himself that there hadn't been any good memories, until he'd completely believed it? Why? Because he didn't want to be happy?

He hadn't wanted to be, until he'd met Betty. She'd changed that. Changed him.

Betty couldn't remember how long she'd lain on the ground after Henry had driven away that day, but she did remember how she'd collapsed. Slowly, like a burning building, one wall and then the other, destroying anything that had ever been inside, and how the shards of her broken heart had stabbed her so deeply, she'd thought she might die right there.

She hadn't died and when she'd managed to lift her head, Jane had been sitting next to her.

"I told him," Betty had whispered.

"I saw him drive away," Jane had answered.

"He hates me."

Jane had leaned down and kissed her forehead. "I don't."

Then Jane had helped her to her feet and walked her home, where she'd had to start living with her decision. For the rest of her life.

Today was the next step. She was at the church, wearing the long white dress that she'd agreed to wear, to please her mother. It wasn't fair of her to take her misery out on others.

Her sisters were wearing new dresses, too, ones they had picked out. Jane's was peach colored and Patsy's was yellow. They both looked so nice, so pretty.

"You look beautiful," Patsy said. "So beautiful."

"Yes, she does." Jane waved a hand over her face. "So beautiful I'm going to cry."

"Don't you dare," Patsy said, "because then I will, too, and we'll both have mascara running down our cheeks."

Betty had been fighting tears all day, but she'd grown used to that over the past weeks, and once again managed to blink them away without affecting her mascara. She was still numb inside, merely going through the motions of living as one goes through the motions of washing dishes, a mere repetitiveness of dunk, wash, dunk, rinse, put aside to dry. "You both know I'm the ugly duckling," Betty said, "and you are the swans." They were in her eyes, they always had been, from cute little sisters, to beautiful young women. She loved them dearly.

"Horsefeathers," Jane said. "Swans are taller than ducks, and you are the tallest."

"Tall?" Betty laughed. It felt good to pretend all was normal. That they could joke with each other. "The three of us are short, shorter, and shortest." Her breath snagged in her lungs as she looked at Patsy and Jane, wondering if her children would love each other this much. Or if she would only have the one child. Henry's child.

No. She couldn't do that. Not now. Not here. This was her child.

"Girls," Mother said, stepping into the little side room of the church. "It's time."

Betty suddenly felt as if she was freezing, from the inside. So cold even her teeth were chattering. She pressed four fingers to her mouth, but couldn't make the chattering stop.

"Jane, you walk in first, and walk slowly," Mother said. "Patsy, you'll follow, and then you, Betty. Your father is waiting to walk you down the aisle." Mother's eyes lit up even brighter. "Smile, dear. There are a lot of people here."

Before Betty attempted to pull up a smile, Jane reached up and flipped the netted veil over her face.

"She is smiling, Mother," Jane said.

Betty wasn't. She might never smile again, but at least the chattering had stopped. She drew in a deep breath, and silently thanked Jane for pulling the veil over her face. No one would notice that she wasn't smiling. That she looked like she was walking to the gallows instead of to the altar to be united in marriage.

She had to become united in marriage because in eight months, she would be having a baby. Her sisters kept reminding her of what a joyous occasion that would be. What wonderful aunties they would make. They would, and it would be a very joyous occasion the first time she held her baby in her arms. That was the thought that kept her going every day.

Her mother left the room, leaving the door open, and Jane stood there, watching until it was time for her to exit.

By the time it was Betty's turn to leave the room, she was trembling so hard she could barely move. She hooked her arm through her father's and started walking. She had to go through with this. That was all there was to it.

There were people sitting in the pews. That had been Patsy's doing, and Betty did appreciate her sister's support. Both Jane's and Patsy's support in this whole farce.

That was what it was. A farce.

The wedding.

Her.

All of it.

Her insides sank deeper and deeper with each step she took toward the altar, where the big cross hung overhead. A shiver coursed down her spine.

Thou shalt not bear false witness.

Her footsteps stumbled. Father grasped her arm, kept her moving forward.

Toward the cross. Toward James.

She had to lie. For her baby. The tiny life growing inside her. The tiny boy or girl who would never know their father.

Henry.

That was the worst farce of all. She'd hurt him so badly. Had seen it on his face, in his eyes. A sob got caught in the back of her throat. Choking her.

She got it out, sucked in air.

She glanced at Jane.

At Patsy.

What had she been thinking?

This wasn't setting a good example.

This was wrong.

So wrong.

What she'd done to Henry was wrong.

So very, very wrong.

Her father stopped. James took her hand, held it as she took her final steps up to the altar. Chills raced over her, and she closed her eyes, wishing at that moment that it was Henry who had taken her hand.

He wasn't holding her hand. James was. It was wrong what she was doing to him, too. All this time, she'd thought about him as a means to an end. An imaginary person who, in an odd sense, wasn't even real. But he was real. He was a good person, too. He'd thanked her about standing up to her father because of the building codes. He hadn't dared to do that. He wouldn't dare not marry her, either. That wasn't fair. He truly didn't deserve to be deceived.

She couldn't do that to him.

She couldn't do this.

This wasn't who she was. This was not her.

It was not.

And if it was, it was not who she wanted to be. Who she would be.

A warmth washed away the chills. The same one that used to appear whenever Henry was near. She pulled her hand free from James. It may be her imagination, but she'd felt a flutter in her stomach, and pressed her hand against it.

The baby didn't want her to do this, either.

Tears filled her eyes, but they weren't sad ones. They were tears of hope. Of finding her true self. She had her sisters. She had her baby. She had a life. Her life. Broken rules or not, it was her life. One that she had control over. She just had to take that control. She'd thought she had been, in some ways, but not enough.

"I object," she blurted out.

The priest frowned and shook his head.

She squared her shoulders, nodded, and louder, repeated, "I object."

"Betty?" James asked.

"I'm sorry, but I can't do this," she told him. "Not to you, and you shouldn't have to do it, either." Glancing the other way, toward her sisters, she repeated, "I can't do this." Looking at the priest, she repeated once more, "I object."

The priest cleared his throat, and then whispered, "You can't object. You're the bride."

"Then I object," Jane said.

"You can't object, either," the priest said.

"I can! I object!"

Betty's heart nearly leaped out of her chest as she spun around, saw the man who had shouted. "Henry," she gasped, and blinked to make sure she wasn't seeing things.

"Who are you?" Father asked, leaping to his feet.

She wasn't seeing things. Well, she was, but it was real, and a wonderful sight.

Dressed in a black suit and tie, with a white shirt, Henry walked up the aisle toward her. He stopped next to Father and held out his hand.

Stunned, Father looked around, and somewhat sheepish, shook Henry's hand.

"I'm Henry Randall, Mr. Dryer." He then nodded at Mother. "Mrs. Dryer."

Mother waggled her fingers at him, and whispered to Father, "It's the man whose house she cleaned."

Betty couldn't contain her mirth and let out a giggle.

"Who?" Father asked.

"Henry Randall," he said, walking the rest of the way to her. "The man who is going to marry your daughter." He reached out, took her hand. "This one."

Father nodded, then shook his head. "Now, see here, Betty's already marrying someone. James."

Henry didn't look back at Father; his eyes never left hers. Those unique blue eyes that she hoped their baby would have.

"I was right," he said. "You were more than a co-incidence. You were the person who would teach me how to love."

Tears of pure joy flowed from her eyes at his statement.

"Will you marry me, Betty?"

She wanted to shout yes, but had gone through so much to convince him that wasn't possible, she couldn't, could she? Just like that? Forget all her worrying? All her reasons? All she'd concluded? Actually, right now, she couldn't even remember what her reasons were. Not a single reason why she couldn't marry him formed in her mind.

"Yes, she will marry you, Henry."

He grinned, but his eyes never left hers as he said, "Thank you, Jane, but I need to hear it from Betty. I tried to stay away, to give you what you wanted, but I couldn't, because I know this is not what you wanted. Is it?"

"No, this is not what I want," she whispered. "I want to say yes, but I don't want to ruin your life." There. She had remembered.

"Ruin my life?" He laughed. "You'll make my life perfect. Complete." He took ahold of her other hand. "I resigned from the FBI."

Her heart nearly stopped. "No. Henry, you can't."

"I already did. I love you more than I love the FBI. I love you more than my one-suitcase life. I love you,

Betty, and I don't want to spend the rest of my life without you."

"I don't want to spend the rest of my life without you, either," she admitted.

"What's going on here?" Father barked. "What are you two whispering about? You can't marry her. You can't object!"

"I can!" someone else shouted.

Betty shifted, to look around Henry, at a man walking up the aisle. A stranger. "Who is that?" she asked.

Henry twisted, glanced over his shoulder. "Uncle Nate?"

"Hello, Henry," the man said.

"Who are you?" Father's shout nearly rattled the windows.

Taller than Father, but just as gray, the man stopped next to the pew and held out his hand. "Nathan Randall, and you are?"

"William Dryer. Owner of Hollywoodland Properties."

The man glanced at her and Henry, and then said to Father, "And father of the bride I presume."

"Yes, I am." Frowning, Father asked again, "Who are you?"

"Nathan Randall, United States Attorney General." With a grin toward Henry, he added, "And Henry's uncle."

Betty was nearly as stunned as her father. While Father shouted the question, she whispered the same question to Henry. "The attorney general?"

"Yes," Henry said. "The attorney general."

Henry turned back to Betty. He'd made it as far as the California border, on the train, transporting Elkin and

Burrows, when he knew he couldn't do it. He couldn't let Betty marry someone else. Anyone else. He also couldn't let another man raise his child. Becoming a father scared him; he didn't know anything about it, but he'd learn. Just like he'd learned to love. He'd let the demons put inside him by his childhood rule his life, and refused to let them keep him from having a future.

He'd thought about all that Betty had said, too, long and hard. Especially when she'd said that his job was the only thing he'd ever loved. She'd been right. It had been because he didn't have to worry about it loving him in return.

Then he'd remembered the last words his father had said to him on the phone. *We love you, Henry.* They'd said that to him hundreds of times, but that morning, on the phone, he'd felt it. Truly felt it.

He felt that for Betty, too, so he'd left the other two agents in charge of the prisoners, gotten off the train at the next stop, called LeRoy, and then bought a ticket back to Los Angeles. He'd arrived in town less than an hour ago and had feared he might already be too late. Thankfully, he hadn't been.

Henry cleared his throat, then shifted, leaned toward his uncle, and whispered, "What are you doing here?"

"What am I doing here?" Nate said loud enough people outside the church could hear.

Henry sucked in air. Nate could be as boisterous as William Dryer was ornery.

"When I get a phone call that the best field agent the Bureau has ever had suddenly submitted his resignation," Nate said, overly loud, "I hop on an airplane to find out why."

"I left you a message," Henry said. He had called his uncle, while waiting for his return train, but hadn't gotten ahold of him and left a message with Nate's secretary that he'd resigned his position because he was going back to Los Angeles to get married.

"An airplane?" William asked.

"Yes," Nate replied, sounding somewhat offended, as he stepped closer. The wrinkles around his eyes deepened as he smiled at Betty. "I now see the reason." He slapped Henry's shoulder. "I'm not only proud of you, Henry, I'm happy for you. So are your parents."

Henry turned toward the back of the church. He hadn't seen them in years, but John Randall was as tall and thin as ever, and Esther was as short and round as ever. They waved at him from the back of the church.

"Are those your parents?" Betty whispered.

"Yes," Henry replied, still not quite believing that his uncle and his parents flew all the way out here because of him. It did make him smile, though, and filled him with happiness.

"They must love you very much," Betty whispered. She then let out a little groan. "Oh, dear, what are they going to think of me? Almost marrying someone else?"

She looked so beautiful in her long white dress, but she was beautiful no matter what she wore, and he loved her, so very much. "I don't care what anyone in this room thinks, except for you." He squeezed her hands. "You still haven't answered me. Will you marry me? We'll make this work. I swear to you, we'll make this work."

"Yes, we will make this work," she said. "And yes, I will marry you."

He wanted to kiss her, but the veil was in the way, and they were in the middle of a church full of people.

"Was that a yes?" Jane asked.

"Yes," both he and Betty answered at once, laughing.

"Bee's knees!" Jane shouted. "Get out of the way, James—make room for the real groom."

"H-he can't marry her," James said.

A hush fell over the room. It was the first time James had spoken.

"Why can't I?" Henry asked, fully prepared to go head to head with James Bauer.

James fiddled with the lapels of his suitcoat. "B-because you don't have a marriage license, and there's a five-day waiting period in California."

"He's right," Betty whispered.

Henry's heart sank at the deflation on her face, in her voice.

"Father," Uncle Nate addressed the priest. "Do you have the marriage license for these two, who *were* going to get married?"

"Yes, sir, I do."

"Let me see it, please."

The priest picked a sheet of paper off a table, carried it down the two steps and stepped around him and Betty to hand it to Nate.

Upon reading the license, Nate pulled a fountain pen out of his pocket and then used Henry's back as a table in order to alter the license right there in front of everyone.

"Is—is that legal?" James asked.

Nate handed the paper back to the priest before he said to James, "You find a judge who won't honor that, you tell him to call me."

Nate made the comment with humor in his voice, but Henry knew the truth in Nate's words. As much as he didn't like James, Henry felt a flash of empathy for the man right now. After all, he was losing Betty. Then again, Bauer hadn't deserved her in the first place.

"You ready?" he asked her.

She nodded, then shook her head. "One second." She stepped back up next to James, spoke quietly to him, and then lifted her veil, kissed his cheek as he nodded, then turned, and left the church. She returned to his side then. "Yes." Smiling brightly, she nodded. "I'm ready."

"Do you mind if I go invite my parents to sit up front?" he asked. They had given him more than he'd realized over the years. Their presence proved that.

"May I join you?" she asked.

"I'd like that."

"Nate." Henry gestured to the back of the room. "Give us a minute."

Nate nodded, but it was Jane who spoke.

"Take your time," she said. "We have some rearranging to do."

He and Betty smiled at each other as they started down the aisle and Jane continued with her rearranging, which included inviting Lane and Nate to stand up as best man and groomsman.

"She has that all under control," he said.

"That's my sister," Betty said.

Esther and John walked forward, meeting them in the aisle, with Esther giving him a motherly hug and kiss on the cheek as she always did whenever he saw her.

"I can't believe you're here," Henry said.

"We hope you don't mind," John said. "When Esther heard you were getting married, well, she really wanted to be here." He nodded. "So did I. We're proud of you, son. Proud to be your parents."

"I'm proud to be your son," he admitted, truthfully, heartfully, and then introduced Betty. "This is Betty, my bride-to-be. Betty, this is Esther and John Randall. My parents."

Betty lifted up her veil. "I'm sure this all seems a bit unorthodox—I'll gladly explain—"

"Oh, darling, there is nothing to explain," Esther said, kissing Betty's cheek. "Henry stole your heart. He stole mine the first day I met him."

Betty looked at him, smiling. "That's exactly what happened to me."

"Well, let's get you two married," John said. "We can talk later." He winked at Esther. "We've always wanted to see California, so we'll be here for several days."

"That's wonderful," Betty said.

"Yes, it is," Henry said. His life was wonderful.

His parents walked back up the aisle behind him and Betty and took front-row seats. Henry's heart had never felt so large, so full, as he took his spot next to her, ready to start the ceremony that would bond him and Betty together, forever.

"Hold on!"

Chapter Fifteen

Henry liked Jane, but leveled a glower on her at her shout to hold up the ceremony. Then, he had to grin as she merely flipped Betty's veil back over her face and winked at him before rushing back to her spot.

"Are we ready now?" the priest asked.

Jane nodded.

Betty nodded.

Henry nodded.

"Good." The priest let out a long sigh. Then, with a smile, he looked out over the guests, and began to speak. "Dearly beloved…"

Henry doubted he'd remember exactly what the priest said, but he'd never forget this day. The day Betty became his wife.

When instructed, he lifted her veil and kissed her with all the love inside him, then laughed, and kissed her again because he'd never be satisfied with just one kiss from her.

There was cake, coffee, and punch served in the basement of the church after the ceremony, and it was the longest hour of his life. Betty was at his side the entire time, and he couldn't wait to be alone with her.

The secretive smiles she kept sending his way told him she felt the same way.

They were standing near the punch table, when Jane asked, "Henry, where is your car? It's almost time for you two to leave. I carried Betty's suitcase outside but couldn't find your car."

He'd bought a suit, and a ring, thinking that was all he'd need. He hadn't thought about a car. He'd turned in the Bureau-issued car when he'd left for Washington, DC, and had used trollies since arriving in town a short time ago. "I don't have a car," he said.

"You don't need a car," Nate said, stepping into the conversation. "I'll drive you to the hotel. I rented the honeymoon suite for you as my wedding gift."

"Thank you," Betty said. "That's very kind of you."

"Yes, thank you." Henry tried to shake off the little quiver that shot up his spine, and did for the most part, but it came again, after the guests had showered them with rice and he and Betty were in the backseat of Nate's car.

"Your parents and I are staying at the Bay Hotel, too," Nate said. "I'd like to buy you both dinner tomorrow evening."

"That would be lovely," Betty said, her blue eyes twinkling.

"You'll still be here tomorrow evening?" Henry asked.

"Yes. I'll be in town for a few days," Nate said.

Henry could guess the reason, but let it go. Today, he was going to celebrate his marriage with his wife. Tomorrow, he'd tell Nate that he wouldn't change his mind. That he wouldn't take back his resignation. Betty didn't want to be married to an FBI agent, which meant he'd never be one again.

They arrived at the hotel, where the person at the front desk told him his suitcase had been transferred to the honeymoon suite. He thanked the attendant and led Betty to the elevator, once again letting go of how his uncle had thought of everything.

As soon as they entered the room, all thoughts of anyone else completely disappeared as Betty slid her arms up and around his neck.

"Thank you," she whispered. "For coming to the church today. For objecting. For being there when I turned around. I'm so sorry that I thought this couldn't happen. I don't know what I was thinking. Why I—"

He kissed her softly, quickly, just to stop her from saying more. "You were scared. We all do things when we are scared, justify things in a way that we think will keep us, or those we love, safe. I did the same thing for years. Didn't even realize it until you pointed it out to me."

"What did I point out?"

"That the only thing I loved was my job." He shook his head. "You were right, I did, because I didn't have to worry if it loved me back, if I was worthy of love."

"You are worthy, Henry, you always have been."

"You made me realize that." He kissed her again. "I'm so glad we both came to our senses."

She nodded and giggled. "In the nick of time."

"I love you."

"I love you, too."

The kiss they shared then was of a man and woman with one thing in mind. They removed their clothes between long, slow, languid kisses that had his pulse hammering and his need screaming for release.

She had so many different smiles. A coy, sweet one.

A teasing, sexy one. An oops-you-caught-me-off-guard one. An I-can't-believe-it one. And an I-love-you one.

He loved them all. Loved the way her eyes shimmered, her cheeks glowed, and her breath caught when he touched her just so.

There was nothing separating them now, not a stitch of clothing, as she lay on her back, golden hair spread out across the pillows and he sat on his knees, looking down at her.

They were both still, eyes locked. There was a smile on her face, the I-love-you one, at the same time there was a serious expression on the rest of her face. He knew what she was thinking because he was thinking the same thing. She'd become everything to him. So dear to him that nothing else in this world mattered.

Her smile shifted, into a teasing one as her eyes glowed even more brightly. She arched her back, upward, toward him.

He ran a hand down her sides, caressing the silkiness of her skin while maintaining his control in order to take this slow, make it last. Make it perfect, because that was what he wanted for her, a perfect life.

She bit down on her bottom lip. "I want you, Henry."

"You have me." She did. She had his heart, his mind, and his soul. He placed a row of tiny kisses along her collarbone.

Their eyes met again as he lifted his head. She pulled his face down for a long kiss, and then whispered, "I want all of you. Inside and out."

He straddled her hips, and half-afraid he might explode at any moment, took ahold of himself and guided his way into her. The heat of her made his hips buck forward and his mouth go dry.

She gasped and wrapped her legs around his.

He could barely draw in a breath of air but managed to say her name. It sounded hoarse, barely a whisper.

She arched upward, and his control was lost. Nearly desperate, he set a fast rhythm that she matched, taking as much as he was giving. This was exactly how it had been before. So in tune with each other, they traversed through the storms building inside each other as smoothly, as joyously, as they had sashayed around the dance floor that first night when they'd won the dance-off.

He should have known then that his life was never going to be the same. Betty, sweet and adorable, and undercover as a flapper, had stolen his heart, and as far as he was concerned, he never wanted her to give it back to him. It was hers, forever.

They hit the crescendo together, gasping for air, muscles tight with tension, and then soared into an ultimate pleasure-filled void as one.

Afterward, as they were both shuddering with aftershocks, they laughed, and kissed, and laughed again.

Betty could stay exactly where she was for the rest of her life, lying naked on a bed and staring at the ceiling and smiling as her heartbeat gradually returned to normal after making love with her husband yet again. She laughed then, because she had been here for hours and hours.

Henry's hand was on her stomach, his palm rubbing small circles right above where their baby was growing.

"When are you due?"

Her smile grew. "May, from my calculations." A hint

of embarrassment had her adding. "Only my sisters know, besides me and you."

"I was stunned when you told me. So shocked I couldn't think, and I'm sorry that I drove away."

"I'm sorry that I sent you away. I should have told you sooner, but…" She covered his hand with both of hers. "I was so scared."

"There's nothing to be afraid of now." He kissed her temple. "I'll get a job here, buy us a house. It'll all be fine."

She bit down on her bottom lip. That sounded perfect, and had been exactly what she'd thought she'd wanted, but now… Now she wasn't so sure. How could that be? She was married to the man she loved. The father of her baby. What more could she want?

"We are going to have to get dressed soon," Henry said. "Go down to the restaurant. Meet Nate."

They had eaten in their room last night, and again this morning. Which had been hours ago. Her stomach growled, and she giggled.

Henry climbed off the bed and tugged on her arm. "Come on. You're hungry."

"I am hungry." She leaped off the bed. The room was so lovely. The walls were painted a pale green, with sheer yellow curtains that matched the yellow of the chenille bedspread. There was even a sink in the room, along with a dresser with a mirror, two chairs, and a small round table that they'd sat at to eat this morning, her wearing only her dressing robe and Henry his pants.

She lifted her suitcase onto the chair and opened it. Her choices were minimal, since she'd only packed one outfit. Actually, Jane had packed for her, and she laughed as she lifted out the powder blue dress. It was one of her favorites.

"What are you laughing at?" Henry asked while splashing water on his face at the sink.

"Nothing." She reached over, pulled a towel off the rack, and tossed it at him before lifting up the dress to pull over her head.

He caught the towel and wiped his face. "That's a pretty dress."

"It's one of my favorites." She lifted a pair of tap pants out of the suitcase and stepped into them, pulling them up under the dress, and then flounced the skirt and tied the waist sash into a bow over her right hip.

"It looks lovely on you." He kissed her cheek as he reached for his own suitcase.

She went to the sink and washed her face, then brushed her hair. By the time Henry was dressed, she'd added the pearl necklace and earbobs that she'd worn yesterday.

"Very lovely." He lifted her hair and kissed the side of her neck. "I must be the luckiest man on earth."

She giggled and reached up, laid her hand on the side of his face while staring at the reflection of the two of them in the mirror. She was the lucky one. So very, very lucky that he hadn't listened to her. She shouldn't have listened to herself.

"Let's go before I take that dress off you and we end up eating in our room again," he said, grinning at her in the mirror.

"I wouldn't mind."

He kissed her cheek. "Neither would I." Grasping her hand, he pulled her to the door. "We'll eat fast."

Laughing, they left the room, and, alone in the elevator, he kissed her thoroughly and whispered in her ear, describing what he would do after they returned to her room. Her cheeks were warm and her heart racing with anticipation when they stepped out of the elevator.

"There's the happy couple," Henry's uncle Nate said, waving at them from the other side of the lobby.

Henry's parents stood next to him, and she breathed through a bout of nervousness.

He squeezed her hand as they crossed the lobby, greeted his family, and then entered the restaurant.

His parents, and his uncle, were very pleasant, and by the time the main course of their meal arrived, she felt very comfortable, and was extremely interested in learning more about Henry.

"He was a top member of the first graduation class of the Virginia State Junior College," John said, full of pride.

"The top member," Esther added. "Henry's grades were always exemplary. In all subjects."

"Henry had a job waiting for him at the Bureau before he graduated," Nate said.

Henry looked at her. "Family had more to do with that than grades."

Both his uncle and father frowned.

"No, they didn't," Nate said. "It was your grades, your attention to detail and intelligence that got you that job." He shrugged. "But I will admit that I was awfully proud to tell people you were my nephew. Still am."

"You worked at the Bureau, too?" she asked.

"Yes, I did, and the Justice Department," Nate said. "Until I was appointed the attorney general."

Betty wasn't miffed or upset that Henry hadn't told her about his uncle, and his position, but wondered why he'd never mentioned it. She wondered why he seemed a bit solemn, too.

"I'm not going to talk business here, tonight," Nate said. "But I do want to talk to you, Henry, before I head back. The Bureau doesn't want to lose you."

She felt the way Henry stiffened and saw how stern his expression turned.

He took a sip of his drink, set down the glass, and squeezed her hand. "I resigned for good reason, Nate. I'm married now. Will have a family soon—someday soon. Agents are more suited for single men."

Her stomach sank. That had been one of her reasons. Not the dangers, but how much he enjoyed his job. How good he was at it. She hadn't wanted him to change. Hadn't wanted him to give up his job for her. She bit her lips together as the bottom one started to tremble. That was exactly what he had done.

"There are other positions besides field agents." Nate picked up his glass. "We can talk about it later."

"There's nothing to talk about," Henry said.

A heavy silence hovered over the table for several long moments. His mother finally broke it.

"Do you have a house, or an apartment here, Henry?" Esther asked. "In Los Angeles?"

"No, I lived in hotels during most of my time here." He looked at her and smiled. "But we'll start looking right away. Tomorrow."

Betty returned his smile and nodded.

"Well, let us know what you find," John said. "We want to assist you in buying one, as your wedding gift."

Henry shook his head. "I can't let you do that."

"Yes, you can," John said.

"It's a gift, Henry," Esther said. "We insist."

Sensing something, although she wasn't sure exactly what, and used to a demanding parent, Betty said,

"Thank you. That is so very kind of you. We will let you know as soon as we find something suitable."

"The government owns a house here in town," Nate said.

"Yes, it's near my parents' house," Betty said, noting how Henry had stiffened again. "It's been abandoned for several years."

"It's still in good shape, isn't it?" Nate asked.

"Yes, other than needing a good cleaning, it's fine." Afraid someone might question how she knew that, she added, "My father has tried to buy it several times."

"Well, let me check into that," Nate said.

"Oh, that would nice, wouldn't it, Betty, to live near your parents?" Esther asked.

"Yes, it would be," she answered.

"Anyone interested in dessert?" Nate asked.

"Not for me, thank you," Betty said, glancing at Henry, who had stopped eating sometime ago. "I'm so full I couldn't eat another bite. It all was very delicious."

"Could we invite the two of you to lunch tomorrow?" Esther asked. "We don't mean to impose, but we haven't seen Henry in four years."

"That would be lovely," Betty answered due to Henry picking up his drink instead of answering.

"Wonderful. Thank you, dear. Shall we say, noon, here?" Esther asked.

"We'll be here," Betty answered, feeling queasy because she had a strong sense that Henry wasn't happy. Happy about anything that had been said. He hadn't been happy since his uncle had mentioned him resigning.

The evening didn't last much longer, and Betty held her breath nearly the entire elevator ride back up to their room.

Henry grasped her waist as soon as the door was shut, and locked. Pulling her up against him, he kissed the tip of her nose. "I'm sorry about that."

"About what?"

"My parents. My uncle."

"They didn't do anything wrong."

He released her and walked over to the window. "Offering me a different job. To help us buy a house?"

"They love you, Henry. Very much. I can tell by the way they look at you." She laid a hand on his back. "It's the same way I look at you. They just want you to be happy." That was what she wanted, too, and had taken that away from him.

Betty's touch melted Henry's insides. He turned around. "I am happy. I'm married to you." He kissed her forehead. "I'm sorry. It's just going to take me a bit to adjust. When John and Esther adopted me, the headmistress said it was because I was an experiment. John had pioneered the junior college in Virginia, and she said there wasn't a better way to prove his idea was successful than to enroll his own son—adopted son—in the school. I believed her. To the point that, upon graduation, I believed he got me the job at the Bureau."

Betty's expression was that of confusion, and disbelief. "Why would you believe that? Your uncle said you got that job because of your grades. So did your parents."

He shrugged. "Because I was young, and scared. She told me it wouldn't work, and that I wouldn't have anywhere to go then."

"She sounds like she was awful. Mean and controlling."

He nodded. "She was. That's why I had to steal food

for the younger children. And blankets. And help them with their classes so they wouldn't get reprimanded." He'd remembered so much more about his childhood, and it all seemed crystal clear now. He felt bad, too. His parents had already given him so much. Including love that he'd never accepted. They'd given him so much more than he would ever have had without them, he couldn't let them keep giving. Not Nate with another job, or his parents by allowing them to help pay for a house. He'd do those things on his own. It was beyond time.

"You were their Robin Hood."

He grinned. "I should never have told you that."

"I'm glad you did."

He stepped forward and slid his hands around her waist. "And I'm glad that you showed me that I love you more than I'd loved the FBI."

She returned his kiss, but he felt she was holding something back. He lifted his head. "What's wrong?"

"Nothing."

The smile she flashed was a feigned one. One that said, *I'm pretending to smile right now because that's what you want to see.* "Something is," he said.

"I—I was just wondering what sort of job you are going to get here."

He shrugged. "What kind of job do you want me to get?" He kissed the side of her neck, right below the ear. He was tired of talking about himself and ready to act upon their love for one another.

"I want you to have a job that makes you happy."

He picked her up and plopped her down on the bed. "I'll show you what makes me happy."

Chapter Sixteen

Habit had Henry jumping out of bed and pulling on his pants at the first knock that sounded on his door.

"What's wrong?" Betty asked.

He flipped the suspenders over his shoulders. "Someone's at the door."

"Wait!" She scrambled out of bed. "Let me put on my dressing robe."

The knock sounded again as she slipped her arms into the oversize blue robe and tied the belt tight around her narrow waist.

She nodded and he unlocked the door. Opened it.

"I'm sorry, Henry," Nate said. "May I come in, or can you come out here?"

"He can come in," Betty said, taking a seat in one of the chairs.

Henry waved a hand and held the door wide as Nate entered the room. "It's the middle of the night."

"I know," Nate said. "I apologize, but I just got a phone call. LeRoy Black's been shot."

An icy wave washed over Henry. "Is he—"

"He's going to make it, from what I was told," Nate said. "But Curtis Elkin escaped."

"Damn it," Henry hissed beneath his breath. "I told them to—" He let that go and asked, "Where?"

"Rockville. Last stop before they would have arrived in DC."

In the recesses of his mind, Henry heard Elkin's laugh, and how he'd said that he had backup. "It's Burrows family and the Tribbianis from New Jersey. Bootleggers. But they've extended their operations west. Elkin had been slipping them information for years, and was prepared to take over the operations out here. It's all in my report."

Nate nodded. "The report was with LeRoy. No one else has read it."

Henry rubbed his head. "How bad is LeRoy?"

"I don't have those details."

LeRoy had been his supervisor for years, and he thought of the last time he'd seen him, how LeRoy had to get home to his wife. Wife. Henry looked at Betty. He was no longer an agent. There was nothing he could do to help. Not the Bureau or LeRoy.

"I know you resigned, Henry," Nate said. "I know it's your honeymoon—"

"No," Henry said. "I can't." He balled his hand into a fist, having never imagined he'd ever feel this torn in two again. He was married, to Betty, whom he loved more than the FBI. He did. He just hated not being able to help a man who had saved his life more than once. Nate knew that. Knew the trials and perils LeRoy and he had been through together. "Even if I could," Henry said. "I would take days to get there. The trail will be cold by then."

"I can have a plane in the air in half an hour," Nate said. "Fly you straight to DC."

It was tempting; he was the only one who knew about

the Tribiannis' connection to Elkin, but no, he couldn't. He looked at Betty again, so his mind would understand all that he had, and all that he couldn't give up. His heart knew it.

"I understand," Nate said, slapping him on the back. "I'll keep you posted."

Henry opened the door and held it for Nate to exit. "Please do. Anything, everything you hear. Let me know."

"I will."

He closed the door and frowned at the sight of Betty putting clothes in a suitcase. "What are you doing?"

"Has anyone ever escaped while you were transporting them?"

"No." His jaw locked tight. He'd instructed the agents transporting Elkin and Burrows to expect the unexpected. To be alert, ready, the entire trip. "Never."

"This LeRoy man, the one who was shot, he's a friend of yours?"

The air left his lungs like a punctured tire at the idea of LeRoy in the hospital. "He was my supervisor, and yes, a friend."

"Then you need to help him." She closed the suitcase. "You need to capture Elkin." She turned, faced him. "Again."

It was his suitcase she'd packed. Closed. "No. I resigned."

"Because of me." She walked closer, cupped his face. "Which was the very thing I didn't want you to do. I said all those mean things about your job, because I was afraid to tell you the truth."

"The truth?"

"I was so in love with you. So in love with you, and I knew you weren't ready for that. You didn't want anyone to worry about you. To be waiting for you to come home." She closed her eyes and a smile formed. Opening her eyes, she rubbed his cheek. "But that is who I fell in love with. That Robin Hood. And that's who I want to be married to."

He grasped her waist. "I did say those things, before I realized how much I love you. I love you more than I love the FBI. More than I loved being an agent."

She kissed him. "I know you do. But that doesn't mean you don't love the FBI. That you wouldn't love being an agent. It just means you love me more."

It was tempting, so tempting, to accept what she offered. To complete just one more assignment. Catch Elkin again, and this time, deliver him to DC himself, but he couldn't. "I can't go, Betty. I won't go. You need me here."

"I do, and I'll need you tomorrow, and next week, and next year, and twenty, thirty, fifty years from now. And I'll be here, me and the baby, and all the other babies that we have together, each and every time you return home from an assignment, because that's when you'll need me. You said we'd make this work, and we will." She smiled and shook her head. "The longer we stand here talking about it, the colder Elkin's trail is growing."

"You don't understand. There's no way of knowing how long catching Elkin could take. How long I'd have to be gone." He was getting too close to saying yes, and change the direction of his thoughts, to why he couldn't go. "We don't even have a house. You can't stay here at the hotel the entire time."

"Looking for a house will give me something to do while you're gone, and I can live at my parents' house. All of my things are still there." She grinned and glanced at her suitcase. "Trust me—everything I own doesn't fit in one suitcase. I can also show your parents the city. Your parents, who—I guarantee—love you. Almost as much as I do."

He'd given up being an agent for her, and that had been the right choice. And now, she was... He shook his head. "You are making this too tempting."

"No, I'm making this right, Henry. We both kept things hidden before, because we were scared, but there's no reason to be anymore. We're married. We are going to have a baby. That makes me so happy, and I want you to be just as happy."

"I am."

She shook her head. "You're justifying, just like you said people do. I did that, too, right up until you walked into the church, and then I couldn't remember a single reason why I couldn't marry you. Except for one. That I didn't want you to change because of me." She hooked her hands beneath his suspenders and pressed her body up against his. "You gave me everything I wanted, and this is the only thing I can give you. Please let me. Please."

In his job, more people had lied to him than told the truth. He knew the signs of both. Right now, she was being completely honest. This beautiful, amazing woman he'd married. "You really mean this, don't you?"

"Yes, I do."

He shook his head.

She cupped his face. "I told Jane that I couldn't marry you, because I thought that would be as if I was trying to be someone I'm not." She smiled brightly. "And Jane asked me, what if marrying you would be my chance to be who I am? She was right. This is who

I am, Henry, the wife of an FBI agent, and I'm very, very proud of that."

His heart swelled in his chest, full of love for this amazing woman. Not because she was giving him permission to be an FBI agent, but because she was right. She had found herself and because of her, he'd found himself, too. "You are wrong about one thing. This isn't the only thing you can give me. You already gave me everything I wanted. You. You are more than everything I ever wanted."

She kissed him, a long, passionate kiss that was full of promises. Future promises. As their lips parted, she said, "Just come home to me, safe and sound."

Betty told herself she wouldn't, but then, knowing that was impossible, gave in to tears as soon as Henry left. Only because she already missed him and would until he returned home to her.

There was no use going back to bed; she wouldn't be able to sleep, so she took advantage of the empty bathing room down the hall, then packed her suitcase and straightened up the room while her hair dried.

It was amazing how good she felt. She missed Henry tremendously, and would until he returned, but that was part of the reason she felt so whole, so complete. It was all because of him. He had rescued her from so many things, including her own misconceptions.

She was afraid for his safety, but she also believed in him. Believed he'd come home safe and sound. The fact that Elkin had escaped was proof that Henry was the best agent. No one had ever escaped under his watch. That made her proud. Everything about him made her proud, especially being his wife.

She was about to leave the room when a knock

sounded on the door. "Who is it?" she asked, already holding the knob in her hand.

"Esther and John, dear," Esther said.

She opened the door.

John, nearly as tall as the door, had silver hair, and Esther, barely past his elbow, had snow-white hair, and both were smiling.

Smiling in return, because it would have been impossible not to, she said, "Good morning."

"Good morning," Esther repeated. "We thought we'd ask if you'd like to have breakfast with us, since Henry left with Nate."

"We are terribly sorry about that," John said. "And we promised Henry we'd keep an eye on you for him."

They were good people; she could feel their love for Henry, and she loved that about them. "That is very kind of you, and I would love to have breakfast with you. Thank you."

"Afterward, we could go look at that house Nate mentioned," John said. "Or other ones, if you're interested."

Delight filled her. "I would like that very much." She pulled the door closed behind her. "And I would love to hear more about Henry. About how you chose him for adoption, and everything, just everything about him."

"Gladly," Esther said while they walked down the hallway. "We would like to learn about you, too, dear. We feel so blessed that Henry found you. As blessed as we felt upon adopting him. That was hard for him, being fifteen and still living in the orphanage."

John slid open the elevator door for them. "Remember how that headmistress tried to make us choose someone else? Someone younger?"

"Oh, do I," Esther said with a miffed pucker. "I was

so angry with her. We had met nearly every child in that place, and Henry had stolen our hearts. He was so easy to like, so polite and studious, and so…"

"Cautious," John said, pulling the door shut and pushing the button.

"Yes, cautious," Esther said. "That's a good way to describe it."

"That's also what makes him an excellent agent," John said. "He was so enthralled with the Bureau, would spend hours talking to Nate about it every chance he got. Nate warned us, they rarely hired young men, that it would be tough for him to get it. We told Henry he could study any subjects he wanted to study, become anything he wanted to become—he was the one who chose law enforcement, the Bureau."

Betty nodded, fully believing that.

"We were careful, though," Esther said, "because of how wary Henry was, since the first day he entered our home, and never pushed anything on him, including our love. He didn't know what love was, growing up the way he had, and I—" She glanced up at John. "We think that scared him."

"I completely understand that," Betty said. She did, and she believed that was why she and Henry were so drawn to each other right from the start. Two lost souls looking for love, yet scared to death to receive it. "Did you know the headmistress tried to talk him out of being adopted by you?"

"No!" Esther said, pressing a hand to her chest.

"Yes," Betty replied. "Despite her efforts, Henry was fortunate that you adopted him."

"No, we are the fortunate ones," John said. "And fortunate again that he found you. That he finally knows the joys of love."

"And we're hopeful," Esther said.

"Hopeful?" Betty asked.

"That the two of you will allow us to come visit," John said, hugging Esther with one arm and looking down on her. "Regularly."

"I guarantee it," Betty said. "In fact, if Henry agrees upon the house Nate mentioned, there's plenty of room for guests."

Henry watched the ground growing closer and closer. He could get used to this type of travel. It had been nerve-racking at first, when he'd flown to DC four days ago, but now, about to arrive in Los Angeles within a fourth of the time the train would have taken, he'd gladly fly to his next assignment and back.

Back to Betty.

Lord, he'd missed her. Her face. Her laugh. Her kisses. Her body.

He'd talked to her on the telephone last night, before leaving DC, as well as every day he'd been gone. She'd sounded so happy, so excited, each time they'd spoken. He had been, too. Just hearing her voice had helped the longing inside him.

During their first call, she'd asked about the house Nate had mentioned, if he would consider buying that one. He'd consider buying the White House if that was the one she wanted. She'd laughed when he'd told her that.

His uncle had looked into the house, and must have done whatever it took, because that was now their house. She'd told him last night that her sisters and his parents had helped her, and that when he arrived in town, that was where she would be. At their house. Their home.

The sun was setting, and it would be dark soon, but

there would be a car waiting for him when he landed and he was certain he'd make the trip across town, to her, in record time.

Just as he'd been sure he'd capture Elkin in record time. He had. Because he'd known where to look, thanks to his interrogation of Burrows when he'd captured Elkin the first time, in Los Angeles.

He'd not only captured Elkin, and delivered him to DC; three members of the Tribianni gang were also behind bars.

That had been almost as rewarding as knowing LeRoy had been released from the hospital and was on his way back to Texas. The bullets had missed any vital organs, and LeRoy would have nothing but a few more scars in a few weeks.

Henry would take over his workload, overseeing field agents, during LeRoy's recovery, and after that, they'd split the area LeRoy had been covering, which made LeRoy very happy.

It made Henry happy too, because he'd be based out of Los Angeles, traveling only when one of his men needed him. It was perfect. He was still an agent, yet also home where he could be a husband, and next May, a father.

Thanks to Betty.

He had so much to thank her for.

So much to love about her.

Lost in thoughts, he had to grab ahold of the seat to keep from bouncing out of it as the tires beneath the plane hit the ground and bounced several times before smoothing out and finally rolling to a stop.

The Bureau-issued car was waiting for him, and he made it across town in record time.

Lights shining in the windows made the house look different. A good different. Homey. Welcoming.

But it was the woman who threw open the door and ran toward the car that made his heart swell. He opened the car door, jumped out, and caught her in his arms in the middle of the yard.

He kissed her until his lungs burned, sucked in air, and then kissed her again. And again.

"I missed you so much!" she said. "So much!"

Her arms were wrapped around his neck, and her legs around his waist. He spun in a circle out of sheer delight and relished her laughter before he kissed her again. Then, he carried her across the lawn and into the house. "I missed you so much."

"I can't wait for you to see everything!"

"I'm looking at everything I want to see," he said, staring at her.

She laughed. "Put me down so I can show you."

"On one condition."

Nodding, she asked, "What?"

"That you show me our bedroom first."

"Deal!"

He released his hold, and she grasped his hand as soon as her feet touched the floor.

"This way!" she said.

They ran up the stairs, laughing.

Within seconds of entering the room, he'd seen what he needed to see. The bed.

Within seconds after that, they were on it.

His fingers fumbled in his rush to get her clothes off, while hers wrestled with his suit. When skin touched skin their fumbling stopped and they stared at one another. The passion, the desire, shimmering in her eyes, sent a wave of something through him. He wanted her as badly as she did him, but what he felt was more than that. He loved her, had admitted that more than once. But until this moment, he hadn't realized how deep, how strong, how powerful and encompassing that love was.

Her smile grew, slowly, sweetly.

"It's amazing, isn't it?"

"Yes," he said, certain she'd read his mind. His face.

"And to think we were both afraid of this," she whispered. "The most wonderful thing on earth and in heaven."

Confused, he kissed her nose. "Afraid of what?"

"Love. We were both so afraid of it, that we kept it locked inside us, hidden away, afraid to share it because then we might never get it back." She stroked his face. "Now we both know that that's how it grows. By sharing it."

His throat went dry, his eyes stung, as he thought of all the love John and Esther, Nate, and then Betty, had shown him, but he hadn't seen it, hadn't accepted it, because it had scared him. He'd never have realized what love was capable of, how it could transform lives, if he hadn't met her. He may be an FBI agent, but she had truly uncovered the greatest secret, the greatest power of the universe.

"It's amazing, isn't it?" she repeated.

"Almost as amazing as you." Becoming a father still frightened him a touch, but he knew, all he had to do was watch her, and learn. He could do that.

She giggled; then her eyes grew serious. "I missed you. So very, very much."

"I missed you, so very, very much."

Henry didn't see the rest of the house that night. That could wait. Showing her how much he'd missed her couldn't.

The following morning, she gave him the full tour, including the basement. All the furniture that had been down there, covered with dust sheets, had been carried upstairs, to various rooms, and other furniture had been purchased. The cupboards were full of dishes and pots and pans, and all sorts of other necessities he'd never known were necessities, other than the food in the pantry and fridge.

Shaking his head, he poured himself a cup of coffee from the pot on the stove. The entire home shone like a new penny. "You must have worked day and night while I was gone."

"No, I had help. My sisters, your parents, my mother, even my father, who, by the way is boasting that I married an FBI agent as if he picked you out himself, and you don't even want to get him started on who your uncle is. That's the most famous person he's ever met." She laughed, then fluffed the curtain on the back door. "I missed you, terribly, but it was fun. Setting up our home." Settling both of her hands on her stomach, she said, "I'm so blessed that you entered my life."

Esther always said that. A chuckle rumbled in his throat as he set down his coffee cup, crossed his arms and attempted to look serious. She was a little nymph. His sea nymph. And the smile on her face said she was hiding something.

"What else do you have to tell me?"

"James helped me, too."

He lifted a brow, only because he could believe it.

"Just with the outside. The way the windows had been boarded up really needed to be repaired, and he's a very good carpenter. Just very, very boring."

"Is he?"

"Yes." Her face was glowing, her eyes sparkling, as

she crossed the kitchen floor and slid her arms around his neck. "Nothing like you. My Robin Hood."

He wrapped his arms around her and lifted her off the floor, so she was the one looking down at him, and kissed her. "I'm glad I'm the one you married."

"Me, too." She kissed him. "So very, very glad."

"Knock, knock."

"We are in the kitchen, Jane!" Betty shouted.

He didn't let her down, was still holding her off the floor, up against him, when Jane walked into the kitchen.

"Hello, Reuben," she said, setting a box on the table.

He laughed, kissed Betty, and then set her down. "What is it with you and that name?"

"Reuben?" She shrugged. "I just like calling you that. It makes you scrunch up your nose."

"It does not."

She shrugged, then punched him on the arm. "I do like how happy you've made my sister."

"Thank you." He picked up his coffee cup and took a sip. "Coming from you, I take that as a compliment. Probably the only one I'll ever get."

Laughing, she pointed at him and winked.

He leaned over, and whispered into Betty's ear, "How did you ever keep that one in line?"

His insides quivered slightly at the smile that appeared on Betty's face. It was another one of those feigned ones. He looked at Jane and then back to Betty.

She grabbed the coffeepot. "More coffee?"

"No." He set his cup down. "What's in the box, Jane?"

She picked the box up. "Just a few of my things. One never knows when one may find adventure on a quick getaway. I'll take them downstairs now," she answered nonchalantly.

A bit too nonchalantly. "Her things?"

Betty stepped over and looped both of her arms around one of his. "Yes, she's going to keep a few of her things in the basement."

He nodded, once, then the shiver returned. "Why?"

Betty kissed his cheek. "Because it will be safer for her to use the tunnel than ride the trolley by herself."

Oh, yes, that was worth quivering over. More so than a mobster with a gun. What the hell had he gotten himself into now?

"I thought you'd agree with me," Betty said.

He lifted her chin and kissed the tip of her nose. If it made Betty happy, then he agreed with it. "I do," he said. "As long as she doesn't sneak upstairs when she's passing through. We don't need an audience."

"She won't. I promise."

"You're sure?"

"Yes."

He'd never get enough of her. "Prove it."

The twinkle in her eye said the challenge was on, even before she tugged on his arm, saying, "All right. I'll prove it. Right now."

Her answer couldn't have pleased him more.

Epilogue

❧❧❧

Betty rolled over and arched her back, trying to stretch out the sting that had awakened her. Her eyes popped open at an entirely new pain. One that took her breath away and had her grasping Henry's arm.

He instantly shot up. "What is it? The baby? Is the baby coming?"

She tried to hold back the whimpers in her throat caused by the pain gripping her stomach, enough to answer, but couldn't, so she nodded.

Henry flew into action, and by the time the pain had subsided enough for her to take an actual breath, he was fully clothed and holding up a dress for her to put on. "Your suitcase is in the car, and my parents are ready to open the doors for us. Let me slip this over your head and I'll carry you to the car."

Betty rested her head against the pillow for a moment, admiring how handsome he was, even in the middle of the night. How he was there for her, even in the middle of the night.

"To hell with it." He tossed aside the dress. "I'll just carry you in your nightgown."

She laughed and patted his worried face. "I can get

dressed. And I can walk. The pain is gone now—I just needed a moment to catch my breath."

"All right, but I'll help you out of bed."

He did, and helped her get dressed, even put on her shoes because her stomach was so large that bending over was nearly impossible. He then helped her down the steps and out to the car.

John and Esther had arrived last week, and were staying for a month or more, to help her once the baby arrived. They both gave her a hug before Henry helped her climb in the passenger seat.

That was when the next pain hit, as he was walking around the car. It again stole her breath away and made her whimper.

"Don't hold your breath, honey," he said, grasping her hand. "You have to breathe."

His reminder helped, and before long, she leaned back against the seat as the pain subsided.

He lifted her hand, kissed the back of it. "I'm sorry, Betty. Sorry that you are in such pain."

She smiled and shook her head. "It hurts, but it's fine. Our baby will be here soon, and I'm so excited to meet him or her."

"I am, too."

She closed her eyes as he drove them toward the hospital. "I hope our baby has your eyes," she said.

"And I hope they have yours."

"I've loved your eyes since the moment I saw them," she said.

"I've loved you, since the moment I saw you."

She laughed. "Isn't it amazing how things work out?"

"Yes, it is," he agreed.

The pain that hit then, the bearing-down pressure, had her screaming rather than holding her breath. It wasn't subsiding, and through the pain, she yelled, "Faster, Henry! Faster!"

He drove fast, and her babies came fast. They didn't even have time to wheel her into the maternity ward or administer ether. One baby was born in the hallway, the other in the elevator.

Later, once she was settled in a room, holding a baby in each arm, one wrapped in pink and the other blue, Henry kissed her forehead.

"When were you going to tell me there were two babies inside you?" he asked, touching their daughter's adorable little button nose.

Betty laughed. "I didn't know there were two of them."

Their son wrapped his tiny fingers around Henry's much larger one. "Well, I have to say, when we do something, we do it right."

"Yes, we do." She laughed as he kissed her, because she was so full of joy.

"Two," Henry said, as if he still couldn't believe it. "I'll buy another crib on my way home today. And another high chair. And another rocking chair. And another—"

"Knock, knock. Hello, darling, Hello, Henry."

"Hello, Mother," Betty greeted. "Is Father with you?"

"Yes, but they won't let him back here." She glanced at Henry. "How did you manage that, Henry?"

He winked at her. "My uncle's the attorney general."

Mother laughed. "Twins! This is so exciting. And look at them, they are so perfect, even being a wee bit early."

"Early?" Betty asked.

"Yes, it's only May, dear." Mother removed her

gloves. "Ask any doctor—they'll tell you twins are always a month early."

Between her mother's wink and the grin on Henry's face, Betty had to laugh out loud. Mother's month-early explanation eliminated any baby scandal considering she and Henry had only been married eight months.

"Knock, knock. It's me, Auntie Patsy." Patting her growing stomach, Patsy added, "And baby."

"And Auntie Jane!"

Tears formed in Betty's eyes at the sight of her sisters. Especially Jane. She hadn't expected to see her. "You made it."

"I told you I'd be here." Jane, looking like she'd just stepped out of a fashion magazine, entered the room. "I flew in last night. I called and told Reuben. But told him I wanted to surprise you today."

Betty looked at the sly grin on Henry's face. "Surprise!" he said.

She laughed, then told her sisters, "Come look at my month-early twins. They are perfect!"

* * * * *

If you enjoyed this story, be sure to read the first
book in the Sisters of the Roaring Twenties miniseries

The Flapper's Fake Fiancé

and look out for the next one in the series,
coming soon!

And whilst you're waiting for the
next book, why not check out her
Brides of the Roaring Twenties miniseries

Baby on His Hollywood Doorstep
Stolen Kiss with the Hollywood Starlet